Vaucluse

Donna Every

Acknowledgements

I would like to acknowledge all the people who helped to make this book about Henry Peter Simmons of Vaucluse Plantation a reality. Mr. Robert "Bobby" Morris, noted Barbadian historian, who shared his great knowledge of Barbados' history with me. Thanks also to John Knox who shared his research about the Quakers with me as well as his copies of old maps of Vaucluse Plantation. Harriett Pierce from the Shiltone Memorial Library at the Barbados museum who introduced me to the Queree tables and information on Henry Peter Simmons. Carlisle Best of the West Indian Collection at the Library of the University of the West Indies (UWI), for allowing me to use their microfilm reader. The Barbados National Library services, for lending the UWI library microfilm of the *Barbados Mercury* on my behalf. Paul Grimwood of Canada who provided exciting information about Henry Peter's life in Upper Canada. My neighbour, Gillian Morris, who helped me to decipher the legal jargon in Henry Peter's will and who shared great discussions with me about the discoveries that I made. And finally, to my editor, Toni Daniel, who did a great job as usual.

I was very fortunate to come across some useful publications that helped me tremendously with background information about the occurrences in the island during the period of the book. One such resource was *History of Barbados: Comprising a Geographical and Statistical Description of the Island; a*

Sketch of the Historical Events Since the Settlement; and an Account of Its Geology and Natural Productions by Sir Robert H. Schomburgk, PhD. The three letters which Henry Peter wrote to the Right Honourable Earl Grey, First Lord of the Treasury of England, also gave me great insight into his views on abolition and provided me with sources from which to create dialogue to support his pro-slavery arguments in the book. All extracts from those letters (written in italics) are from the actual letters and are not figments of my imagination.

I must also acknowledge the work of Dr. Thomas Rolph of England who wrote extensively about his visit to Vaucluse in 1833 and his and Henry Peter's subsequent trip to Canada. It was from his extensive writings titled *A brief account, together with observations made during a visit in the West Indies and a tour through the United States of America in parts of the years 1832-3; together with a statistical account of Upper Canada* (quite a mouthful) that I gleaned valuable information. I have incorporated many of his observations into the book either in the form of extracts from his journal (written in italics in the book) or by interweaving it into the dialogue. I give full credit to his work. One of the treasures that I was delighted to find in his publication was the reason Henry Peter changed the name of the plantation from Yorkshire Hall to Vaucluse, which you will find out as you read. Dr. Rolph's work provided significant details about the social life in Barbados at that time without which the book would have been lacking.

Last, and by no means least, I need to acknowledge the hand of God in this work. He dropped many gold nuggets into my lap that brought the pieces of the puzzle together, even as he taught me that I won't always have all my questions answered and I need to learn to be okay with that. I'm still learning.

Author's Note

I have discovered that there is a major difference between writing historical fiction as I have done in the past *(The Acreage Series)* and fictionalising a historical figure. While both are based as accurately as possible on historical information, with historical fiction you have the artistic license to create the characters the way you want. However, when you are writing about a person who existed, the challenge is to capture the character of that person in order to represent (re-present) them as true to character as possible. That is done by researching what they said, what they wrote and what they did, but it can be a challenge when limited by the information that is available, so some aspects of the character are arrived at by deduction.

Nevertheless, I hope that, based on my extensive research over two years, I have been able to re-present a fairly accurate picture of the main character, Henry Peter Simmons, who bought Vaucluse Plantation (formerly Yorkshire Hall) in 1816 and owned it until his death in 1843. Although the book is titled *Vaucluse*, it is primarily the story of Henry Peter Simmons in the period that he owned Vaucluse Plantation, though at times he was referred to as an absentee planter. Vaucluse was the reason he was able to reside in England and, in later years, to purchase a substantial amount of land in Ontario, Canada and live there for a time.

While not an easy task, I was able to characterise

him more accurately than some of the other characters in the book such as Molly Harry who was named in his will as "a woman on my plantation" and who was the mother of his two coloured sons. The reason being that, of course, as a slave, there would have been very little information about her other than her estimated date of birth, her position on the plantation and when she died. So, I have taken greater artistic license with her character.

While I believe his children played an important part in his life and helped to reveal some of the character of Henry Peter, it has been impossible to find specific information about them and so I have been limited in my writing about them.

Then there is Isabella Young, the mysterious "friend" who Henry Peter left an annuity of £400 in his will and instructions that she was to have the use of his plantation and its contents for as long as she chose to live in Barbados. This was another challenging aspect of the story, since she was already married, significantly younger than he was and seemed to have left her husband to come to Barbados and live at Vaucluse. Was theirs a love interest or did he see her as a daughter?

Finally, while the book focuses on Henry Peter Simmons and his life at Vaucluse and beyond, I could not have written it without including the dramatic events of the rebellion of 1816, since the state of the country at that time would have impacted on all the planters, including Henry Peter. Of even more significance is the fact that the rebellion was largely planned at Simmons (aka Harrow/Allens), the plantation owned by the Simmons family and by John Simmons (Henry Peter's brother) at the time. John

Simmons is another interesting character. I could not locate any record of his birth, but he died in 1828 and was said to have been 47. If that is accurate, he would have been born around 1781, but his father, Henry Peter Simmons Sr., died in November 1779. It is possible that he was actually 48 and not 47, in which case he could have been conceived just before his father died. Another source suggests that he was born around 1778 which would make more sense as his brother Philip was born in 1774, Henry Peter in 1776 and their sister Ann (who later died) in 1779.

I must caution my regular readers who know me for writing romance novels that this is not a romance novel. It is about how people deal with oppressive systems which, in this case, is slavery. For the oppressors, it benefits them, and therefore they prefer to maintain the *status quo*; some people are largely unaffected by it, and are therefore somewhat oblivious to the oppression, while those who suffer under it daily are often prepared to give their lives to destroy the system. All these groups are represented in *Vaucluse*.

I hope that this book manages to capture the complexity of the character of Henry Peter Simmons while demonstrating that there is not simply one story of slavery, but that whatever the story, slavery was an oppressive and dehumanising system.

Sincerely
Donna Every

Vaucluse Timeline

1776	May 17 - Birth of Henry Peter Simmons Jr.
1778	Birth of John Simmons - Brother (Estimated)
1779	Birth of Ann Simmons - Sister. (Died in 1782)
1779	November - Death of Henry Peter Simmons Sr.
1784	Birth of Mehetabel Ann Edey (Wife of John Simmons)
1785	Marriage of Ann Simmons (Mother of Henry Peter) to John Allen Olton Sr.
1790	October - Birth of John Allen Olton Jr. (Stepbrother of Henry Peter)
1800	Brother Philip Simmons dies at 26
1801	Birth of Thomas Rolph and wife Frances (Estimated) – he visited Upper Canada with Henry Peter in 1833 and settled there for a time
1801	Estimated birthdate of Molly Harry (mother of Henry Peter's sons)
1804	June 22 - Ann Olton (Henry Peter's mother) dies in England
1805	October 10 - John Simmons marries Mehetabel Ann Edey
1807	Mary Thomas Simmons born to John and Mehetabel

1809	December 23 - Henry Peter Simmons born to John and Mehetabel
1810	Mary Ann Simmons born (Estimated) – coloured daughter of Henry Peter
1810	John Allen Olton Sr. dies and leaves Allens/Harrow Plantation to his son John Allen Jr.
1811	Henry Peter in Parliament representing St. Philip
1812	Isabella Akers (friend from HP's will) baptised (HP would have been 36)
1813	Henry Peter in Parliament representing St. Philip
1813	October 17 – Philip Cadogan Simmons born to John and Mehetabel
1815	Harry Simmons conceived (coloured son of HP) – about Oct (Molly Harry would have been14, Estimated)
1815	Charles Kyd Bishop takes out a small mortgage from Henry Peter Simmons using Reed's Bay as security
1815	John Simmons buys Harrow/Allens from his stepbrother John Allen Olton Jr.
1816	John Simmons buys Four Square Plantation
1816	Henry Peter and John Simmons buy Yorkshire Hall Plantation
1816	John conveys Yorkshire Hall to Henry Peter who changes the name to Vaucluse. Vaucluse has 435 acres and 190 slaves

1816	February 3 – Ad in the *Barbados Mercury* offering a reward for a missing slave who was suspected to be at Vaucluse, formerly known as Yorkshire Hall
1816	Henry Peter Simmons and Philip Cadogan Simmons baptised
1816	April 15- The Great Rebellion (now known as the "Bussa" rebellion)
1816	June 6 - Charles Kyd Bishop dies
1816	Harry Simmons born to Molly Harry – about July (HP 40; Molly 15, Estimated)
1817	May 26 - HP in Liverpool and manumits three slaves – a Mary Joseph, a coloured slave; a Mary Simmons and an Eliza Simmons, two coloured slave girls
1817	May 31 - First Slave Register. Vaucluse's prepared by Henry S. Cummings – Harry Simmons listed as 10 months Vaucluse has 229 slaves
1817	September 25 - Henry Peter and John Allen Olton Jr. buy Dunscombe Plantation
1819	March – HP manumits William Richards (his slave who was said to reside in Liverpool)
1819	June 15 - HP, John and family sail to Bristol, England on the Venus. Arrive July 10
1819	John Alleyne Simmons born to Molly Harry (HP, 43; Molly, 18, Estimated)
1820	March 5 - Henry Peter's coloured sons baptised under the Church of England.

	Vaucluse has 252 slaves. Register prepared by Henry Peter
1820	July 13 - John and Mehetabel Simmons mortgage Four Square Plantation to George Gibbs and Robert Bright of Gibbs, Son & Bright of Bristol. Appeared before Henry Bishop Chief Judge for St. Michael
1822	February 23 - Henry Peter transfers the mortgage of Reed's Bay to Thomas Lee and company
1822	February 26 - John and Mehetabel Simmons add Simmons as security to the mortgage made to George Gibbs and Robert Bright of Bristol for Four Square Plantation. Sealed by Charles Thomas Alleyne acting as attorney for Gibbs and Bright
1824	Alexander Richard Simmons born to John and Mehetabel
1825	Henry Peter takes out a mortgage for £1500 on Vaucluse with Margaret Goodridge as the mortgagor
1826	Molly Harry recorded as dead in Vaucluse's Slave Register – 25 years old. Slave Register at May 22 lists Vaucluse as having 281 slaves. Prepared by William Doyle as manager
1827	February - Henry Morris Simmons, son of Mary Ann Simmons, baptised (Grandson of Henry Peter)
1828	February - John Simmons dies suddenly

1828	August 28 - John Allen Olton Jr. married Mary Anne Sibun in England
1829	Mary Ann Simmons holds slaves Mary and Cubbah Grace (in trust) from a Henry Piggott
1829	Henry Peter gifts Mary Ann Simmons a slave girl Mary Williams (10) in trust for Henry Morris Simmons (a minor)
1830	March - Margaret Goodridge assigns the mortgage over Vaucluse to James Neil and Henry Peter takes out a further charge of £500 and signs an indenture over Vaucluse for one year to James Neil. Vaucluse was then 580 acres with 280 slaves, although only 272 slaves were included in the document as security. 8 slaves (including his two sons) were not listed among the slaves assigned in the mortgage
1831	HP sells 6 acres of land from Vaucluse with dwelling house and buildings to William Doyle, his attorney at the time, for £513
1831	August 11- Great Barbados Hurricane which destroys most of the island
1832	Mary Ann Simmons returns Mary and Cubbah and buys Tibby (18) at a public sale
1832	Caroline Gresham (who becomes the wife of John Alleyne Simmons) born
1832	Slave Register at May 18 – Vaucluse has 285 slaves. Prepared by Henry Peter
1833	Thomas Rolph visits Barbados

1833	April 17 - HP and Thomas Rolph depart Barbados for Canada via the US
1833	May 8 - HP and Thomas Rolph land at Cape May (New Jersey) and travel by land to Philadelphia, arriving on May 10
1833	May 13 - HP and Thomas arrive in New York
1833	HP and Thomas arrive at Ancaster in Upper Canada (date not determined)
1833	November - HP buys 70+ acres in Ancaster with plans to develop and sell small lots
1834	Isabella Akers marries Edward Young in Rochester, Kent
1834	HP gifts a slave girl, Sarah Frances (10), to his daughter Mary Ann Simmons who then owns 3 slaves – Tibby (20), Agnes (1½) and Sarah Frances (10)
1834	Final slave register (March 31) shows that HP emancipated his two sons, John Alleyne and Harry, as well as three other slaves – Henry Wellington (coloured), Margaret Ann (coloured) and Sam Fleming (black) – before emancipation date somewhere between 1832 and 1834. Vaucluse has 295 slaves. Prepared by Joseph Bayley as attorney
1834	August 1 - Emancipation Day. Start of Apprenticeship period
1834	September - Henry Peter begins to sell lots in Ancaster

1835	Henry Peter leases Vaucluse for five years (July 1,1835 – July 1, 1840) to George Hewitt. Vaucluse now 582 acres. All labourers apprenticed except David (servant), Bess Hagar (washer woman), Cam (cook), Sarah (elderly woman), Molly Grace (called Molly Harry in the document - girl aged 8).
1835	June 29 - Henry Peter arrives in New York en route to Canada with a Harriett Simmons (Lady), Mary Rolph (Lady) and David Simmons (Servant)
1835	HP continues to sell lots in the village in Ancaster, donating two of them – one for a school house and one for a library – plus 250 books of literature and history
1839	June 20 - Mary Ann Simmons marries James Baber Esq. in Hellingly, Sussex, England
1841	November 5 - HP makes his will, naming his sons as executors
1843	February19 - Henry Peter Simmons dies at Vaucluse.

Prologue

March 24, 1815
Residence of Henry Peter Simmons
St. Philip, Barbados

Henry Peter Simmons dropped to his bed and pressed a shaking hand to his chest in a futile effort to ease the tightness there. His other hand came up to grip his forehead, trying in vain to still the pounding in his head. Sweat moistened his hand, but he was too weak to even wipe it on the sheet. He gasped for air as his airways constricted, threatening to cut off his breath. A rough cough forced its way from his mouth, clearing the mucus obstructing his throat and giving him a small measure of temporary relief. He could hear himself wheezing with each breath and fought against the panic that was threatening to overcome him.

He opened his mouth to call his housekeeper, Betsy Jane, but he had no strength and his voice refused to cooperate. Frantically, he pushed a jug on the table beside his bed to the floor, hoping that the thud on the wooden floor and the shattering of it would bring help. He did not have long to wait before he heard steps hastening towards his open door and Betsy Jane rushed into the room.

"Master Simmons, what's wrong?" She looked at him worriedly.

"Doctor–," he managed to gasp.

"Yes, sir," she replied, flying back the way she had come.

One part of Henry Peter's mind idly wondered if he would be alive when the doctor came. He had sent one of the slaves for the doctor when he had first begun to feel short of breath earlier. He only hoped that he had been at home and would make haste. Under the hand holding his chest he could feel his heart racing as if it was trying to pump what little air he could take in around his body as fast as it could. Shadows began to darken the corners of his room as the sun started its descent, and he felt as if death itself was skulking in those corners waiting to take his life.

Deep regret that he had not accomplished all that he had wanted to in his life pierced his heart with an almost physical pain. He had spent two terms in the House of Assembly, but what had it accomplished? He had bought and sold several pieces of property, but he had not yet achieved his ambition to own a sizeable plantation, and now he had the means to do so he would not have the opportunity. Would he even live to see his fortieth year? This was his last thought as his eyes drifted shut.

***

The words "Help me sit him up!" together with someone pulling him into a sitting position jerked Henry Peter back to consciousness.

"Get me a coal pot!" the voice commanded again.

"A coal pot, doctor?"

"Yes, as fast as you can and empty the coals out!"

Henry Peter forced open his eyes to find the concerned face of the doctor peering at him.

"What is wrong with me? What are you doing?" he rasped.

"Mr. Simmons, I sat you up to assist with your breathing," the doctor explained patiently. "From the sound of your wheezing I would surmise that you have bronchial asthma."

"Bronchial asthma?" Henry Peter repeated.

"Save your breath. You can talk once I've got it under control. Thankfully, your boy told me you were having trouble breathing so I brought some stramonium and a mixture of mustard oil and camphor which I will massage into your chest."

The doctor pushed up his shirt and began to work the mixture across Henry Peter's chest, matting the hair on it.

"What's that for?" he wheezed.

"It will help to loosen up the phlegm and ease your breathing. I've sent your housekeeper to get a coal pot. I will burn the stramonium in it for you to inhale."

"Will that cure it?" Henry Peter was beginning to feel some relief in his chest as the mixture began to work.

"No. There is no cure for asthma, but there are

medicines you can take to help when you feel an episode coming on."

"No cure?" Henry Peter repeated, appalled.

"But you can live a long life, if you take certain precautions. First of all, if you have feather pillows get rid of them. I would also recommend that you move to an elevated place on the island with plenty of fresh air. Maybe St. Joseph or St. Thomas, if you can, and that you keep medicines handy. Some doctors prescribe opiates to help, but I do not like their addictive properties."

Henry Peter's face looked grave. He had a disease that had no cure? How could this happen to him? He had been healthy all his life. Would this bronchial asthma be the death of him?

Betsy Jane appeared with the coal pot and gave it to the doctor who set it up on the bedside table. He poured some seeds and leaves in the place of the coals, lit them and stirred them until they began to burn and give off smoke which he fanned into Henry Peter's face. Henry Peter breathed in deeply, willing to try anything to restore his breathing to normal. He couldn't afford to die yet; he still had much to do.

Chapter 1

Sunday, October 15, 1815
Simmons Plantation, St. Philip

"John! Mehty! Congratulations! I cannot believe you have been married ten years already." Henry Peter Simmons hugged his sister-in-law and kissed her on the cheek before slapping his younger brother on the back affectionately.

"Thank you, HP," Mehetabel said warmly, taking the gift that he proffered. "And thank you for making the effort to come when you have been feeling so poorly."

"Yes, thank you, brother," John added. "I hope that you are much improved."

"It goes and it comes. The doctor says that it might improve with a change in my living conditions and with the right medicines," he divulged with a grimace.

He hated the episodes that, from a few months ago, gripped him from time to time, stealing his breath and leaving him weak the next day. One had come upon him only last week and had forced him to put off a visit to the Chancery Court with John to sign papers for their purchase of Yorkshire Hall Plantation in St. Thomas. He hoped that the high elevation of the indebted plantation would reduce his attacks.

"I'm glad that there is hope," Mehetabel smiled.

"Then you can focus on joining us in this wonderful state of matrimony," John teased. "You're nearly forty with no sign of a wife. Have you no plans to beget some heirs?"

"I still have plenty of time, God willing. I'm yet in my prime and I believe I have proven that I'm quite capable of siring offspring."

"Yes, well, I'm talking about ones that you can leave your property to, especially since you are about to buy Yorkshire Hall, which is a considerable investment."

"I can always leave my property to you if I die without any heirs."

"All right, gentlemen, no talk of dying tonight please. Let us join the rest of our guests," Mehetabel interrupted, heading to the formal sitting room. "My brother Frere and his wife Elizabeth are here, the Wiltshires from Bayleys, and the Draytons from Yorkshire. I've also invited Rebecca Connell, who is of marriageable age," she reminded him quietly over her shoulder.

Henry Peter scowled as he brought up the rear. Mehetabel never tired of trying to marry him off and

Rebecca Connell was the latest woman she was trying to interest him in. She didn't understand that he was content as he was. The last thing he needed was a woman putting demands on his time and requiring constant attention. Besides, he had no desire to marry only to die early like his father and his brother Philip and leave his wife with a plantation to run. It would only end up in Chancery Court as theirs had. And now with this asthma he was more convinced than before that he should stay clear of the bonds of matrimony.

"Henry Peter is here," Mehetabel announced cheerfully, entering the room.

Henry Peter was greeted politely, if not warmly, by the other planters. He was well-known for speaking his mind with no thought of who he would offend and as such he was treated with reserve by those who knew only of his reputation. However, no one could fault his business acumen and for that he was well-respected. He lifted Rebecca's hand to kiss the smooth skin, showing that he could be quite gallant when he chose to be. She blushed prettily and caught her breath. She was quite attractive with her dark hair and creamy white skin (he could see that she successfully avoided the sun), but he could not honestly say that she aroused any interest in him. Especially since he knew that her father had no substantial holdings.

His eyes scanned the room that had a fresh look to it since he had last visited. John had bought the plantation from their stepbrother, John Allen Olton, earlier that year and it seemed that Mehty had done a few basic improvements since he had visited, rather than replacing all the furniture. Mehty had good taste and was not extravagant in her spending. She also had a good head for business and had partnered with him and John in several land purchases. She was a good balance for John, whom he worried about on occasion in terms of taking on more than he ought to sometimes. He had had to help him out of financial trouble more than once. Yes, John had done well in marrying Mehty. Not only was she good for him, but she came from a reputable family, the Edeys. The Edeys had married into the Frere family, one of the old established families in the island with vast holdings of land.

"Dinner will be served shortly," Mehty announced.

"The slaves are having a little celebration tonight as well," John told them.

"I thought I saw rather a lot of activity by the slave yard when I came in and they were rather dressed up," HP observed. "I don't know how you stand the noise of all that drumming and singing," he grumbled.

"Some of mine are here as well, I believe," John Wiltshire informed them. "They seem to come over quite often."

"I don't understand how you allow your slaves to be all over the island like that," William Drayton interjected. "We don't indulge that kind of thing at Yorkshire. They're likely to be planning a rebellion or something."

"Hardly," John scoffed. "Our people are content. Besides, we haven't had any major trouble on the island in over a hundred years, nor are we likely to."

"I hope you're right," Rebecca shivered dramatically. "I still hear stories about the last rebellion and what they planned to do to the women after they got rid of the men."

"This is not appropriate pre-dinner conversation. Let us eat before we all lose our appetites," instructed Mehetabel. "Philly has probably had the girls working hard all day to prepare our meal, so let us enjoy it and no more talk of rebellion."

***

Slave Yard
Simmons Plantation

The rhythm of the drums coming from the clearing just behind the slave huts set the feet of the men and women dancing with abandon. The jewellery around the necks of the women bounced against their breasts as their bodies jerked in tune with the music while the men's feet kicked in a dance created by the beat. Clapping hands and raised voices provided accompaniment for the drums. They knew that on many plantations this was not allowed, which made their enjoyment all the sweeter.

Behind a nearby tree a group of men gathered together, their voices muffled by the music and the shouts of the dancers. In the shadows, a little way from them, a figure crouched listening.

"James Bowland from River tell me dat' he read in one of dem newspapers from Englan' dat dey stop traders from getting slaves out o' Africa eight years now and dat people over dere saying slavery should be done with all together," John announced.

He was a ranger on the plantation and often roamed the island carrying and bringing messages from slaves on other plantations.

"I hear the master talkin' about somet'ing dey is to vote on in the House of Assembly next month," one of the slaves from Bydemill said. "I t'ink it is somet'ing to do with freein' we."

"Simmons' brother come out of the House last year so he ain' goin' be dere to vote. Not dat he did gine vote to free we. Dem old planters did ownin' slaves too long to change now and de ones dat now comin' up want the same t'ing," Jackey told them authoritatively.

He was the chief driver on the plantation and often arranged for the meetings like this one under the guise of a dance or celebration.

"Dis plantation ain' the wors' and we could come and go as we like, but dem ain' know dat we want to be free to live we own lives like dem?" he continued. "The' t'ink that we want dem to own we forever? Dis island belong to we more than it belong to dem. We is de ones who mek de money for dem to live up in dese big houses all o' dese years."

"The' better vote right next month," Bussa, the chief driver at Bayleys, said. The original accent of his mother country, Africa, was barely noticeable after being captured and brought to the island over twenty years ago. "I don' plan to spen' another crop season with somebody ownin' me. Wunna born here, not me. I could still remember what it like to be free and do as I please. Wake up when I want to, go sleep when I want to, go wherever I want to and plant my own land. I was my own man," he said fiercely. "I got to be free again or the' got to kill me for tryin'!"

There were murmurs of agreement.

Charles Ward listened attentively from his place in the shadows. He was not much of a talker, but he knew how to listen well. As a mason on the plantation, and being hired out sometimes, he heard a lot but kept it to himself. He had been born at Simmons, or Harrow as it was also called, when Henry Peter Senior was alive, and he was the same age as Henry Peter Junior. In fact, he had played with the boys in the yard as a youth. Now that John had taken over the plantation he sometimes hired him out to do mason work and allowed him to keep some of the money he earned. He was saving to buy his freedom, but it seemed like the horizon; something that could never be reached. He wondered how much money information could sell for. Was it easier to buy freedom or to fight for it? He had not decided as yet.

"I gine sen' word by John next month to let wunna know when next we could meet," Jackey told them. "Nanny Grigg say she goin' to listen out to hear what de master and mistress say 'bout the vote next month and I gine sen' word. Or if anybody hear anything firs', sen' a message."

They nodded their assent. Their grave faces were in stark contrast to the exuberant ones of the nearby dancers and drummers who seemed content just to have a few hours of entertainment every few weeks. Did their hearts not burn for the taste of freedom too?

***

Yorkshire Hall Plantation
St. Thomas

Molly Harry finished drying the last plate and tiredly put it in the wooden crate after wrapping it in old newspaper. The mistress had instructed that all her dishes and cutlery were to be washed and packed away into crates. They did not know what was happening, but she seemed to be preparing to clear out the house. The next day they were to start on the sheets and towels, leaving out only what was being used that week.

"Girl, I tired enough," sighed Hannah, one of the cooks, coming into the room.

"Not like me," said Hagar who was a few years older. "I can' wait to see my bed tonight."

"You hear that the plantation gettin' sell?" Hannah asked her. Molly's ears pricked up.

"Who you hear that from?" demanded Hagar.

"Jack hear the lawyer talkin' to the mistress 'bout it in the office when he was outside cleaning the windows. He say he hear that the court sell it out because it owe 'way a lot of money and somebody name' Simmons buy it."

"That must be why she got we washin' and packin' 'way all o' these things."

"What goin' happen to we?" Molly asked, her brown face wrinkling with concern. She was a good-looking girl with smooth brown skin, soft curly dark hair and a voluptuous figure which belied her age.

"We goin' get sell with the land and the house," Hannah said, shaking her head at the thought.

"I hope the Simmons man is a good master," Molly said worriedly. "Mistress Mary Ann is a good woman."

"That is de truth. She try she best since Major Hugh dead these seven years but she ain' know not'ing about runnin' no plantation. Not that he did know much either. It was she father, Master James Straker, that left the plantation for she. Before you born the Major was in the regiment and then he was in charge of the customs. He didn' accustomed to ownin' no plantation," she told Molly Harry with authority.

Molly Harry nodded, but had no idea what "customs" was. She could barely remember the Major as it was.

"You ain' got to worry though," Hannah continued. "You pretty, so you will get through. Unless we get a new mistress and she ain' want you in the house too close to the master. 'Cause you would be out in the field quick so." She snapped her fingers.

"I hope they don't send me out in that hot sun," Molly Harry said. "I been workin' in the house from the time I was small, and I don't know not'ing 'bout field work. And I ain' able for that kind of work."

"Girl, make use of what you got and the new master bound to keep you in the house," Hannah advised her and laughed at her puzzled expression.

"Girl, how old you is though?" Hagar asked.

"I ain' know fo' sure. I think I 'bout fourteen or fifteen."

"Either way, you really ain' know not'ing 'bout men. That is a good t'ing though," Hagar assured her.

"I don' know 'bout that," Hannah disagreed. "If you know, nobody can' take advantage of you."

"When you is a slave you ain' got no advantage at all," Hagar corrected her.

Molly didn't have any idea what they were talking about, but it seemed that her life was about to change in some way.

***

"That was wonderful, Mehty," Henry Peter praised, leaning back in a comfortable armchair and patting his rounded stomach in appreciation of the vast quantities of food he had just consumed. His dark hair contrasted with the pale blue fabric of the chair while he stretched his long legs in front of him onto a matching patterned rug. His chest was beginning to feel a bit tight, but he did not want to concern John and Mehty. It was the blasted asthma. It was a good thing he had got one of his boys to drive him over in the carriage. The other guests had left and he would soon take his leave after he'd had a chance to talk over the purchase with John.

"Yes, the meal was wonderful and it was altogether a pleasant evening, love," agreed John, covering his wife's hand where it lay between them on a love seat.

"Thank you, gentlemen. I know that you are

dying to talk about your latest venture so you may now do so to your heart's content."

"Thank you for your permission, dear," John said drily, teasing her. Henry Peter looked on them tolerantly tonight as it was their anniversary. He was happy that John had made a good match with Mehetabel, for more reasons than one, but sometimes their open admiration of each other could be quite annoying. He really had no desire to marry, so he wasn't sure why it annoyed him at times. Could it be that he was beginning to feel that something was lacking in his life? Surely not.

"I am sorry that the bloody episode kept me from our appointment last week, John."

"Do not be concerned, HP. We can go in and sign this week."

"I sent a message to the attorney at Yorkshire Hall that I want to ride over on Monday morning and have a look around the plantation. I want to see it again before we sign the papers. After all, this is our biggest investment to date."

"*Your* biggest investment, since I'll be conveying my share to you once the transaction is finalised."

"Thank you, brother."

"You have done the same for me on other occasions."

"That is what brothers are for. It's times like these that I think of Philip." Philip, their older brother, had died fifteen years earlier.

"I know what you mean," agreed John nostalgically.

"We will have to meet the obligations of the plantation, but I am convinced that I can turn a tidy profit in spite of that," Henry Peter asserted. "Furthermore —" He was interrupted by Mehetabel clearing her throat not too subtly.

"Are you hinting that it is time for me to leave, Mehty?" Henry Peter teased her.

"Not at all, HP," she denied politely.

"I don't know why I am not convinced," he said drily. "Nevertheless, I shall take my leave. It is, after all, your tenth anniversary and I am sure you will want some time to yourself."

"I will certainly not try to dissuade you, brother," John assured him with a smirk.

"John…" Mehetabel protested weakly, a blush staining her cheeks.

"All right, I will leave you youngsters to enjoy the rest of your anniversary," Henry Peter teased, getting up and taking a minute to catch his breath. "I'll let myself out."

He kissed Mehetabel on the cheek and shook John's hand before heading out to the hallway.

The house was deserted and he could still hear the sounds of the slaves singing and dancing in the slave yard. Why wouldn't they be dancing and singing? They had everything they needed given to them – food, clothing and shelter. They didn't have the responsibility of looking after hundreds of lives and making sure that the plantation produced enough to cover its expenses and make a profit on top of that.

He was looking forward to the challenge of running Yorkshire Hall. It had not done anything to speak of in the last few years, but it had great potential, as the land in St. Thomas was among the best in the island. He would turn it around. And leave it to whom? Maybe he should think about getting married and producing some heirs as John said. After all, he wasn't getting any younger. Next May would see him reach his fortieth year, if he lived. What did he have to show for it apart from a few acres? Well, he had Mary Ann too, but he couldn't leave his property to her; after all, she was only his coloured daughter. At five years old she was a pretty little coloured girl, but he needed some legitimate sons to carry on his name.

Chapter 2

Monday, October 16, 1815

In spite of the time he had gotten into his bed the night before, Henry Peter was up just before the sun, as was his habit. He enjoyed this time of the day when everything was fresh and unspoiled by the noise and activities of people and only the sound of the birds broke the silence. It would take him about two hours to reach Yorkshire Hall on horseback, but he didn't mind. He loved to ride, and he would take his time and enjoy the trek from St. Philip to St. Thomas, cutting across the ravine in St. George to make his way to the plantation.

He felt somewhat better this morning. The crisp morning air always loosened the tightness in his chest and he had not had an episode, thankfully. The

18

doctor had sent back a vile tasting concoction which he said would help him. He preferred not to know what was in it and he did not find that it was very effective anyway. All it did was make him empty his stomach several times and it was that which made him feel better. He hated the feeling of not being able to breathe properly, and he would be glad to get over the annoying illness. If the doctor was right and changing his environment would help him, then living at the plantation in St. Thomas, which was in one of the highest parts of the island, would hopefully improve his health.

The sun was now casting a short shadow in front of him, but the day was yet cool. His horse plodded surefootedly along the path that was overgrown in some areas as the rains had been quite abundant that year. He had been riding for nearly two hours when his eyes saw in the distance the hills that marked Yorkshire Hall. They were covered with lush trees from the darkest green to the palest. As he drew nearer, the verdant soil boasted of its richness by bringing forth an abundance of beautiful flowers, shrubs and bushes. He urged his mount to the top of a gently sloping hill that had been cleared of some of its trees and looked down at the plantation that would soon be his. It gave him a feeling of peace that banished any remaining tightness in his chest. He took a deep breath of the pure, clean air. This spot on the island would be his retreat; somewhere to go out from and come back to. Somewhere that would ease the restlessness in him and hopefully heal him.

Vaucluse – closed valley. The word settled gently into his mind from somewhere outside of himself. He frowned slightly as he sought to remember where he had heard it before. The memory resurfaced in a few minutes, replacing the frown with a reminiscent smile. It was the favourite retreat of the poet, Petrarch, whose story and poems he had read years ago. He tried out the name on his tongue and it felt right. Yes, this would be his retreat, *his* Vaucluse.

***

Yorkshire Hall Plantation House

"I hear that the new owner out there lookin' at the plantation," Mary Ann, one of the cooks, announced coming into the kitchen with a handful of herbs. "The gardener tell me that he see the solicitor, Mr. Cummins, and Mitcham, the driver, showin' he 'round the place."

"I wonder if that is why the mistress clear out this mornin'. She must be ain' want to see somebody lookin' 'round the place to buy it," Hannah reasoned.

"What he look like?" asked Judy Ann, another house slave, ignoring Hannah's observation.

"I ain' know. Wha' you want to know for? All I care 'bout is if he is one of them masters that does beat the slaves for anyt'ing the' do or anyt'ing the' ain' do, or if he is a decent one."

"Girl, I start prayin' for a decent one from last night when I hear that the plantation gettin' sell and I know that God goin' hear me," Hagar chimed in.

They were interrupted by Jack rushing into the kitchen. "The solicitor say he headin' to the house soon. He say to tell everybody to line up 'pon the veranda so that the new massa could see we."

"Oh loss. Molly Harry, run and fin' the rest," instructed Bonny, the oldest slave.

In a few minutes, all the house slaves were lined up on the veranda, from the oldest to the youngest, to meet the man who would own them and the plantation in a few months' time. There were mixed feelings among them as they stood waiting. The older ones were resigned to their fate as they had seen several owners come and go. Judy Ann, a buxom girl, was eager to see if she could catch his eye and increase her status among the slaves by becoming his woman. Molly Harry's stomach was seized with anxiety because of the uncertainty about what a new master would mean. All eyes were downcast as the two men approached, although they cast surreptitious glances across the yard, trying to catch a glimpse of their new master. Soon their feet came into their vision as the men mounted the steps.

"This is Mr. Henry Peter Simmons," announced the attorney without pre-amble. "He is to be the new owner of the plantation. Mr. Simmons, these are the house servants and cooks. Tell Master Simmons your names."

"Bonny, Massa Simmons."

"Hagar, Massa Simmons."

"Hannah, Massa Simmons."

"Nanny Kay, Massa Simmons."

"Jack, Massa Simmons."

"Mary Ann, Massa Simmons."

"Judy Ann, Massa Simmons," she said, raising her eyes boldly to look at him.

"Molly Harry, Massa Simmons." Molly glanced sideways and saw that the eleven-year-old, Mary Reeves, standing next to her was squirming with shyness and seemed to have been rendered speechless.

"Can you speak, girl?" Henry Peter asked her.

"She is Mary Reeves, Massa Simmons," Judy Ann said, drawing his attention to her and giving him a brazen look.

"Very well," Henry Peter acknowledged.

"I am sure they all know their duties and will serve you well," Mr. Cummins ended, emphasising the last part as a warning to the slaves. "The master will also be bringing some of his own slaves to the plantation, so make sure you help them to settle in."

Molly chanced a quick glance from the new master's slightly muddy brown boots to his face, to find that his eyes were on her so she quickly lowered hers. She had enough time to notice that it took a long time to travel from his feet to his face which was only a little reddened by the sun, and that his hair was long and dark. He could not be described as a good-looking man, but he had a face that you could not help but notice and something about him felt powerful. Right now a vexed look crossed his features. What was he vexed about? Had they done something to annoy him already? Did that mean he would be a hard master to please and quick with the whip? She could feel his eyes burning into her and she trembled.

Henry Peter frowned, annoyed with himself. He had come to take an inventory of the plantation and see the condition of the slaves he was buying, not to be distracted by young slave girls, like the one Judy Ann who was obviously sizing him up. The main thing he was interested in right now was how much he was paying the Chancery Court for them.

He knew exactly the measure of Judy Ann and he had no plans to encourage her. That was not his nature anyway, at least not to the extent of some of the other planters he knew. The other one, Molly Harry, was quiet and submissive, the way a slave should be. If he felt inclined to seek physical release, he would more likely choose her. She didn't look like she would make any demands on him.

"Molly Harry is it?"

Molly Harry's heart lurched and her eyes flew up in distress to meet his for the second time. What had she done? She searched her mind frantically but could think of nothing.

Henry Peter could see the fear in her widened eyes as they encountered his. She looked like an animal when it knew it had been seen by its predator and was paralysed by fear, but she had no cause to fear him. He was not a harsh master. After all, he was well schooled in the methods of Henry Drax and he knew how best to get the most out of his slaves. It was the uneducated brutes that some used as managers who foolishly misused their slaves.

"Yes, Massa Simmons?" she answered tremulously.

"Come and show me around the house, girl. Thank you, Mr. Cummins. I've seen all that I need to see today."

***

Molly separated herself from the others and silently led him inside on shaking legs.

The other slaves just as silently filed out to the kitchen when they were dismissed. Hagar's eyes were drawn to the retreating figures of Molly and the new master as she led him towards the room that housed the office and library that was situated near the back of the house. She sent up a silent prayer for Molly Harry that Master Simmons would not take advantage of her.

"How come he ask Molly Harry to show he 'round the house?" asked Mary Reeves innocently once they were outside.

"You only now talkin'?" taunted Judy Ann, taking out her jealousy on her.

"Because she does work in the house," Hannah answered, cutting her eye at Judy Ann.

"But all of we does work in here," she reasoned.

"I woulda show he the house and anyt'ing else he want to see," Judy Ann claimed boldly.

"Girl, hush you' mout'. You ain' glad that Hanibal want to marry you? He does be eyein' you every time he in the yard."

"Wha' I want wid a field slave? He can' give me no coloured children or not'ing," she scoffed, making Hannah shake her head in disgust.

"That is why the massa ain' ask you to show he the house. He must be look at you and done size you up. Molly Harry is a sweet girl. I only hope that he is a decent man and don' try to tek advantage of she when she showin' he the place."

"Any of them decent?" scoffed Mary Ann. "Once we belong to them the' feel that they could do as the' like to we."

"Well, Molly Harry ain' belong to he yet," Hagar said hopefully.

"You t'ink that would stop he?" Mary Ann sucked her teeth.

"Lord, have mercy," Hagar implored the Almighty.

***

Molly was very aware of Master Simmons walking behind her down the corridor. She took a shaky breath and opened the door to the office, stepping back to allow him to enter the room. Henry Peter gazed around the room with satisfaction. It was a good size, with a large desk to one end and a sitting area at the other. Bookshelves stood empty, ready to receive his considerable collection of books. A window behind the desk and two others along the wall filled the room with light, making it a good place to work or to read during the day. He could see himself spending many hours in here, lost in his books or writing, something that he enjoyed.

It was a good thing that the girl brought him here first instead of wasting his time looking at the living room or the dining room, although he would look at them as well. Mary Ann Dalrymple would be taking most of the furnishings with her, so he would have to replace them with his, but it looked like he would have to acquire some more. Maybe he would get Mehetabel to help him as he really had no inclination to go shopping for furniture. He supposed that is where a wife would have been useful.

He turned back towards the door where Molly was waiting patiently with her head bent. She stepped back as he approached to give him room to pass.

"You may as well show me the living room and dining room now and any other rooms down here."

"Yes, massa."

The plantation house was a good size and he soon realised that he would have to spend some money to furnish it as it deserved. He'd also seen some areas that would need a bit of maintenance, as there had obviously been no extra money for the Dalrymples to keep up the place. He was so excited at the challenge of turning the plantation around that he belatedly realised he had not once felt any tightness in his chest since he'd been there. That was surely a sign that Vaucluse was good for him and would be the place he would settle down.

"Has your mistress moved out her things from the upstairs rooms yet?"

"No, massa. I think she say that she would do that by the end of the week."

"In that case, I will come back on Saturday and see the rest of the house. You can show me the bedrooms then."

"Yes, massa." Molly Harry chanced a quick glance at him, but he was already moving to the door. She was relieved that he seemed happy with what she had shown him and she felt as if she had passed her first test with the new master.

***

"Molly girl, you alright?" Hagar asked when she joined them in the kitchen.

"Why she wouldn' be alright? She didn' gone long enough for not'ing to happen," Judy Ann said, sounding pleased.

"Yes, I alright. I only showed the massa downstairs. He said that since the mistress t'ings still upstairs he would come back Saturday and see the rest when she move out."

"I glad to hear that," she said.

"Wha' you glad to hear? That only mean that she get 'way today but mark my words, she ain' goin' be so lucky when he come back," Mary Ann prophesied.

"Why you does got to be so though?" Hagar asked her, annoyed. She could see Molly Harry beginning to look worried.

"Wha' you mean, Mary Ann?" asked Molly Harry in an anxious voice.

"Sorry if I frightenin' you, Molly Harry, but I talkin' from wha' happen to me. It is only since I did here that I ain' had no trouble with the massas or the overseers. You lucky that you born here because it ain' so bad, but I live' at two of the wors' plantations in the island. The stories I could tell you would mek you cry."

"Well, don' worry with none of them now," advised Hagar warningly.

Molly was not foolish. She knew what went on between men and women and she had heard about how some masters and overseers lay with the women slaves, even if the women had husbands or a man that they lived with. But she did not think that the new master was that way. He looked too decent. But then again you couldn't always go by looks. She hoped he wasn't looking for nothing like that from her, but if he was to demand it, there was nothing she could do to stop him. She belonged to him. He was paying money for her like he was paying money for the horses and cattle on the plantation, so he could do what he liked with her.

"I ain' frighten," Molly assured her. "Massa Simmons ain' seem like that kind of man to me. I don' t'ink he interested in that kind of t'ing." She said it to assure herself as much as to assure them.

Mary Ann cackled and even Hagar had to smile at Molly's innocence.

"Girl, I never meet a man who didn' interested in that kind of t'ing. I sure he ain' no different. You mark my words."

Chapter 3

Simmons Plantation

"So, how did the trip to Yorkshire Hall go?" John asked Henry Peter once he had settled down in an armchair with a glass of brandy.

"Good. I saw a good portion of the slaves and they look to be fairly well cared for, all things considered. There are more women than men and a lot of children, so I'll be good for labour for several years," Henry Peter told him.

"Sounds good. What state of repair are the house and outbuildings in?"

"They are not the worst but will need maintenance. I only saw some of the rooms inside the house, but I will see the rest once Mary Ann Dalrymple moves out. I did not think it appropriate to be going through her bedrooms with her personal things still there." John nodded in agreement, taking a sip of his brandy.

"You seem keen to sign the papers and get your hands on the plantation," John teased.

"I certainly am," Henry Peter smiled. "There is something about it that draws me. The air is fresh and pure, and the land is covered with the most abundant foliage. My lungs feel practically healed already just from being there."

"Now, *that* I am glad to hear."

"In fact, I have decided to change the name from Yorkshire Hall to Vaucluse," Henry Peter announced.

"Vaucluse? That's a far cry from Yorkshire Hall. Where did that come from? It doesn't even sound English."

Henry Peter chuckled. John was never the scholar and hated to read unless it was something that interested him, like business. He, on the other hand, read all kinds of books, journals and pamphlets. He firmly believed that knowledge gave power.

"You are right there. It is not. Vaucluse is a place in France. It is where the poet Petrarch built his retreat in the fourteenth century."

"Oh, that would account for me never having heard about it. I have never even heard of this Petrarch fellow. Vaucluse," he repeated. "I like it," he announced at last.

"Glad to hear that. Not that you have any say in the matter. Once you convey your share to me you are free to go and buy whatever else takes your fancy."

"To tell the truth, I have my eyes on Four Square Plantation, but I am rather concerned about the

Imperial Registry Bill that they're voting on in the House of Assembly next month. It has already been passed in England and I hope that our parliamentarians aren't pressured into passing it here. Don't know why you did not run for another term. We could certainly use your vote to make sure that it doesn't pass."

"I'm not concerned; we have enough people who are of the same mind as us concerning this bill. The politicians in England are under pressure from the abolitionists so they want to appease them by trying to make us register all our slaves."

"What will registering them prove?"

"If we're forced to register them, they can see if we are somehow violating the Abolition law by buying new slaves or see if an inordinate amount of our slaves are dying because of ill treatment. While some of the islands are suffering because of the end of the slave trade, we will be all right. We have enough that we don't need to bring in new slaves from Africa or anywhere else because ours are breeding and replenishing our stocks very well. All we need to do is make sure that they are in good health and able to reproduce."

"I just hate the idea that they want to control what we do here! We've been successfully lining the pockets of the motherland very well for almost two hundred years and now this weak lot of politicians are letting the masses pressure them into changing the status quo. I pray that I am not alive to see slaves emancipated in Barbados. That would be the end of life as we know it in the island."

"I do concur with you there. If we do not have access to the labour of the slaves without having to pay them how are we to make a profit from our plantations? As it is, having to spend money to clothe and feed them certainly eats into the profits, as you would know. We know first-hand what it is to have to go to the Chancery Court and our family is only one of many. I, for one, never intend to lose Vaucluse to the Chancery."

"We've all suffered because of the poor economy and the debt that has resulted from it. It is a shame how many plantations have been handed over to the Chancery. Still, it has worked in our favour with Yorkshire Hall... I mean Vaucluse," John amended.

"Yes, indeed. The fact that we're managing to get it for nearly six thousand pounds less than what it's worth makes me a very happy man," HP said with satisfaction.

John chuckled in agreement.

"Me as well. But as I said before, HP, who will you leave it to? Or are you planning to sell in a few years? My Henry Peter and Philip may inherit it if you don't do something soon."

"As long as they have good business minds it would be in capable hands, so I am not concerned," HP assured him.

"You just need the right woman to make you an honest man and give you some heirs."

"I am an honest man and if I haven't met the right woman by now I probably never will. Anyway, do you want to accompany me to Vaucluse on Saturday?"

"I would love to, but some of Mehty's relatives are coming to pay us a visit. They want to see the children."

"Wonderful," HP said sarcastically. "This is

exactly what I'm trying to avoid. Family duties getting in the way of business."

"I am sure that you don't need me there anyway."

"That is true. I am getting one of the girls to show me around and I will also take the opportunity to see some more of the plantation. No point in me riding all that way just to see the house."

"You have your eyes on one of the girls already?" John asked, surprised. He was not one to associate with his slave women, but it was common knowledge that a lot of planters did, even Henry Peter had sired a daughter through one of them.

"Not really, although one should be able to fully appreciate one's assets," Henry Peter said. "After all, that is the whole point of having them. Is it not?"

***

Yorkshire Hall Plantation

Henry Peter pulled on the reins of his horse at the top of the same gentle hill and surveyed the land that would soon be his. In the few visits he had made, the sight of the verdant land had not failed to cause his heart to lift and his chest to ease as he breathed in the clean air. In the distance he could see the slaves working in the fields, planting canes in one field and something else, root crops of some sort, in another field with the drivers hovering close by with their whips handy. What he could see from that vantage point was only a fraction of the four hundred and thirty-five acres he was acquiring. Rather than feeling any anxiety at the thought of the amount of money he was putting into the purchase of the plantation, excitement caused his heart to accelerate. He was finally about to own a sizeable plantation and join the major land owners in Barbados. He turned the horse and headed towards the plantation house.

His eyes moved over the house and outbuildings, assessing what needed to be done and working out in his head how much money he was likely to have to spend to bring them to a better condition. The girl that had been too shy to speak when the slaves had introduced themselves looked up at his approach and ran into the house, dropping the broom that she had been using to sweep off the veranda. No doubt she was going to announce his presence. He should probably let the manager know that he was here. He would get one of the slaves to seek him out after he looked around the house.

As he dismounted and tied his horse to the hand rail, one of the older slaves he had seen earlier that week waddled out of the door to greet him. If her size was any indication, food was not a problem on the plantation; at least not for the house slaves. Her name escaped him, but then there had been about ten of them telling him their names that day. He would soon get to know them when he took up residence in a few months. There was one that he remembered though: Molly Harry, the one who had shown him around the house.

It wasn't that she was the prettiest of the ones he had seen, or even the most endowed, as many of these slave women seemed to be, but there was something about her that drew him to her. She seemed uncomplicated and would not disturb his peace. If he decided to lie with any of the women on the plantation, it would probably be her.

"Good mornin', Massa Simmons," the woman greeted him.

"I've come to look over the rest of the house. Has Mistress Dalrymple moved out all her belongings?"

"Yes, massa."

"Good. Now where is that girl Molly Harry? She is to show me around," he told her, heading for the door as if he owned the place already.

"She comin', massa. I sen' Mary Reeves to fin' her."

"Good. I don't have all day. I want to see some of the fields as well before the sun gets too hot."

"Yes, massa," she said, looking anxiously towards the staircase.

Molly Harry appeared as if the old slave had mentally willed her there. Her hair was covered with a handkerchief as it had been the other day and she wore a dress that may have been a dark blue when she first got it but was now faded. It stretched tightly across her bosom and her ankles and bare feet peeped out from beneath the hem as if she had grown since she got it. She hurried down the stairs towards them, her eyes intent on looking anywhere but at him.

"Good mornin', Master Simmons," she greeted breathlessly, as if she had been running.

"Mornin', Molly Harry. I'm ready to see the rest of the house."

Molly Harry glanced up at him in surprise. He had remembered her name. Henry Peter smiled slightly at her look of surprise. She wasn't the only one surprised, although for much different reasons. The quick response of his body at the sight of her surprised him too. It had obviously been too long since he'd been with a woman. He hadn't planned on trying out his assets today, but he had come to see exactly what he was paying for, after all.

"Lead the way," he invited with a gesture.

Molly Harry looked somewhat uncertainly at the older slave who nodded slightly before she turned to lead him up the stairs.

"No one is to come upstairs while I am looking around," Henry Peter instructed the old slave over his shoulder.

"Yes, massa," Bonny replied resignedly, throwing a quick sympathetic glance at Molly Harry. She did not know if Molly Harry understood what that meant.

"How many rooms are up here?" their new master asked nonchalantly, as if he had not just made an announcement that would impact Molly Harry's life forever.

"Four, Massa Simmons." Molly Harry had heard from John, who heard him telling the attorney, that he was not married so she wondered what he would do with all those rooms.

"And there is a master bedroom, of course?"

"Yes, massa."

"Good, that is the only one I really wish to see today."

Molly did not understand why he would come all the way to the plantation to see just one room, but he was the new master. He could do whatever he liked.

Molly turned right at the top of the stairs and hastened to a door at the far end of the hallway and opened it, stepping back to let him pass. She had just finished cleaning it when Mary Reeves came to tell her that the master was there. The bed was stripped bare since the mistress had taken all her linens.

Henry Peter surveyed the room with pleasure. He approached the window that overlooked the front of the house and was greeted with a wonderful view of the driveway bordered by flowers and shrubs that the gardener was tending. There was another window overlooking the south side of the plantation. He turned and surveyed the large four poster bed that was now bare of all its linens. The room was otherwise empty, but he would bring his own furniture to finish the room.

"Come in and close the door, Molly Harry," he instructed. "I won't bite." Molly obeyed but stayed near the door.

"Have you lived on the plantation long?" he asked.

"I born here, massa."

"You have family here?"

"No, my mother dead when I was small and I don't have no other family that I know about." Molly Harry wondered why he was asking her these questions. Masters, as far as she knew, did not take any interest in their slaves.

"Tell me, Molly Harry, have you ever been with a man?"

"Been with a man, massa?" she asked, puzzled at the change in his questions.

"Lain with a man," he explained, more patiently than was his custom.

"No, Massa Simmons," she replied with a slight tremor in her voice, knowing where his question was leading.

"Good. After today see that you don't lie with anyone else. You will be for my exclusive use.

Understand?"

"Yes, massa," Molly Harry agreed quietly, although she was not sure what exclusive meant.

"Come over here. I have a sudden desire to sample one of the assets I'm acquiring with Vaucluse. Remove that awful dress and let me see what you look like without that handkerchief covering your hair."

***

Molly Harry sat under a tree on a little hill behind the house. She had come out there to get away from the searching eyes of the older house slaves and the cut eyes she was getting from Judy Ann. Although she had not been upstairs with Master Simmons very long, Bonny would have told them that he had said nobody was to come upstairs while he looked around and they all knew what that meant. After they had dressed he had gone downstairs, gotten on his horse and rode off, she assumed to see the rest of the fields as he had planned to.

She was still in disbelief that the master had lain with her and in broad daylight at that; he had not even waited until night time. She had not taken what Mary Ann and Hannah had said to heart. She had not thought he was interested in that kind of thing, especially with her. After all, Judy Ann was much prettier and filled out her dresses more than she did, but for some reason the master had chosen to lie with her. There had not even been any sheet on the bed, but he had not seemed to care. She could not say that he was rough with her and she had not felt much pain when he had finally joined his body to hers after touching her in all kinds of places that no one had ever touched. Revulsion came over her as she remembered the feel of his body pressing hers to the mattress and the sounds that he had made towards the end. It made her want to empty her stomach of what she had eaten early that morning.

Uncharacteristic anger took its place at the thought that the master could do with her whatever he liked. Hannah was right. They were just like the house and land that he had bought. She was no more than the desk he would write on in the office or the bed that they had just lain in. He could order her to lie with him and she was expected to obey. She did not know his ways well enough to know what would happen if she refused and she did not want to find out. Not that she would refuse. She was not to lie with anyone else either. Not that she was interested in doing so, for it had not been something she enjoyed. Thankfully, it was over fairly quickly and only the stain on the cloth that she had used to wash afterwards and the shame on her face told the tale of what had happened.

What had made him single her out of all the slaves on the plantation? Should she be happy about that? Judy Ann would have been, but instead she was ashamed. She had tried not to meet the eyes of Hagar and the others when she came downstairs. She felt as if she had done something wrong. It was true that she had not tried to stop him, but neither had she encouraged him. She wondered if he would want to lay with her all the time. It seemed so, because he had told her not to let any other man touch her. Was she special somehow? If so, she was sorry.

A sudden thought dropped into her mind, chasing

away all the others. Suppose the master got her with child? She wondered if it was possible to get pregnant from lying with a man just once. Would the massa be vexed if she was, even though it would not be her fault? After all, she had not asked him to lie with her; she had not even looked at him the way Judy Ann did. She laid her hand over her flat stomach as if it held a secret it would tell her. If a child had taken root there it would be a few weeks before she would know. She hoped not. Or maybe it would be a good thing, if it stopped the massa from lying with her.

She stood up to go back to the house and the coins he had given her jingled in her pocket. They were five coins. She had never had that much money in her whole life! She would save it to buy some cloth from the market to make a new dress. She wondered if he was the kind of master to let his slaves go to the market. She hoped so.

Chapter 4

Saturday, January 27, 1816
Vaucluse Plantation

Henry Peter put down the *Barbados Mercury* newspaper he had been trying to read since it was failing to hold his attention or take his mind from the fact that he could feel an episode coming upon him. He had moved into Vaucluse that week and although he did not have to physically move his belongings himself, he had spent several days going through the books and papers in his office and instructing his housekeeper which ones he wanted to pack and which she could throw away. The dust had not done him any good.

Roaming the cane fields of the plantation under a blistering sun that made it feel more like July or

August than January just made it worse. The wind brought some relief and caused the cane arrows from the mature canes to wave a welcome to him but riding through them had been foolish. The doctor had warned him that the arrows might be one of the triggers for his episodes, so he should not have gone near the mature canes. What was he to do? Canes were a part of his life; a major part. He was a stubborn fool, determined not to live by avoiding everything that might or might not affect him. But now he would pay for it.

He took long, deep breaths, trying to remain calm. He hated the feeling of helplessness that came upon him with these episodes. The last set of medicine the doctor gave him had not helped much and he had wheezed through the night after taking it, not knowing if each breath would be his last. He had been weak and drained the next day. Philip had died very early, four years short of his thirtieth year. Was he to be next? Would he even live to see his fortieth birthday in four months' time?

Standing, he pressed his hand firmly to his chest, as if the pressure would ease the tightness, and tiredly walked inside, pausing at the bottom of the stairs to catch his breath before he attempted to mount them. He sensed a presence at his side and turned in annoyance to see who it was. He did not like anyone to see him in his weakness.

"Massa Simmons, you feelin' alright?" It was Molly Harry, looking very concerned.

Some of his annoyance faded, but he didn't want to admit to his weakness. "I'm fine, Molly Harry. I think the cane arrows have affected me a little. I'm going to lie down."

"Yes, massa," she said quietly and turned away towards the back of the house, as if she knew he would not want her to witness him dragging himself up the stairs.

The hallway seemed a lot longer than the first day he had walked it and he was relieved when he opened the door to the master bedroom, stumbled across to the bed and practically collapsed on it. Crisp white sheets covered the bed, unlike the day when he had made Molly Harry his on the bare mattress. She had neither rejected nor accepted him; she had allowed him to do what he wanted.

He had not even touched her since he moved to the plantation. Not that he had not wanted to, but he had been too tired from spending days on horseback visiting the vast holdings with the overseers and inspecting the outbuildings and the workshops to observe the work of the masons and carpenters. Now this confounding illness was coming upon him and rendering him incapable of lying with her. Perhaps it would not be a bad way to depart the earth, he thought wryly.

A quiet knock at the door several minutes later surprised him as he could not imagine who would intrude upon his privacy.

"Who is it?" he asked brusquely, and then had to catch his breath.

"Molly Harry," came a soft voice through panels of wood.

"Come in." He softened his voice marginally.

The door opened quietly and she stooped down and picked up a small pot with a cover over it before coming in and pushing the door shut with her foot.

"What's that?" He looked curiously as she set

down the pot on the side table and lit a lamp.

"It is somet'ing to help with your breathin'."

"What makes you think I need help with my breathing?" He knew he sounded defensive even as the words left his mouth. However, his breathless voice made a liar of him.

"You looked so to me. Sorry if I wrong."

"What is it?" he asked, not admitting anything. "And how do you know that it helps?"

"It is something that one of the nurses used to make for the mistress' son. The cane arrows used to make he sick too. It have in leaves and seeds from a plant that you does get from some other country. You does burn them and breathe in the smoke.

Henry Peter wondered if it was the same thing the doctor had used on him. He hoped so. If it didn't kill him it might make him feel better. Anything to loosen this tightness in his chest which was causing him to gasp for breath as it grew worse.

He sat up and Molly Harry placed a pillow on his lap, put the hot pot with the burning leaves on it and removed the lid so that the smoke could escape. She stood quietly next to the bed and waited on him.

"Sit down, Molly Harry. I feel like you're hovering over me," he complained fretfully.

Henry Peter obediently breathed in the smoke and after a few minutes he could feel his chest easing. He took deeper breaths, hoping to hasten the process, but that made him cough. Molly disappeared and soon re-appeared with half a glass of water which he sipped gratefully and handed back without a word. By the time the mixture had burnt out his chest was looser, but he felt exhausted.

"I'm done," he announced.

Molly Harry took the pot from him and placed it on the floor before propping the warm pillow behind him as he leaned against the bed head. Henry Peter sank back against the pillow gratefully and felt the warmth from it soothe his back. Molly silently took off his boots and socks and turned back to take the pot. She knew he would be more comfortable without his work clothes on, but she was not bold enough to offer to take them off.

"Thank you, Molly Harry," he said drowsily. "That helped me a lot."

"I glad, massa," she said shyly and quietly slipped out of the door.

Henry Peter felt sleep closing in on him, but he welcomed it without the fear that he would not awaken because his breathing was a lot easier than it had been earlier, thanks to Molly Harry. She was a good girl. He had chosen well.

***

Molly Harry woke with the sun the next day. She rose quickly and washed before dressing for the day. She was glad that the sickness she had felt in the morning for the last few months had now passed. What she feared had been confirmed a few weeks after Master Henry had lain with her. She didn't know how to tell him so she kept it to herself, although only yesterday Hannah had asked her when she would tell him. Anyway, he had not moved in long so she had not had much opportunity to speak with him. The night before he had not felt good so she had not wanted to tell him anything then.

The master was usually up early and her habit was

to wait until he appeared at the table before she brought his breakfast so that it would be hot. She did not know if it was his usual custom to be up so early or if it was because he had been going to bed nearly as soon as he came in from the fields every day. He had not called for her to come to his room since he moved in and she wondered if he was no longer interested in lying with her. To tell the truth, she was glad, although that might mean she would not get any more coins to spend at the market.

She was surprised that he was not at the table yet and wondered if he was still feeling sick, or worse. Suppose he had gotten worse during the night? Suppose the mixture she had given him to breathe in did not agree with him after all? He had seemed a lot better when she left him. She glanced up the stairs, undecided about what to do. Should she dare go to his room? Straightening her shoulders, she gathered her courage and mounted the stairs.

Stopping outside the door, she listened for noises on the other side, anything to suggest that he was awake. She heard nothing. She knocked quietly and waited for a few moments. Nothing. She knocked a bit louder and still nothing. In her distress, she pushed open the door and stopped abruptly as she saw the master, on his side, still dressed in his clothes. She watched him carefully to see if he was breathing and let out a breath that she did not even realise she was holding when she saw that his side was moving up and down.

Tiptoeing from the room, she closed the door quietly and went down to prepare some warm water for him to wash with and to put his breakfast on a tray. She wasn't sure if he would welcome her waking him up or if she should just leave him to sleep.

Half hour later, accompanied by Judy Ann who volunteered to carry up the warm water, she took up his breakfast on a tray. This time her tentative knock was answered by a gruff command to come in. The master was awake and was propped up against the back of the bed. Although he seemed to have slept all night, he still looked tired and irritable.

"Good mornin', Massa Simmons," Molly Harry greeted him quietly.

"Good mornin', Massa Simmons," Judy Ann parroted, swaying her hips as she took the pitcher of water to the wash stand.

"What's this?" he asked grumpily, gesturing to the tray that Molly Harry put down on a side table.

"Your breakfast, massa. Since you didn' come down I thought you might still be feelin' —"

"Enough, Molly Harry," he cut her off abruptly, casting a warning glance at Judy Ann, not wanting her to carry back tales to the other slaves. Molly hung her head in shame, heading for the door. Judy Ann followed with a smirk on her face.

"You stay, Molly Harry," he softened his tone slightly. "You go," he ordered Judy Ann gruffly and gestured for her to leave. She flounced past Molly Harry and closed the door with a bang.

Henry Peter frowned at the noise, swung his legs over the side of the bed and ran a hand across the stubble on his chin. He seemed to have to make an effort to get up, cross over to the wash stand and pour water into the basin to wash his face. Molly thought that she saw his hand shake a bit with the effort to lift the pitcher, but she knew better than to offer help. She waited awkwardly, not sure what she should do.

After washing quickly, he stumbled back to the bed and lay back against the pillows. Molly hovered uncertainly, waiting for further instructions.

"Bring the tray, Molly. I will try to eat since you have gone to the trouble of preparing it."

"You not feelin' no better, massa?"

"My breathing is easier today, but these episodes leave me tired. I don't want any talk of this with the house servants," he added sternly. "You understand?"

"Yes, Massa Simmons." Molly wondered if this was a good time to tell the master about the baby he had put in her belly. She was not sure how he would react.

Henry Peter took a sip of his tea, which he soon discovered was peppermint rather than the black tea he usually drank. He grimaced.

"What is this, Molly Harry? Where is my regular tea?"

"Sorry, Massa Simmons, but I thought this would make you feel better. I could go and brew some of the one you like," she said, hurrying to the door.

"Don't bother," his voice stopped her. She turned back, avoiding looking at him while she fidgeted with her new skirt.

"What is the matter, Molly Harry? You have something you want to say? Well, out with it."

"Massa Henry…I expectin'," she confessed quickly before she lost her courage.

"Expecting?" Henry Peter's eyes flew to her belly. That was the last thing he was expecting to hear. He could see no difference as the full skirt concealed any swelling.

"Yes, massa," she confirmed, waiting fearfully for

his reaction.

"Well, that is good news, Molly Harry. And after only that one time? I still have it!" he chuckled.

Molly didn't know what it was that he still had, but she let out her breath when she saw that he was not upset.

"It's a little sooner than I would have liked, but there are still several months before you are due, from the looks of things." He paused and then asked: "Are you sure it's mine?"

"Yes, Massa Simmons. You told me not to let anybody else touch me," she said in an offended tone. Henry Peter smiled slightly at her tone. At least she had a little spunk in her. He was beginning to wonder.

"Good. Maybe it will be a boy this time."

This time? Molly wondered. What did he mean by that?

Chapter 5

Barbados Mercury
Saturday, February 3, 1816

    A Reward of £10 will be given for apprehending and lodging in the cage or delivering to the subscriber, a yellow skinned woman named Sally - she is about 5 feet and 6 inches high, pitted in the face with small pox, has bad fore teeth, the first joint of her right forefinger is injured and she is from 45 to 50 years of age; she is a good washerwoman and is likely to be employed in that capacity; is well-known at the Castle, about Polgreen Land, the King's House and Collymore Rock. She is likely harboured at the estate of HP Simmons called Vaucluse, formerly Yorkshire Hall, where she has connections. All persons are forbid harbouring her and masters of vessels taking her off the island. A further reward of £10 will be given to any person or persons who will convict any white or free coloured person of having harboured her. J. Manning

Henry Peter threw down the newspaper in disgust. How dare this Manning person publish such an outrageous accusation without even coming to speak to him? He was sure that no slave was being harboured at Vaucluse. Surely, one of the overseers would know or they would hear talk from the slaves. She should be easy to spot since, to his knowledge, none of his slaves were pockmarked from small pox. And imagine offering a reward to anyone who would convict any white person (him included, it would seem) for harbouring her. As if he would condone such a thing.

The *Mercury*, of late, seemed inordinately full of notices of slaves missing from their owners. He'd seen several notices for one negro slave named Primus who seemed to have been missing for quite some time. Now in today's paper, Sarah Pinheiro was missing three of hers and Mary Picket two. There was obviously a reason why their slaves were running away, including this Sally woman. Perhaps that injured forefinger had something to do with it. He wouldn't be surprised if her master had broken it himself. Thank God that none of his had run away, at least not in the two weeks since he had moved in.

To think that he was having a perfectly splendid day up to that point. He had gone to a cockfight at Agard's house that afternoon and won a good pocketful with the cock he'd bought. The black and red bird had been undefeated until the last match when tiredness had probably caused his defeat, but not before he had filled his pockets nicely. And now this! He wondered if there was any truth to Manning's claims. After all, he had nearly two hundred slaves. It would be easy for one to hide out among them. Pushing himself to his feet, he crossed to the door, opened it and shouted: "Molly Harry!"

Before he had settled back in his chair properly Molly Harry appeared through the open door. She always stayed near when he was in the house in case he needed anything.

"Yes, Massa Henry."

"Molly Harry, do you know of any slave named Sally who could be hiding out here on the plantation?"

"Sally, massa?"

"Yes, Molly Harry. Sally." Why did he get the feeling that she was stalling? The fact that she did not meet his gaze was no clue, for she seldom did so anyway. To tell the truth, he had not been there long enough to know all his slaves or even to see all and he had several hundred acres, so he couldn't say for certain that the woman Sally was not on the plantation somewhere. That was quite annoying. It was not that he thought Manning would dare to charge him, but he did not want his plantation being known for harbouring other people's slaves. That could lead to poor relations with other estates rather quickly.

"You have not answered me, Molly Harry," he continued in a harder tone after receiving no response.

"I…I see a strange woman when I went to hang out you' clothes this mornin', massa. I don' know who she was and she run when I call she. I don' know if she is the Sally you mean." She glanced at him quickly to see if he believed her.

Henry Peter levelled a stare at Molly Harry and

saw her visibly squirm under his scrutiny. She was obviously not telling him the whole truth. Was she protecting someone?

"There is an advertisement in the newspaper for a runaway slave named Sally who has marks in her face from small pox. Her owner believes that she is being harboured here at Vaucluse because she has connections here. If any white or coloured person is found harbouring her they will be charged. Do you understand what that means?"

"Y-yes, massa," her voice quivered.

"That is nothing compared to what I will do to anyone that *I* find harbouring her," he threatened angrily. Molly Harry did not answer, but he could see her trembling slightly. If that was any indication of her guilt, she obviously knew something.

"Send someone to find one of the overseers and tell them that I want all the men and women assembled in the yard when they come in. I will get to the bottom of this."

"Yes, massa." She disappeared as quickly as she had come in.

***

Molly Harry rushed into the kitchen out of breath.

"Wha' happen with you, Molly?" Hannah asked concernedly.

"I just come from sendin' one of the boys to carry a message to Thorpe. The massa want to talk to all o' we when the rest come in this evenin'."

"Oh loss, 'bout wha'?" she asked cautiously.

"I t'ink it 'bout the woman that in Judy Ann hut," she whispered, looking around fearfully.

"Tha' is she mudda. She run from she master because he brek she finger for washin' for other people. You could believe that? And he still expect she to wash fo' he with the brek finger!" She shook her head in dismay.

"The massa say that the newspaper got in somet'ing 'bout she and say that if anybody hidin' she they goin' get charge'. He real vex! I had to tell he that I see she in the yard, but I ain' tell he nothin' 'bout Judy Ann."

"Lord, have mercy! The' gine be trouble 'bout here today."

"Wha' to do?" Molly Harry asked fearfully.

Before she had a chance to reply, Thorpe's voice could be heard shouting at the slaves to gather around.

"Molly Harry!" The master shouted from the back door. "Find the house slaves and tell them to join the other slaves in the yard."

"Yes, massa," she replied, poking her head through the door before moving to obey on shaking legs.

"I gine help you," offered Hannah. "I gine find Judy Ann and tell she to get rid of she mother from 'bout here before she get fin' out. Tha' girl is get me vex, but I still wouldn want to see not'ing happen to she."

Minutes later Molly Harry and the other house slaves stood on the fringes of the gathering watching Master Henry as he stood on the veranda looking out at his slaves. He seemed to be inspecting each one, particularly the women, as if he was either trying to identify the one who was believed to be hiding at Vaucluse, or maybe to see if anyone looked guilty.

The silence in the yard was evidence that the slaves knew something serious had happened. In all the years that Molly Harry had been alive she could not remember ever seeing everyone gathered to hear from a master. The smell of fear was thick in the air, mixed with the sweat from the day's toil.

"I have been here barely two weeks and today I opened the newspaper to see that this plantation has been accused of harbouring a slave woman named Sally. She is described as being yellow skinned with pockmarks in her face from small pox. Has anybody seen such a person?"

Silence greeted him.

"She is said to have connections here. Is anybody here connected to this Sally?"

Again, no one broke the silence.

Beside Molly Harry the house slaves tensed and a few of them darted surreptitious looks at Judy Ann who kept her head down. Molly Harry noticed her shaking and in spite of everything, compassion moved in her. She hoped that no one would betray her.

"There is a reward of ten pounds for anyone who returns her to her owner."

There was murmuring among the slaves for £10 was a lot of money.

"However, if a white or free coloured person is found helping her, they will be charged. That means if she is found on my plantation, I could be charged. Now I ask again, does anyone know of this Sally? This is the last time I am asking. If I find that she is being hidden here, everyone will get a flogging, even if it takes the whole week!"

"Oh loss," murmured Hannah next to Molly

Harry. "Wha' I tell you?"

"I ain' teking no licks for Judy Ann. She is Judy Ann mudda." A voice pierced the silence. Everyone looked around to see who it was. It was Lydia, a field slave who made no secret of the fact that she was after Hanibal who wanted to marry Judy Ann.

Judy Ann looked in disbelief towards Lydia with a mixture of fear, hatred and anger on her face.

"Thank you. You can all go," the master said. "Except you, Judy Ann. You harboured your mother who belongs to someone else and brought trouble on this plantation that I have barely owned for a few weeks. Vaucluse is not to be known for harbouring other people's slaves!"

Molly Harry and the other house slaves moved from around Judy Ann and walked slowly towards the back of the house, leaving her alone and vulnerable. Each one shuddered when they heard the master tell Thorpe, "Send two men to search for the mother and if they find her tell them to take her to the cage. And give Judy Ann ten lashes for the trouble she has brought on me and Vaucluse when you have seen to the mother."

He turned and walked back into the house, ignoring Judy Ann's pleas for mercy.

***

Molly Harry and the other slaves retreated to the yard at the back of the house mournfully. Although Judy Ann was a troublemaker no one would wish a beating on her.

"I sorry enough for Judy Ann," Mary Ann said at last as they sank down on benches in the yard. "I know what a beatin' feel like and I wouldn't wish tha' 'pon my wors' enemy."

"Molly Harry, go quick and beg the massa to spare Judy Ann," Hannah urged her.

"Me?" Molly Harry looked horrified. "Why he would listen to me?"

"'Cause you is the one that does look after he and he chile in you' belly."

Molly Harry's conscience tugged at her. She didn't know why they thought she could get the master to change his mind. She might be carrying his child but what was she to him? He had seemed happy to hear that she was with child and he called for her once during the week since then, but would he listen to her?

A scream rent the air, causing her to jump. The others looked at her accusingly until, without another word, she rushed through the back door and headed for the master's office.

"Master Henry," she gasped, rushing through the door. She stopped abruptly, realising that she had barged in without knocking.

"What is it, Molly Harry?" he asked, putting down the paper he was reading. She hesitated and before she could open her mouth, another scream reached their ears. She glanced towards the window frantically and back at the master.

"Master Henry, you could spare Judy Ann?" she finally asked fearfully.

"Why would I do that?" he asked calmly. "She exposed this plantation and me to the threat of the law by harbouring another man's slave."

"But …" Molly Harry trailed off, not sure what to say. Another scream from Judy Ann caused her to shiver in fear.

"You care to tell me why you did not say that Judy Ann was hiding her mother?"

Molly Harry's head snapped up and she froze. Would the master order a flogging for her too? She wished that she could read his face, but he showed no sign of his thoughts. He did not even seem to hear Judy Ann's scream that shattered the silence. There was a pause as if Thorpe was giving his hand a rest.

"M-massa, Massa Henry…" she started, not knowing what she would say. He waved his hand dismissively.

"Don't bother to lie, Molly Harry. I will let this one go, but never let me find out that you know something like that and do not tell me. I expect unwavering loyalty from you. Understand?"

"Y-yes, massa," Molly agreed, somehow understanding exactly what he meant even without knowing the words he used.

"All right, you can go."

She hesitated, still trying to find the words to cause him to change his mind.

"And if Thorpe is still at it, tell him I said he can stop." He picked up the paper again as Molly Harry left the office running with her "Yes, massa" trailing behind her.

***

"Thorpe like he stop," Hannah whispered in relief. They had not heard any screams for the last few minutes.

"Praise the Lord," Hagar exclaimed. "I did prayin' that Molly Harry would get the massa to stop the beatin'."

"Who tell you that he listen to she? When last you hear a master listen to one of he slaves?" Mary Ann scoffed. She stopped talking when Molly Harry ran into the yard breathlessly.

"The massa send me to tell Thorpe to stop the beatin', but Judy Ann back look bad," she cried.

"Oh loss, come and help me get she to she hut, Mary Ann," Hagar commanded, getting tiredly to her feet.

"Well, you surprise me fo' true, Molly Harry," Mary Ann said, getting up. "I never thought you would be brave enough to beg the master for mercy for Judy Ann, far less that he would listen. I surprise' he ain' order a beatin' for you for not tellin' he that Judy Ann did hidin' she mudda."

"All of wunna did know too," Molly Harry accused, catching her breath.

"Yes, but we ain' up in he like you."

"He didn' too happy 'bout it," she admitted, "but he only tell me don' let it happen again."

"Well, you like you got he bewitch'. For now anyhow. Mek sure you keep he happy so that you don' fin' you'self at the wrong end of a whip like Judy Ann," she advised. "If you want a little potion to keep he so, I could mek somet'ing for you."

Hannah sucked her teeth. "You better be careful *you* don' fin' you'self like Judy Ann if you don' stop with tha' talk," she threatened. "You know them people don' like none of that obeah t'ing 'bout they plantation."

"I ain' got no use for obeah," Hagar told them. "I trustin' in my God."

"Tha' alright for you, Hagar. You old. But Molly

Harry got to look out for she self and she child. Just because she got the master now it don' mean it gine always be so. Molly Harry, you best do what you could to keep he before he start sniffin' 'round the next young girl 'bout here. Especially when you get big as a sow."

"Mary Ann, lef' the girl," Hannah interrupted. "And try and go and help Hagar with Judy Ann. I goin' and cut some aloes to put 'pon she back."

"I goin'. Molly Harry, don' mind them. You might be carryin' the master child but don' think he gine say that it belong to he and don' look for no special treatment. Them massas does get nuff children from the women 'pon they plantations and don' look back at them. So when you ready come to me," she advised, finally following Hagar.

"Don' mind she. He might be different," Hannah assured Molly Harry when Mary Ann left. She lowered her voice. "I hear talk that he got a daughter from one of he slave women and he ain' shame to let people know that she is he daughter."

Molly Harry looked at her in surprise. The massa had a daughter from a slave woman? That was what he meant when he said maybe it would be a boy this time? The thought of that made her feel sick inside, like when she had the morning sickness. She wasn't sure why she felt like that. What did it matter to her if the master lay with another woman? It wasn't anything to do with her.

Maybe Mary Ann was right. The white men only wanted slave women for one thing. She would not get her hopes up and she would not look for any special treatment. But he had listened to her when she begged for Judy Ann. Maybe he was different.

Chapter 6

Bussa left the slave yard at Bayleys flanked by King Wiltshire, Dick Bailey and two slaves both named Johnny. The sun was beginning to set and once they kept a good pace they would get to Simmons Plantation just as it was getting dark. The darker the better, because they didn't want the white folks to see them meeting. He knew that Jackey would have organised some dancing and entertainment from early in the evening to cover up the real reason for them being there.

He had not wanted to leave his wife Phibbah, but going to this meeting was more important than what he wanted. Even now he could see in his mind the crisscross of the lash marks across her back that were starting to scab but were still raw. He had come in from the fields the evening before to find her lying on her stomach across their bed with the flesh torn from her back which was caked with blood. The old slave, Bertha, who was tending to her told him that Thomas, the manager who was the devil in the flesh, had personally given her thirty-nine lashes.

Bussa knew, as certain as he knew his name, that Thomas had done it to remind him who was boss at Bayleys. As a head driver on the plantation he enjoyed certain privileges and he had the respect of both the slaves and many of the planters in the island. Edward Thomas was white, uneducated trash and he showed it every time he opened his mouth and spoke to the slaves, usually with a threat of punishment or with instructions to deliver it if he didn't choose to do it himself, which he often did.

He was yet to find out what he had whipped Phibbah for. Not that Thomas needed a good reason, as if there could be any good reason for one human being to do to another what he had done to Phibbah. But then, they did not think that black people were human beings like them. To them black people were savages and beasts. He scoffed angrily to himself. He knew of tribes in Africa that were well-ordered, where women held positions as leaders, something that was unheard of in Barbados. Their craftsmen produced items of the highest quality, made of gold and other metals, the likes of which the white man could not produce, and they called them savages?

His hands clenched at his sides and he ground his teeth as he forced the image of Phibbah from his mind. It had taken all his self-control not to rip out

Thomas' heart. The only thing that stopped him was because he knew he would find no heart in that breast and he also knew that there was more at stake than the satisfaction it would give him to kill the poisonous snake.

The group passed well below Mapps Plantation and soon marked Sandford as the half-way mark of the two-mile journey. None of them spoke as they made quick work of the distance. After all, this was not a social outing or a nice Sunday evening stroll; they were there to discuss what they would do now that the House of Assembly had rejected the Registry Bill. They had gotten together only once since November for their Christmas festivities, so this was a very important meeting. The time for talk had finished. It was time for action.

That brought back to Bussa's mind what Nanny Grigg, the only woman in the group, had said when she turned up at the meeting they had at Simmons after they had gotten word about the vote. From the time he had met her their spirits had connected. Although she had been born in the island, she somehow understood freedom in a way that a lot of the creoles did not. Maybe it was because she could read so she knew what was happening in other islands and what was going on in England from newspapers that were in the house.

She had reminded them that the slaves in Saint Domingue had gotten together and rebelled against the French people who were ruling them and took over the island, gaining their freedom. Then she had looked them in the eyes and told them fiercely that if they wanted freedom they would get it, but they would have to fight for it like the slaves in Saint

Domingue. He had felt her words deep in his belly. The desire to fight that had almost been lost to him under the yoke of slavery rose up in him again and it was then that he had vowed silently to get freedom, if not for himself, then for his brothers and sisters, even if he had to die to make it happen. After all, if he died trying, then death would emancipate him from slavery.

The thought caused him to set his face like flint as he walked, glad for the cool evening breeze that dried up the sweat on his brow before it had time to trickle down his face. Looking up, he could see the palm trees signalling Simmons in the distance and they cut through a cart road in the cane fields that were now almost as familiar to them as their own at Bayleys. They came up at the back of the slave yard and headed for the tree that had become their meeting place.

The shadows that shrouded them were co-conspirators with the men who had already gathered under the big breadfruit tree, hiding them from any curious eyes. The night had been well chosen to make sure that there was no moon to reveal who was meeting. Not that the Simmons or their overseers would venture into the slave yard at that time of night. They had not the slightest thought of what was being planned right on their plantation.

Jackey was already there with John and another slave from the plantation named Robert. There was no sign of Nanny Grigg tonight, but he could make out James Bowland from River, Mingo from Bydemill and King William from Sunbury. He and the others from Bayleys joined them. There were no jovial greetings. Instead they nodded to each other with an air of sombreness about them.

These were only some of the men who were committed to the rebellion. The others were in nearby parishes but lived too far away to make the trek at that time of night. However, their plans would be communicated when they met up at the market or when John made his rounds to the other plantations. Apart from the ones in St. Philip, men from Ayshford and Sturges in St. Thomas and Haynesfield in St. John were ready to take a stand. All were serious and trusted one another. There would be no betrayals before their plans were carried out, like the ones they had heard about in the past. They had no knowledge that Charles Ward was once again hidden in the shadows listening to their every word.

"How you, Bussa? We hear that dog Thomas give yo' wife a beatin' yesterday. How she is?"

"She gine be good. I gine deal wid he when the time come," Bussa promised. They all nodded in agreement.

"Alright, leh we start," Jackey said. "Whoever comin' mus' be here by now. Bowland, tell the rest what you find out."

"I see in one of them newspapers from England that people over there up in arms because we House of Assembly reject the Registry Bill," James Bowland shared. He was one of the few slaves among them who could read the newspapers that took weeks to come from England.

"We been talkin' 'bout this t'ing since last year when they ain' pass tha' bill. We shoulda know that they didn' gine give we freedom so easy, no matter wha' the people in England sayin'," Jackey declared bitterly.

"Well, as Nanny Grigg say, if they ain' givin' we freedom, we gine have to take it!" hissed Johnny Cooper.

"We can' wait for Englan' to put pressure 'pon the planters. We got to do somethin' we self. The time come for we to act!" declared Bussa.

"Yes, we got to get freedom for we people," agreed King Wiltshire.

"We got a lot of people who ready to rise up and fight, and the ones who frighten I willin' to get them to join with we," John added.

"You got to mek sure that they more frighten for we than for them massas because we can' tek the chance for none of them to talk!" Jackey charged him.

"Tonight, we got to decide what we gine do and when is the best time to do it," James Bowland pronounced. "We got to do somet'ing to mek Englan' sen' in people to see what happenin' in Barbados."

"If the' sen' people or not, we got to get we freedom now!"

"Nanny Grigg couldn' come out tonight, but she say to tell wunna that the way we will get we freedom is to set fire," Robert said.

Jackey said: "She right. This is what we could do. Burn down the canes and brek up property and cause nuff 'ruption and then kill off as many of them as we can."

"Wha' weapons we gine use?" someone asked.

"We gine have to use the tools we does work wid and brek in the big houses and get what guns we could put we han' 'pon, but them gine still got nuff more guns than we," Jackey said.

"The' got more guns than we and each parish got soldiers in it, plus the ones from Englan' that 'bout here to stop the French from tekin' over some o' them other islands," James informed them with authority.

"We ain' got as much weapons as them, but I prefer to dead fightin' for freedom than to keep livin' as a slave," Bussa declared.

"Alright. Well, we could do it 'round Easter. Tha' would give we nearly two months to finish plannin'. Wunna could come by my plantation Good Friday for a dance and we could talk more then. John, you gine have to get word to all the rest from the other plantations to come by me to mek the final plans," King Wiltshire from River said.

"We got to fight! Even if we don' live to see freedom weself, we got to mek sure that we women and children know what freedom is for demselves," Bussa concluded.

Silence reigned as they came to terms with that thought and then they nodded, almost as one man. They were committed to this cause. The year 1816 would forever be remembered as a year that slaves in Barbados rose up and made their case for freedom heard, not by talking, but by taking action.

The time had been well spent and they bade farewell to the men from Simmons as they left to make their way back to their own plantation yards. The journey and the meeting had taken time that they could have been relaxing, for they knew that before they were long in their pallets it would be time to get up for another day of hard toil. However, to these men leisure and sleep were not priorities; freedom from slavery was what they lived for and were prepared to die for.

***

Bussa opened the door to the hut that he shared with Phibbah. It was quite sizeable, befitting his status as the chief driver. He went to the table and picked up the jug that was covered with a cloth, poured some water into a cup and drank it. Old Bertha must have filled it up before she left, as she had come to stay with Phibbah while he was out. She was still weak from the beating and was in bed but would have to be back at work the next day.

He heard her stirring in the back room and soon her voice reached his ears. "That you, Bussa?"

"Yes. I just come back," he said, bending his head as he stepped through the door to the back room.

"How it went?"

"Good. How you feelin'?"

"You know how."

He had got his fair share of whippings when he first came to the plantation as they tried to beat the spirit out of him, so he knew.

"You want anyt'ing to eat or drink?" he asked her.

"No. Bertha give me something before she left not too long ago." She waited for him to tell her about the meeting.

"We plannin' for after Easter."

"Lord, have mercy. Wunna really doin' this thing." It was a statement, not a question.

"Phibs, you know how I feel 'bout this. I done tell you that I can' live like this no more, especially after what happen to you yesterday. I prefer to be dead than to be a slave the rest of my life. The rest o' we feel the same way."

"I know. But Bussa, wunna ain' got no guns like

them soldiers. How wunna gine fight them and expect to win?"

"We got to fight. We can' tek this no more. Sometimes you does reach a point that you can't live the same way no more. We reach there. We got to do something to make way fo' the people who comin' behin' we."

She didn't quite understand what he meant by that, but she knew that there was no talking him out of their plans and, to tell the truth, she would not try. She had married a strong man who had worked his way up to being the head driver on the plantation, a position of responsibility and trust. She was proud of him and what he had achieved.

She knew that what drove him now was the passion to be free from slavery. She wanted to be free too, never to have to experience a whipping like what Thomas had given her the day before, but that did not mean she liked what they were planning. Every time he went to one of their meetings the dread in her belly increased. She feared that they would get caught planning their rebellion and be executed before they had time to do anything. But he assured her that no one would betray this cause. She also feared that he would get killed during the rebellion and that was only slightly better.

Before he left that night he had told her that they had to do something to get their freedom. It looked like a lost cause, but even if they did not win the battle, to her, he was already a hero for trying.

***

John handed Henry Peter the conveyance papers he had brought with him and sat down in front of the desk in his office. He looked around appreciatively at the changes that HP had made in the month or so that he had taken up residence.

"It's all yours now, brother."

"Thanks, John. I feel good about Vaucluse, although I've already had trouble here this month."

"What happened?"

"One of the slaves was harbouring her mother from another plantation. It was in the *Mercury*. Did you not see it?"

"Tell the truth, I usually skip over all of the notices about missing slaves and see what the merchants are selling and what ships are leaving. So, what did you do?"

"I had her whipped, of course. I can't encourage that kind of thing here, especially since the subscriber was offering a reward of ten pounds to anyone who would convict a white or free coloured person for harbouring her."

John nodded in agreement.

"Not that she got all the lashes I had ordered. Molly Harry begged for her."

John's interest piqued at that.

"Who is Molly Harry?"

"She's one of the house girls. I had an episode soon after I moved in and she mixed up something for me to breathe in that helped."

"I'm glad to hear that. I know you don't like

anybody fussing over you when you have one of your episodes, so I am surprised that you told anyone you were sick. Were you that bad?"

"I did not have to say anything. Molly Harry is very sensitive to my needs. She just seems to know the right thing to do," he said thoughtfully.

"Sensitive to your needs, eh?" John smirked at him. "And I would wager it's not only when you need medicine."

"Now you say that, she told me she is pregnant. Seems like she should have the child by July or so."

"Pregnant? And the child is to be born in July? You only just moved here, HP. Surely it cannot be yours."

"I'm perfectly capable of working out dates, John," HP said drily. "I assure you that when I visited the plantation in October I must have gotten her with child."

"My God, you didn't waste any time getting acquainted with the slave girls. You certainly don't seem upset about it."

"Why should I be? She's of good childbearing age and should have a healthy child to add to the numbers. If it's a boy, better yet."

"Well, we do have to keep them reproducing because, thanks to England, we can't get any slaves from Africa. The fact is, if it was up to them, we would be forced to free the ones we have as it is. They don't realise how well we treat our people. They have proper food, shelter and clothing unlike the ones in some of the other islands. I even let mine travel around and invite others over for dances all the time."

"Yes, that keeps them contented. They really

wouldn't know what to do with themselves if they were free. We have a hard enough time keeping our plantations going with all the competition from other countries producing sugar now and, to make it worse, there is talk that they've started getting sugar from beets. How on earth would these poor slaves manage to earn enough money to live on if they were free?"

"I don't know why those folks in England think that they know how to treat our people better than we do. I would thank them to stay out of our business and pay us better for the sugar we ship over there. After all, the levies we have paid on our sugar over the years, not to mention the goods we have bought, have made the mother country rich and powerful. Why don't you run for St. Thomas in the House of Assembly now that you own Vaucluse so that you have some say in these matters?"

"I think two terms are enough for me. I will leave that to Thomas Williams. I want to focus on making this plantation into one of the biggest and best in the island apart from Simmons, of course," he joked.

"I have no doubt that you will, brother. You obviously inherited HP Senior's brilliance."

"Since we never really knew him, we assume that because he studied at Cambridge he must have been brilliant."

"True. I'm not sure how brilliant he was at running the plantation because it ended up in Chancery. It was unfortunate that he died so early and left it to Mother to deal with."

"It was already in debt when he took it over so that did not help."

Their father had died in 1779 when Philip, their older brother, was five and HP was three, leaving their mother with a baby, Ann, who had been born just a month before his death and John nine months after. Ann had not lived but three years.

Their mother had not had an easy time of it. It had been a relief for all of them when she married John Olton six years later and he bought back Simmons or Harrow, as it was also known, from the court, restoring their childhood home and giving them a father figure. He and their mother had gone on to have several other children, but John and Henry Peter had always been close and more so after the death of their brother Philip.

A tentative knock at the door interrupted them.

"Come in," Henry Peter called, somewhat impatiently.

"Excuse me, Massa Henry." Molly Harry said, hovering by the door.

"Yes, Molly Harry. What is it?"

"Hagar send me to tell you that your lunch ready and to ask if Master John staying for lunch."

HP looked at John who nodded even as he looked Molly Harry up and down, seeing that the full skirt was unable to hide the swelling of her belly. So, this was the girl who had caught HP's eye. She was very young and quite attractive, but he couldn't see what HP saw in her. Whatever it was, HP was looking better than he had for some time so something was agreeing with him. He wasn't sure if it was Molly Harry or if it was Vaucluse. Maybe it was a combination of the two.

"Yes, tell her to set the table for two of us. We will be there shortly."

"Yes, Massa Henry," she agreed before closing the door behind her.

"So, that was Molly Harry," John stated as soon as the door was closed. "She seems young and healthy. She should be able to deliver a healthy child."

"Yes, I hope so. She's not that far along, but I've given instruction for her work load to be lightened."

"You know how that kind of thing causes problems among the slaves," John cautioned.

"There will be no problems of that nature here because if it gets back to me the person will have to answer to me."

"It's true that we give our slaves a lot of liberty, but that doesn't mean we're afraid to discipline them when we have to. They will soon learn that about you."

Chapter 7

Good Friday, April 12, 1816
River Plantation, St. Philip

The music and dancing provided the usual cover for the voices of Jackey, Bussa, Cain Davis, Johnny Cooper and the other men who had come to the Good Friday dance at River Plantation. While their masters thought that they had come for the celebration, they were putting the final plans in place for the rebellion which was to take place the following week.

"We got to start to burn the canes and brek up the buildings Monday mornin'," Jackey instructed. "Then when the white people confused and frighten we gine put them out of the' misery."

The others nodded in agreement. Their faces were set and there was no fear in their eyes. They were prepared to die for their freedom. According to one of the more religious slaves, even if they were like Moses who saw the Promised Land in the distance but never got to enter it, it would be enough for them to know that others would live in it.

"When we tek over we could get rid of tha' man Governor Leith and put we own governor in place. Joseph Francklyn would mek a good governor," Cain Davis suggested. The others nodded in agreement with Cain who was a respected member of the group, being one of the few who could read and write. Joseph Francklyn was a free coloured man whose father was the Justice of the Peace and owner of a small plantation in St. Philip. Unlike many of the coloured people, he sided with them in their desire for freedom.

"Yes, he is a good man, but we ain' get there yet. We got to get we freedom before we could mek he the governor. We got to meet by me Sunday to go through the plans one more time before Monday."

"We got to get we hands 'pon some guns 'cause they ain' gine be expectin' we to fight wid guns," Johnny Cooper said.

"The' ain' gine be expectin' we to be rebellin' a' tall," someone chuckled.

"They think that once the' let we have a little get-together every now and then, and let we go to the market, that we happy. Them ain' realise that it ain' dance we want. All we want is the right to live the way we want to. I would like to see the master face when he see all of he canes gone up in smoke," Jackey smiled.

"Yes, we got to tek we freedom. Nobody tellin' we where to go or what to do. Nobody droppin' a whip cross we back any time the' feel like it," added Bussa angrily.

This time they joined the other slaves in celebration, not because it was Good Friday and a day off from work, but because it would be the last Good Friday that they would be slaves, whether or not they succeeded in their rebellion.

River Plantation House

"The slaves seem to be having a grand time tonight," complained the mistress. "I would like to be able to sleep, but all I can hear is that infernal noise of their drumming. Isn't it against the law for them to play those drums?" she asked irritably.

"It keeps them happy, dear, and that keeps us safe," her husband assured her. "Although we've got laws to govern them, don't forget that they outnumber us by nearly five to one and it's even more than that here in St. Philip."

"If you are trying to frighten me I assure you that you have succeeded beyond your expectations," she grumbled.

"Don't be silly, dear. We're perfectly safe. In fact, I'm so confident of that that I don't even lock the doors and we have quite a lot of valuables in here. So do not let your rest be disturbed. If you want, I can go down and tell the lot of them to stop the celebrations and go home," he offered.

"That won't be necessary. Best to let them enjoy themselves, lest they begin to turn on us and accuse us of all manner of abuse and neglect." She turned on her side and pulled a pillow over her head to block out the noise.

Simmons Plantation House

"It's very quiet tonight," Mehetabel sighed contentedly. "For once our plantation is not hosting some slave gathering or the other."

"Hmm," murmured John, half asleep already.

"I swear that Jackey keeps more socials than we do," she went on. "I mean it's all very well and good to keep them contented and they do bring their own victuals, but I don't understand why all the activities have to take place here. You really are a good master, John," she praised. "You look after the slaves well."

"Hmm," he said again.

"I wonder if they appreciate how well they have it here. And HP is also very good to his. Granted, he didn't have that many before, but now that he's bought Vaucluse he will have his hands full. He told me that there are nurses and everything for the ones that get sick. Where else in the British Empire can slaves boast of such good treatment?"

This time there was no answer. John had obviously succumbed to sleep. Rather than taking offense, she smiled indulgently. He was working hard to build back up Simmons. He had done well to buy it from his stepbrother after it had been given over to the Chancery Court following his father's death. But she worried that he was over-extending himself as he now also had Four Square to manage. She hoped that he didn't feel the need to prove anything to anyone, least of all to her. She was happy with what they had and with their marriage, which was a true partnership, unlike many on the island.

As far as she was aware, he did not go sniffing around the slave women either, which was a rarity for a white man on the island. Even HP was not immune to the dark women. He already had a coloured daughter, Mary Ann she believed her name was. Unlike some of the other planters, he didn't disown her or pretend that she was not his; he even gave her his surname. She didn't know what to say to HP; she certainly couldn't understand his aversion to getting married. She would have to increase her efforts to find him a good wife who could be his partner as she was John's. If she didn't, he might end up with only slave children as his heirs. Lord forbid!

Sunday, April 14, 1816
Simmons Plantation Yard

Jackey, John and Robert, Mingo and his men from Bydemill and John Barnes and his group from Gittens squatted on the ground and whispered among themselves. Tonight they were taking a chance meeting since there was no dance with music to cover their planning. Anticipation raced in each man as they went over the plans one last time to take over their part of the parish. Their whispers fell into silence almost at the same time that a familiar smell teased their noses. It was a smell that was usually accompanied by dread for all plantation owners because it meant loss of profits. It was the smell of burning canes.

They stood as one man, heads swerving in different directions to find the source of the fire. Towards the east the sky was orange, confirming their worst fears. There were canes on fire. Not that they were concerned about the loss to the plantation whose canes were burning; they were concerned about the timing of the burning.

"Tha' look like it could be Sandford canes that burnin'!" one of them exclaimed.

"How tha' happen?" John asked angrily. "We ain' suppose' to start burnin' 'til tomorrow. Something like it happen at Sandford. Wha' we is to do now, Jackey?"

"Look, the' like the got another one further out," Mingo interrupted. "I wonder if that is Bayleys."

"Or it could be Mapps," someone else suggested.

Towards the south, in the direction of Congo Road, they saw the same tell-tale orange in the sky.

"Some of the men like the' start too early. We gine got to go ahead. Head to the cane fields and let we start burnin' these and then we gine brek up the place!" Jackey instructed.

The men obeyed without question. The anticipation that had been stirring in them before became adrenaline that rushed through their veins, propelling them into action. The time for talking had finally given way to the time for action.

Bayleys Plantation
St. Philip

Bussa, King Wiltshire and Dick Bailey met Johnny Cooper and John Ranger in the yard as they all rushed from their huts. Each of them wore puzzled looks on their faces at the crackling of flames that could be heard a mile away. Other slaves rushed about, adding to the confusion. They could see flames in different parts of the parish.

"Somebody start early!" Johnny announced unnecessarily.

"Well, we gine have to join in," Bussa declared. "Burn the canes, brek up the windows and doors of the big house," he instructed.

"Wha 'bout Thomas house?" Dick Bailey asked.

"Lef' tha' to me. That is the first place I headin' once we get these canes burnin'."

"I comin' wid you. I got to get piece of tha' action!"

"Alright. Bring down Bayleys!" Bussa shouted and took off for the fields like a man half his age.

Simmons Plantation

"John, I smell canes burning," Mehetabel announced, sniffing the air. She dropped her book and stood up as John hastened to the window of the living room where they were reading before going up to bed.

"It looks like our fields," John said in disbelief. He had bought the plantation less than a year ago; he could not afford to lose his first crop to fire. He was just about to rush to the door to round up the slaves to help put out the fire when he was met in the hallway by a timid-looking house slave named Jane Ann. Her eyes were wild and she was barely coherent.

"Massa John, Jackey and the rest burnin' the canes and the' plannin' to brek up everyt'ing and then the house," she stammered, trembling.

"What do you mean Jackey is burning the canes?" John asked incredulously.

"He say that it is them time to tek over and they want freedom. They did plannin' this ever since."

"And nobody thought to tell us about it?" he shouted, making the girl tremble even more.

John turned to Mehetabel who now stood behind him, her face white with fear.

"Go up to the children's room and lock yourself in. Push something behind the door," he instructed.

"What about you? Where are you going?" she asked in a panic.

"I'm going to my office to get my gun. I will come up soon. I have to be able to protect you and the children in case they break into the house."

"But, John…"

"Do as I say, Mehty!" he snapped at her. She backed away with a shocked look on her face before turning to hurry up the stairs. He was sorry, but he had no time for discussion or disobedience now. He would apologise for his harsh tone later. If he was alive.

***

The Barbados Mercury
Tuesday, April 30, 1816

It is unnecessary to state to our readers in this Community the occasion of that suspension of our labours which has taken place since the 15th of this month: - it will be long and painfully imprinted on their minds – but those of our subscribers, who reside in the neighbouring Settlements, will no doubt be desirous of knowing the cause of it. We shall therefore endeavour to perform this unpleasant duty, although we feel considerable difficulty in the attempt.

At so early an hour as two in the morning of Easter Monday, this island was placed under Martial Law in order to quell a perfidious league of Slaves in the Parishes of St. Philip, Christ Church, St. John and St. George; who, in their mad career, were setting fire to fields of cane, as well as pillaging and destroying Buildings on many Estates, and otherwise pursuing a system of devastation which has seldom been equalled.

The inhabitants of this Town were apprised of these nefarious proceedings through the personal exertions of Colonel J. P. Mayers, of the Royal Regiment of Militia, who, upon receiving the intelligence, instantly proceeded from his Plantation and having, on his way, acquainted Colonel Codd, in command of the Garrison of St. Ann, the troops were immediately called to arms and put in readiness to march in the route of these incendiaries.

This promptitude on the part of the Commandant was followed by his kindness in supplying the St. Michael's Militia with some arms that were required, and likewise with ammunition, so that, by day-break, they were ready for service; upon which the Flank and some other Companies, headed by Col. Mayers, were soon afterwards despatched, and on their march they joined a large body of Regulars commanded by Col. Codd, with which they proceeded to the scene of desolation.

The Life Guards, too, were sent in that direction and, being divided into squadrons, they frequently fell in with parties of the insurgents, some of whom they killed, and dispersed the rest; and, from the facility from which this Body conveyed intelligence to the troops, it was found to be a most essential Corps on this calamitous occasion.

The enterprising spirit of Colonel Best was conspicuous in this affair; for, with the Christ Church Battalion, he was on duty in the very midst of the rebellion and contributed in a great degree to their dispersion in that neighbourhood soon after its commencement, but in effecting which several of the Insurgents were shot.

Those troops from the Garrison, as well as the Militia, were, upon approaching the Thicket (one of the Estates principally concerned in this outrage) sent in divisions in different directions with the hope of discovering, before night, those places to which the rebellious had retreated upon perceiving their advance: - in the performance of this duty, the troops surprised many parties of them,and some of whom lost their lives in attempting to escape.

Besides those that were killed on the following day, many were taken prisoners, and upwards of 400 have been sent on board of vessels in the Bay to await the result of their trial agreeably to the tenor of the annexed Proclamation, which was issued by His Honour President Spooner: - Barbados by the Hon John Spooner, President and Commander in Chief of this Island, Chancellor Ordinary and Vice admiral of the same.

Silent tears rolled down the cheeks of Nanny Grigg and dropped onto the newspaper she had sneaked out of the house to read. She shook her head in disbelief at the tragedy. Pictures of the faces of those that had been killed or arrested flashed through her mind: Jackey, John, Bussa, King Wiltshire, Davis, Robert and so many others. The soldiers would probably soon come for her by the time they tortured confessions out of Robert and any of the others who used to gather there.

She had told them to fight for their freedom, but Barbados was nothing like Saint Domingue that she had read about. From what she understood, that country had a lot of mountains and places that the slaves could hide and attack the white men. Had she done wrong in telling them to fight? They all knew that there were militia in each parish, plus the soldiers in Bridge Town and at the Garrison. But they still decided to fight. It had been their decision.

She wiped her cheeks and drew in a deep breath, straightening her shoulders which had sagged under the weight of guilt. Yes, they had decided to fight because it was better to fight and be killed than to be alive and a slave. If the soldiers came for her she would not go anywhere with them; they would have to kill her right there in her house.

One thing was sure though, the men had managed to disrupt the whole island and shake up the planters. That brought a slight smile to her face. She had heard that some of the old people had died of fright. Serve them right. They had two days of fright compared to nearly two hundred years that her people lived in fear. England would be forced to send out people to look into what had happened and prepare a report for their parliament. Surely, freedom would follow soon after.

A knock at the door jumped her. Were they here already? But no, they would never knock at the door of a slave.

"Who dat?" she asked guardedly.

"Charles Ward," a quiet voice answered. She got up to open the door, peering around cautiously before stepping back to let him in.

"Wha' you doin' 'bout here, Charles? How you manage not to get carry 'way?" she asked suspiciously.

"I did fightin' at Bayleys, but when I see that the'

bring out we own people to fight against we and that we didn' had no chance, I hide and manage to escape and come back here."

"So, Simmons don't know that you did fightin' too?"

"No. He tell me that he glad I didn' join in and he got me helpin' to fix the buildings that get brek up."

"So, Bussa dead?" Nanny Grigg asked sadly.

Charles nodded.

"Jackey too and John, and I hear that them carry 'way Robert."

"I feel sorry for he. By the time the' done with he, he gine wish that he did dead with the rest. You know that the' goin' get he to talk and then the' gine come for we."

"He ain' know that I did at Bayleys 'cause he did at Lowthers and I didn' had not'ing to do with the plannin'. Simmons t'ink that I backin' he because we use to play together when we did small. All o' this time he lendin' me out to work and keepin' the biggest share of my money and stoppin' me from buyin' my freedom. He get off easy, but the rest of them gine pay for Jackey, John and the rest one of these days."

Nanny Grigg smiled. "I might not be here to see it, but I could go happy knowin' that justice goin' get serve."

Chapter 8

Vaucluse Plantation

"My God, Henry Peter, the talk all over the island is that this whole thing was planned at my plantation! People are acting as if I am responsible!" John reported, stunned.

"Yes, I've heard the talk, but you know how people love to talk on the island," Henry Peter consoled him. "It is not as if slaves from other plantations were not involved as well. I heard that they sometimes met at River as well."

"That is all right for you to say; your slaves were not involved. But people are blaming me for allowing mine too much freedom and encouraging them to have dances and such like."

"As long as your conscience is clear, that is all you

need to be concerned about. I don't waste my time with the opinions of others and neither should you. I, for one, don't blame you and if anyone says such nonsense to me I'll set them straight."

"Thanks, HP."

"Do you have any idea of the cost of the damage?"

"I have not fully worked that out yet, but it is looking like it will be over five thousand pounds. I lost about half my sugar crop in fires and a lot of the property was damaged badly. And that doesn't even include the men I lost in the battles with the militia. Two of my drivers were killed; one was my chief driver as well. Several of my other slaves have been taken in for questioning and I don't imagine I'll see them again."

"That's probably for the best," HP assured him.

"I know, but I still can't believe that my men would turn on me like that, after all I have done for them." He shook his head in disbelief.

"No good turn goes unpunished," HP said cynically. "At least your insurance will cover most of it. You do have insurance, right?"

"Yes, thank God."

HP nodded in agreement.

"How is Mehty doing? I'm sure she must have been terrified."

"She is much better now. Naturally, she was terrified. So was I, to tell the truth. I thought they would break into the house and slit our throats, so I got my gun and I was prepared to defend us against anyone who dared to come near. They could easily have killed us, had they wanted to."

"I'm certainly glad they didn't. It seems that they

had the opportunity to kill many of the planters but instead they concentrated on causing damage, especially to the property of the lower classes, I heard."

"Yes. It seems that they took out their vengeance on a lot of them."

"Mehty must hate seeing the reminder of their rampage every day. You are welcome to bring her and the children here until the house and outbuildings are repaired."

"Thank you, HP, I'll do that. I know she would be glad to get away from the plantation for a while."

"Good, then that's settled. What concerns me is not only the destruction that they wrought but the rebelliousness that has been loosed. We can no longer trust them."

"Yes, and my overseer tells me that they have been very hostile since the rebellion and have the worst attitude. They seem to be angry that the rebellion failed and that so many of them were killed."

"Yes, we've seen that here too even though, as you say, mine were not involved."

"My house slaves are not quite as bad, but I don't even know which of them I can trust. I feel as if I'm taking a chance every time I eat a meal."

"Well, as I said, you are all welcome to stay here for a while. I think it should be safe enough. I have certainly not seen any difference in the attitude of my house slaves."

"Be careful that you don't get too complacent. I never would have thought that mine would turn on me. You better watch out that Molly Harry doesn't try to slit your throat one night after you fall asleep."

Henry Peter laughed. "Not likely. I don't think Molly Harry has a rebellious bone in her body. She does what she's told and without complaint. She's a good girl and she seems content with her lot in life. Once I give her a few coins she is happy."

"I wish they were all like that," John said. "Then we would have no fear of anyone trying to upset the status quo."

"Indeed!" agreed Henry Peter.

***

One Week Later

Mehetabel settled the children in the room that they were sharing at Vaucluse. She had been glad when John told her about HP's invitation to stay because every time she smelled the burnt canes or saw the broken windows of their house or the smashed in doors of the stable and outhouses she was reminded of the rebellion.

She was shaken that their own slaves harboured such resentment as to turn against them. Hadn't she told John only a few nights before the rebellion that he was a good master? How dare they try to destroy the plantation he had worked so hard to acquire mere months before? And after all he had done for them, the freedom he had given them to come and go. Ungrateful wretches!

She quietly closed the door and turned to walk downstairs to sit in the living room with John for a while. Henry Peter had said that he was not feeling the best and he would go to bed early. He had come up when she brought the children up. She feared that all the cane fires of the week before and the ash that was still in the air were taking a toll on him and stirring up his asthma. She felt sorry for him; after all, he was such a fit man otherwise, then to be afflicted with this illness that they did not even know how to cure.

She paused as she saw the slave girl called Molly Harry opening the door to HP's room. When she had caught a glimpse of her earlier she could see that she was pregnant, although with a few months to go by the looks of her. Mehty had not given it another thought except that she absently noted that the girl was rather young. Now, seeing her entering HP's room, she began to speculate. Could the girl be pregnant with Henry Peter's child? She didn't see how that could be, as he had only moved to the plantation about three months ago and the girl looked at least six months gone. She certainly hoped not. She hastened down the stairs to find John.

"John, you know the slave girl that Henry Peter called Molly Harry?" she began. John looked up from the newspaper he was reading.

"What about her?"

"She is with child," Mehetabel announced, sitting next to him on the sofa.

"So I noticed," John replied absently, continuing to read.

"She looks barely more than a child herself!"

"That is none of our business, Mehty." He turned the page of the newspaper.

"Well, I just saw her going into HP's room," she continued. "And you know how he hates people to fuss over him when he's not feeling himself. Do you think there's something going on between them? Could it be his child?" she finished in a whisper.

He lowered the newspaper. "If you're so curious, ask him."

"I could not! It would not be proper. I don't see how it could be his child, though, as he's only just moved in a few months ago."

John shrugged and returned to his newspaper without giving her an answer. One did not discuss these things, especially with one's wife. At least HP was not married, as were many of the other planters who had children from their slaves or mulatto mistresses. Anyway, in a few months it would be known, or speculated, who the father was. They should be gone by then so that he would not have to answer any more of Mehetabel's awkward questions. She probably would not like the answers anyway.

***

"Massa Henry?" Molly Harry whispered as she closed the door behind her.

"What, Molly?" he answered impatiently. Molly knew that tone from the last time he felt poorly. She knew that he did not want to let anyone know that he was beginning to feel sick, but she had known that it would be coming on soon, with all the ash blowing around the place.

"You want me to bring you some of that potion I mix up for you to breathe in last time?"

He sighed resignedly. "Yes. It seemed to help."

"OK, I already start to burn the leaves so I goin' bring it up."

"Be quick about it."

Molly quietly let herself out of the room and left Henry Peter alone with his thoughts. Molly was turning out to be a great asset; worth every pound he had paid for her. He had been ashamed to discover from the plantation's ledgers that she was about fifteen, but although she was young she always seemed to know what he needed. In the three months that he had been living there she saw that all his needs were met, very often before he even had to ask. When it came to his more basic needs he still had to tell her to come to his room as she was never as forward as to push herself at him. But that was good because he wanted no demands put on him. She always came willingly when he summoned her to his room and she pleased him in any way he wanted. What more could a man want?

Perhaps he should do something for her. He would have a new hut built so that when the baby came she would have more room. He wondered where she lived now and with whom? Probably with one of the other house slaves. It was not as if they talked about such things. They rarely talked anyway. After all, what did one talk about with a slave? Did they even think beyond what they would eat and the clothes that they would wear and where they would sleep? He thought about the ones who had led the rebellion. He had heard that most of them were the "elite" slaves on their plantations; the ones who were trusted with responsibilities. They obviously had enough thoughts to plan a rebellion, even if it was doomed to fail from the beginning. Surely that proved that they were not very intelligent. How did they imagine they would run the country? They probably couldn't even run their own lives, if given a chance.

Thank God for slaves like Molly Harry who were happy to be taken care of. She was surely a lot more content than those ones who could read. He always knew that teaching slaves to read was dangerous. No doubt the source of their discontent stemmed from the things they read in the newspapers.

Reading about the revolution in Saint Domingue which was all over the papers when it happened, the abolition of the Slave Trade and all the agitating against slavery that was going on in England could do no good except make them wish for things that they could not have. At least not if people like him had anything to say about it. If they had to pay them to work, how would they ever make a profit?

The door opened again and Molly stooped down to pick up the hot saucepan. He had one of those strange feelings that he had seen this before. Even her clothes were the same as what she wore then. He noticed that the skirt was clinging to her burgeoning belly and the blouse, which had been tight before, was now straining as her breasts grew larger in anticipation of the child. He would have to see that she had some new clothes. He was almost ashamed that he had not thought of it before. She did not ask him for anything, so it pleased him to give her some clothes that fit. He would arrange to have some bought from Richard Maltby who had recently advertised in the *Mercury* that he had brought in a shipment of negro clothes. He would also get William Richards and another of the carpenters to build a hut for her.

Molly Harry arranged the pillows against the bedhead behind her master and put another one across his lap before setting the saucepan down on it and arranging it so that he could inhale the smoke. The wheezing in his chest concerned her.

"You goin' soon feel a lot better, massa," she assured him.

"Sit down, Molly," he commanded. She sat at the foot of the bed. "Are you feeling all right?"

"Me, massa?" she asked in surprise.

"Yes, I mean with the baby."

"Oh. The first months, before you move' in, was the worse. I had the sickness in the mornin', but I good now."

"Are you getting enough to eat? I should have told the cook to make sure you get extra portions."

"I alright, massa. I gettin' plenty of food." She was surprised that he was asking her these questions. But then again it was his baby in her belly so maybe that was why.

"I will make sure that Betsy Jane gets some new dresses for you and you should see one of the nurses to make sure that the baby is growing well."

"Yes, massa. You feeling any better?"

"Yes, I am, Molly. Even with all this talking I don't feel as out of breath as I usually do."

"I glad you feelin' better, massa. I don' like to see you sick," she added compassionately.

"You mean to say that you would not rejoice if I keeled over?" he teased her, catching her eye.

"Keeled over?" she repeated, puzzled.

"Dropped dead," he clarified.

"No, Massa Henry!" she exclaimed horrified, making his smile.

"So you would not have set fire to my plantation and help the other slaves to cut my throat?"

"No, massa! I would never do that. You been

good to me."

"I'm very glad to hear that, Molly Harry. I can sleep a lot better at night knowing that. Here. Put this saucepan on the floor and come and lie with me."

She put down the bowl and started to unbutton her blouse.

"No, not that tonight, Molly. Believe me, the spirit is willing, but the body is weak. I just want some company tonight."

"Yes, Massa Henry." She obediently re-buttoned her blouse and lay down next to him when he moved over to make room for her.

Molly lay awkwardly next to the master. She didn't know what to do with herself. He had never asked her to lie with him without wanting her body. Eventually, tiredness lulled her to sleep, taking the awkwardness with it.

Henry Peter was thankful that his chest no longer felt tight. He was grateful to have found Molly Harry on the plantation, who knew how to treat his asthma. Maybe that had been Providence. The fact that he found her youthful body appealing and satisfying, even as her belly continued to swell with his child, just went to show that fortune was smiling on him. He wondered if it would last.

Chapter 9

July 29, 1816
Vaucluse Plantation

Molly Harry squeezed Hannah's hand tightly as she felt her belly tighten again. She had been in labour since the night before and she was beginning to feel tired. At first there was only a slight tightening of her belly and she could bear that quite easily, but it had gotten worse and worse, especially in the last hour. She knew that she was squeezing Hannah's hand too tight, but it was either that or scream with the pain.

"It gine soon be out now. I could see the head. Push hard when you feel the next tightenin' comin'," the midwife instructed her. Molly Harry didn't know if she had the energy to push hard or even push easy, but then she felt as if something was easing. She could feel the baby wanting to come out and she felt the urge to push. She wanted it to come out too. Not only because in the last month she had been very uncomfortable, but she was also anxious to see what the child would look like.

The midwife put her hand on Molly's belly and felt the strong contraction. "Push now!" She commanded.

"Push, girl," Hannah encouraged her.

Molly Harry pushed with all her remaining strength and felt a surge of relief as the baby slid from her body into the waiting hands of the midwife.

"It is a boy!" she announced, putting him on Molly Harry's now flaccid belly. She cut the umbilical cord and shortly after dealt with the afterbirth.

Molly Harry lifted her head weakly to stare at the pale-skinned baby on her belly. He was the colour of the tea that the massa liked to drink with a lot of milk in it. His body was covered with a white greasy cream and his dark hair was slicked down against his head. She laid her hand gently and reverently on his head and looked down into his brown eyes. She had a son.

"How come he not cryin'?" she asked anxiously, realising that he was silently looking back at her.

"All of dem don' cry when they born," the midwife assured her. "Let me clean he off and I goin' show you how to nurse he just now."

Molly Harry gazed on her baby with a look of amazement on her shiny face. A single tear rolled from the corner of one eye and ran in front of her ear and into her hair.

This was the baby that had rolled about in her belly many days causing her to put her hand on some spot that was sticking out, as if by doing so she would calm him. The first time Master Henry had seen the baby move he had been just as surprised as her. He had laid his hand on her belly and stared at it in amazement. She knew that the baby was not his first child, so she wondered if he had not seen such a thing before.

She was quickly brought back to the present when Hannah helped her to sit up and the midwife put the swaddled baby against her breast and showed her how to get him to latch on. She felt the tug on her breast all the way in her belly. The baby's pale face contrasted with her brown breast and she briefly wondered if he would stay that colour or get darker. Would the master let her keep him or would he sell him one day? A man would not sell his own son, would he?

"I got to go and let the master know how it turn out. He been askin' how you doin'." Hannah's voice intruded on her thoughts. She supposed that everyone knew that the child was the master's. After all, he had had a new hut built for her, so it was no secret that she was his woman. A tired smile crossed her face. She was a woman, the master's woman, and she had given him his first son.

***

"Master Henry," Hannah knocked at the door of his office. The door opened quickly, as if he had been waiting for the knock.

"What news, Hannah?"

"Molly Harry got a son. All two of them doin' good." She saw the unasked question in his eyes. "He light brown; coloured."

He nodded his thanks.

"Tell her I will come and see them soon."

"Yes, massa."

Henry Peter sank into the chair behind his desk. He had a son. Molly Harry had given him a son. He pulled out the heavy plantation register from the bottom drawer, opened it to the last page and wrote.

July 29, 1816
Birth
Coloured boy named… (He paused and thought for a moment) … *Harry*

Harry Simmons. His son. His slave. After all, he took the status of his mother, but he would not be treated as the other slaves because his blood ran in his veins, as well as Molly Harry's.

Life and death were constant. Only last month his friend Charles Kyd Bishop had died. They had been in the House of Assembly together. He and his wife Mercy had eight children and the last one had just been born, a month after Charles had passed. He would have to pay her a visit and see how she was doing. Hopefully she wouldn't lose Reed's Bay, but at least they had Orange Hill.

He pushed back his chair and quickly made his way to Molly Harry's new hut at the edge of the slave yard closest to the house wondering what the boy would look like. He smiled as he remembered how excited she had been when he told her that he was getting William Richards and Windsor, two of the carpenters, to build it for her. When it was finished, and she walked around in it, she had come to his office with tears streaming down her face, making his heart lurch in his chest, as he had thought that something was wrong with the child.

"What is wrong, Molly?" he had asked, looking her up and down anxiously.

"William Richards finish the hut and he just show me it," she had explained. "Thank you, Massa Henry. I never expect I would ever get anything so in my life."

As he reached the hut, Hannah was looking out and pushed open the door to let him in. It was very humble but, compared to the other slave huts, it was a good size and comfortable. There was a front room with a table and two chairs at one end and a rocking chair he had had specially built under a window on the other side of the room. There was one big room in the back but with a partition to create a smaller room within it where she could put the baby. He had gotten one of the carpenters to make a cradle as well and a proper bed for Molly Harry. His child would not live in the house, but he would still live in a fair amount of comfort. They could always add on to it as he got older.

Molly Harry was lying on the bed holding the baby who was asleep. She looked up as the master came in and smiled proudly.

"I hear that it is a boy," HP greeted her.

"Yes, massa. He real sweet." Henry Peter moved closer and peered at the sleeping baby. He didn't particularly resemble him or Molly Harry. His hair looked soft and straight, at least for now, and his skin was pale brown.

"He is certainly a good-looking child," he agreed. "How are you feeling?"

"Real tired, but real happy too," she smiled again.

"I'm happy too, Molly Harry."

As he looked down at his son something stirred in him. His daughter Mary Ann was six years old and now he had a son, Harry. Both coloured. He would give him all that he could and make sure that he became a strong man.

"I will take care of both of you. You will never have to worry about him."

"Thank you, massa. I know that you goin' do that if you say so. You does always do what you say."

***

Monday, May 26, 1817
Liverpool, Lancashire, England

"Mr. Parry and Mr. Jeffries," announced his housekeeper, Mrs. Pounder. She stepped back to allow the men to enter the library of the house that her master had rented, closing the door behind them.

Henry Peter had arrived in Liverpool two weeks earlier aboard the ship John Tobin, named for its owner, a wealthy ship owner from that city. Crossing the Atlantic was not his favourite thing to do. After all, what did one do for nearly four weeks trapped on a boat with nothing but the vast ocean to gaze upon for days on end? However, he had been making the trip for several years, escaping the Barbadian society from time to time, for the freedom of the English society and the ready acceptance he found among both the peerage and the gentry as a wealthy planter from the West Indies.

The house he had rented on this occasion was a solid-looking two storey townhouse of the red brick that was so common in the countryside of England. Over the years of coming to England he had made several friends as well as business acquaintances and he now welcomed two of them.

"William, Edward. Good to see you again," he said, rising to shake their hands in greeting.

"Same here, Henry Peter," answered William Parry. He was a very good-looking man, about the age of Henry Peter, who was rumoured to have been something of a scoundrel before he met his wife and became reformed. Edward Jeffries was quite the opposite. He was a tall thin man, a few years older than both men and was known for his serious nature and disapproval of anything remotely suggestive of fun. Both were merchants who shipped goods to Barbados, which is how Henry Peter had first made their acquaintance and they had become good friends.

"We always enjoy getting together when you're here and we never tire of hearing about Barbados," William continued.

"Indeed," agreed Edward in his somewhat formal manner.

"You must come and visit the island and my plantation one day. I would be delighted to show you the sights. Have a seat. One of the servants will bring us some refreshments shortly."

"So, what business brings you to our part of the world this time?" asked William.

"I am actually here to rest and enjoy the mother country, to tell the truth, as I quite enjoy the climate here at this time of the year," Henry Peter told him. He found that being in England seemed to help his asthma; at least he had never had an attack when he was in the milder climate. "I'm here for about two months."

"Wonderful."

"However, while I'm here I plan to manumit three of my slaves, one female and two girls, which brings me to the reason I asked you here today, apart from your interesting company, that is."

"I knew that you could not just be resting. Like me, you always have business on your mind," William smiled.

"How can we be of service?" asked Edward.

"I would like you to witness the deeds of manumission for me, if you would." He crossed to the desk where he had just laid down the papers and gathered them up once again, handing the deeds to the two men to read. William held the papers a fair distance from his face and began to read out loud:

"To all people to whom these Presents shall be made, I, Henry Peter Simmons, late of the Island of Barbados, but now residing in Liverpool in the county of Lancashire, Esquire have manumitted, enfranchised and forever discharged and by these presents do manumit, enfranchise and set free my coloured woman slave named Mary Joseph, now resident in the island of Barbados…" He paused.

"This is rather magnanimous of you, if I may say so, HP. But why here rather than in Barbados?"

"It's significantly less costly to manumit slaves here." Henry Peter answered him. "And I would not lay claim to being overly magnanimous. I'm simply rewarding her for 'meritorious services and divers other good causes and considerations' as it says in the deed."

"You are being too modest, I am sure," joked William. "I cannot help but wonder what meritorious services your coloured slave Mary Joseph has performed." William cast his eyes on the document again before smirking at him. Henry Peter rolled his eyes.

"I am sure that is none of our business, William," Edward said stiffly.

"And what of this mulatto slave girl, Mary Simmons?" added William as if he had not heard him. "What 'other good causes and considerations' do you have for freeing her?" he asked, reading the other document he had been given. "I cannot help but notice that she bears your surname." He was a good enough friend for Henry Peter to take no offence at his questions.

"Well, since I have asked you gentlemen to bear witness to these deeds of manumission, I can hardly fault you for asking questions. Well, you anyway, William. I hope I do not shock your English sensibilities, Edward, to hear that Mary Simmons is my coloured daughter and Mary Joseph is her mother."

"What about my sensibilities?" asked William in mock offence. Henry Peter ignored him.

"We are now required, thanks to pressure from your parliament, to register all our slaves so I thought this would be a good time to manumit them before the register is required for this year."

Edward stuttered, "Y- your daughter? And her mother? Oh! Yes, well…" he trailed off, unsure of what to say. William smiled at Edward's discomfiture.

Henry Peter smothered a smile of his own. He did warn Edward that he might be shocked. What was common place in Barbados was not something that was spoken about in polite company in England. Then again, what he was doing was not very common place in Barbados either. A few planters manumitted their slaves from time to time, although usually in their wills, and fewer still openly acknowledged their offspring. But he was no hypocrite.

"And this other one, Eliza Simmons?" asked Edward, almost reluctantly, looking at the paper in his hand. "I see that she also carries your name."

"Yes, some negroes take the surnames of their masters, but I do not lay claim to Eliza. However, I have owned her from birth and she is one that I took with me to Vaucluse."

"That is truly generous of you, Henry Peter," acknowledged William seriously.

"I am nothing if not generous," agreed Henry Peter in jest. "Now, if you gentlemen could affix your signatures to the documents, I would be in your debt. And to show my gratitude, I would like to offer you a glass of my finest brandy and a good Barbadian meal."

"That sounds splendid," Edward agreed, his composure now restored.

"I am grateful to you both. And as I said, you are welcome to visit my plantation any time you wish to experience Barbados for yourself," Henry Peter offered. "It is far different than what the abolitionists are purporting with their vicious rumours."

"Perhaps that is so on your plantation, Henry Peter. But can you say that for all?" Edward asked.

"No, of course not. I can only speak for those that I know of. However, the supporters of the Slave Trade Abolition Bill paint us all with the same brush," Henry Peter retorted angrily.

"What have you got in store for the rest of the year?" Edward changed the subject, sorry that he had gotten Henry Peter started.

"John Allen and I are getting ready to make an offer for a plantation called Dunscombe. It is just a short distance from Vaucluse."

"Very good," approved William. "Is it sizeable?"

"Certainly nowhere the size of Vaucluse, but it has 175 acres and about 141 slaves. Quite a high proportion of slaves per acre. I don't see how it could be profitable. Vaucluse has 495 acres, but we only have 195 slaves. We may bring over some of the Dunscombe slaves to boost our numbers, but more likely we will sell them off, for that number of slaves is preposterous for such a small plantation."

"Perhaps that's why the owners are selling out. They have obviously not done a very good job of managing the place efficiently," suggested William.

"That too, but John Farrell lives here and very likely does not want the bother of having a plantation in Barbados, which is fine for John Allen and I."

"You're becoming a veritable land baron," William mused approvingly. "But who will you leave it all to?"

"You're as bad as my brother and his wife. I have plenty of time to think about heirs later. Right now, I am focusing on capitalising on the great market for sugar by getting my hands on as much land as I can. I certainly hope I have a good few years to enjoy before I have to worry about that," laughed Henry Peter.

"Where is John Allen today? He is staying with you, is he not?" William and John got along very well.

"He has gone to friends to have them witness some manumission documents for him as well."

"Who is he manumitting?" Edward asked.

"One of his negro women and three children," Henry Peter answered.

"I will ask no more questions," Edward said drily.

"Ask no questions, hear no lies," HP quipped with a smile, making Edward shake his head. He could not understand the way of these planters from Barbados.

Chapter 10

September 22, 1817
Vaucluse Plantation

Henry Peter closed the ledger for the plantation
and picked up the copy of the slave register for
Vaucluse that his attorney, Henry Cummins, had
prepared in his absence. In spite of the Imperial
Registry Act being rejected in the House of Assembly
almost two years before, the government had
succumbed to the pressure from both anti-
abolitionists and the British government to force all
owners to set up registers to record information
about their slaves. It had not helped that St. Lucia and
Trinidad had complied years earlier.

He had bought a copy of the Registry Act and
several sheets of the printed schedules that were being

109

sold to record the information, but they had sat untouched for several weeks. Before he left for England he had run into Conrade Howell, the treasurer, who had advised him that if they were not completed and sent into the parish representative by the end of May there would be a charge of twelve shillings and six pence for each slave owned. He had not been joking either, for he had put an advertisement to that effect in the *Mercury* and Cummins had saved a copy and filed it in the Slave Register.

PUBLIC NOTICE
Barbados.
I do hereby give Notice to all owners or possessors of any slave or slaves, wind-mills, cattle mills, pot kilns, four or two wheel carriages, or any land, in this Island, that they are required, some time before the first day of June next, to give in, or cause to be given in, to one or other of the Representatives of the Parish, where such slaves, &C. may be, a true and exact account of the same, in default of which, the person so neglecting will have to pay for each and every slave twelve shillings and sixpence; for each wind-mill, fifty shillings; each cattle-mill, twenty five shillings; each pot kiln, fifty shillings; each four wheel carriage, five pounds; each two wheel carriage, fifty shillings; and each acre of land, eightpence, over and above whatever the tax may be for the present year, which forfeitures I am bound to demand from every defaulter.

CONRADE A, HOWELL, Treasurer.
Treasurer's Office, May 19, 1817.- 2n.

He was too diligent about money to ignore the warning and throw away the £150 which he would have to pay, seeing that he now owned over two hundred slaves, so he had instructed Cummins to complete the tedious task before the due date. Cummins had compiled the list of all the slaves at Vaucluse as at May 1 using the records that were kept by the plantation and by physically carrying out an inventory of the slaves, noting their gender, their name, their colour, where they were employed on the plantation, their age and where they were born, as required by the Registry Act. Henry Peter did not envy him for having to write that information for 229 slaves and then make a copy for the plantation to keep, but that was what he was paid for. And well, too!

Among the names that had been written was Harry's. Male, coloured, 10 months old and Barbadian. He was now a year and a quarter and walking about. He had darkened a little bit since his birth and his hair was no longer straight, but had started to curl, though not as tight as Molly Harry's. He looked more like Molly than him, but he had the Simmons' forehead.

Opening the journal again, he flipped back a few pages to where Molly Harry had been listed. Female, black (she was too dark to be classified as coloured), house slave, sixteen and Barbadian. She was not sure when she was born since her mother had died when she was very young, but it was around 1801. Judy Ann was on the same page and had the exact information as Molly Harry but that is where the similarity ended.

A knock at the door interrupted his thoughts.

"Come in," he called. Molly Harry poked her head around the door.

"Massa Henry," she began. "The money that you

give me yesterday gone! Eliza tell me she see Judy Ann sneaking out of my hut. I feel that she t'ief it!"

He sighed. He had decided to send Judy Ann to the fields after the incident with her harbouring her mother. However, that probably made her resent Molly Harry even more, from the complaints that he got about her. The last thing he needed was strife between the slaves, and Judy Ann was clearly a strife maker. He would let the drivers deal with her in the fields or else he would sell her. He had other issues with which to concern himself.

"All right, Molly. I will have Judy Ann's hut searched."

"Thank you, Massa Henry," Molly Harry smiled. "You alright, massa? You look tired."

"I am tired, Molly," he answered, rubbing one shoulder absently.

"Let me do that for you, massa," she said, coming around behind him to rub his shoulders. Henry Peter groaned aloud with pleasure as Molly kneaded the knots in his shoulders.

"That feels wonderful, Molly."

"Wha' you been doing that got your shoulders so hard, massa?" Molly Harry asked.

"Working on the books for the plantation and looking at the register that Cummins prepared. Look, here is Harry's name." He pointed to the place that the attorney had written Harry's information.

"I can't read, massa." Henry Peter realised that he had forgotten that she could not read. He didn't know why because it was rare to find a slave who could read.

"I forgot that, Molly."

"I want Harry to learn how to read and write,

though. I don' want he to be like me." She sounded wistful.

"Don't worry, Molly Harry. I will make sure that Harry has every opportunity. He will learn how to read and write and do much more than that," he promised.

"Thank you, Massa Henry," Molly Harry said. She didn't know what "every opportunity" meant, but she knew that her son would learn to read and write. Master Henry had said so.

Henry Peter remembered thinking, not too long ago, that teaching slaves to read was dangerous and yet here he was promising Molly Harry to make sure that Harry would learn to read. But then Harry was not just any slave; his blood ran in his veins. That made him different.

***

September 29, 1817
Roberts House, near Haggatt Hall, St. Michael

The shouts of the men drowned out the flapping of feathers as two angry cocks jumped at each other before falling in a tangled heap to the sand of the cock pit. The spurs attached to their feet sought the flesh of the other and with each darkening of the sand by blood cheers erupted.

Men were dressed from the fanciest clothing to the plainest, telling the story that all levels of the island's population were represented here. There were even some free coloureds. As long as they had guineas to buy a cock or two and some more to bet they were welcome.

A loud eruption signalled that the slightly bigger cock had struck a fatal blow and two of Roberts' slaves moved into the ring to remove the dead bird and capture the victor, returning it to its owner who stood by ready to grab it and make his way to the man counting out money to those lucky enough to have bet on the winner.

Roberts regularly put on matches at his house near Haggatt Hall on Fridays and Saturdays and was well- known for offering good fighting cocks for two guineas a piece. Henry's was not up to fight just yet and was being restrained by one of the slave boys he had brought with him.

While he waited for the next match, Henry Peter looked around and spotted his friend John Thomas Lord who had served with him as the other representative for St. Philip in the House of Assembly a few years back. He and his brother, Samuel Hall Lord, were making their way over to him. Talk had it that Samuel lured ships into the reefs off his plantation and when they crashed into the reef and he would then strip them of their treasure. Henry Peter didn't know him well enough to make a judgement about that. The island was full of rumours and folklore anyway. Then again, he was currently charged with perjury and forgery and awaiting trial, so maybe there was something to it. Anything was possible.

"Henry Peter, I've not seen you in months," John greeted him.

"John, Samuel, good to see you. I've been in England for a while."

"Oh yes, I know how you disappear to England ever so often. What brings you back now?"

"John Allen and I came in to sign papers for our purchase of Dunscombe."

"Oh yes, I heard that John Farrell was selling."

"We were fortunate that he was willing to sell."

"I do miss your presence in the House of Assembly," John told Henry Peter.

"Sorry, old boy, but two terms were more than enough for me," HP assured him. "Good to see that you're still batting away at it, but I'm hardly here so it makes no sense."

"Yes, I know. I have to say I enjoy the politics and we need to make sure that we're well represented, otherwise those aristocrats would continue to rule the island, to their advantage, of course."

"Well, I for one am glad that you are representing our interests."

"I don't know about "our interests" as you're now a major land owner since you bought Yorkshire Hall," Sam interjected. "You're practically one of the aristocrats now and you likely move in those circles in England."

"As you do when in England," Henry replied. Sam Lord had entered the London and Bath societies in 1804 when he first went to England and spent several years there, returning to Barbados after periods in England. "I am by no means an aristocrat," he continued, "but Yorkshire Hall, or Vaucluse now as I have changed the name, was quite a significant property that I was happy to acquire."

"Oh yes, I think I saw something like that in the *Mercury* a while back. Some chap claimed that a slave was being harboured on your estate, Vaucluse, formerly Yorkshire Hall," Samuel reminisced.

"Yes. That was rather unfortunate and I would

hardly confess to harbouring a slave on my estate."

"Speaking of slaves, I hope you handed in your Slave Register before you left for England," John told him, changing the subject.

"Damned nuisance that! Thankfully, it was handed in before the time. I thought you all had thrown out that bill. How is it that the House gave in to the pressure from England?"

"We lost the motion to the aristocrats. As you know, they have considerable property and connections in the great motherland, so they did not want to create any problems for themselves there. Many of them have started to leave the island anyway so they will not have to deal with the tedious chore of registering their negroes going forward," John groused.

"Well, my attorney Henry Cummins prepared mine this time. I cannot say that I envied him that task, especially since I recently bought eighty-three slaves from Philip Crick to add to those at Vaucluse."

"Philip Crick from Bath Plantation?"

"Yes. I know it better as Mount Edge."

"Why was he selling?"

"I have no idea nor did I ask him"

"Well, that's quite a number. How many are you up to now?"

"I've got about 260 or so at Vaucluse. John Allen and I are planning to sell off some from Dunscombe and Francis Barrow and John Leslie are interested in acquiring them."

"Good for you!"

"Yes, but not for Cummins. He's had quite a job with Vaucluse. However, he managed to get it done and assured me that he submitted it before our dear treasurer, Mr. Howell, had the opportunity to charge for late filing, as he threatened to do in the *Mercury*."

John chuckled. "Yes, he is rather enthusiastic about his job and the coffers could certainly do with some revenue, so we have no complaint."

"As registrar as well, he will certainly get some additional revenue from recording all that information," HP noted drily. "At least, from my understanding of the process, we do not have to do a complete filing each year. We can simply bring forward the numbers and add births and subtract deaths."

"Yes, that is correct. In fact, any changes, whether it be a sale, a purchase, a manumission or a gift."

The sound of Roberts announcing the next fight and inviting bets interrupted their conversation. They assessed the birds that were being pitted against each other and, deciding that they looked too evenly matched, chose to hold their bets for another fight.

"Did you hear what happened to Samuel Gollop?" John asked, moving a little way from the action.

"Can't say that I did," admitted HP.

"It was in the *Mercury*, probably when you were in England. Apparently, he was travelling between Upper Grays and Hannays about eight o'clock one night and three negroes jumped out of a cane field, dragged him from his horse and stole three dollars from him."

"Bloody daring," HP remarked, "but I can't say I'm surprised."

"Me neither," agreed Samuel. "After that attempted rebellion last year they've gotten more daring and troublesome than ever. Brother, looks like you may have to pass a law to increase the size of the parish militia."

"Or get them to actually do the work they're paid to do," inserted HP. "Speaking of work, let me see if my bird is ready to earn me some money today."

"Maybe I'll put a guinea or two on it, HP," John said. "You seem to have the luck of the devil."

"Or is it that the devil looks after his own?" chuckled Samuel.

"I'm sure you are closer kin to him than I am," responded HP with an answering smile as they made their way towards the cock pit.

***

Molly Harry buttoned up her blouse and handed Harry to Eliza to play with while she got a broom and a cloth to go up and clean Master Henry's room so that it would be in order when he got back from the cock fight. She would then have a bath in the big tub that he had given her so that she would be ready for him if he called for her as he tended to do when he came back after a successful time at the cock pit.

Her eyes trailed after the two of them, smiling as Harry tried to wiggle to get down from Eliza's grasp. He was a good-looking boy and very busy all the time, especially now that he was walking. His skin had darkened only a little with his hair remaining soft and curly so far. He was still nursing, although he was at the age where he could eat solid food now, but she was not ready to wean him yet. Besides, the nurse had told her that when she weaned him her monthlies would start again which meant that she could get with child if she lay with the master. Then again, he had been away for a few months so there was no danger of that before. She had missed him, but she had Harry to keep her busy.

"Molly Harry, you ain' goin' stop breastfeeding tha' boy?" Mary Ann asked, interrupting her thoughts.

"When I good and ready," she retorted defensively.

As soon as the master returned he had told her it was time enough to wean Harry and she had promised him she would do it soon, but this was one time she disobeyed him. She loved the closeness to her son that nursing him gave her and she was not ready to have another child. She did not want to take the chance in case another one came as easily as the first.

"Well, I sure the massa must be good and ready for you to stop so that he could get he share," she chuckled, making Molly Harry feel guilty.

"Anyhow, the midwife tell me that when I stop nursin' he all the time my monthlies will come back and I could get pregnant again."

"And you ain' know that the' got t'ings to stop you from gettin' pregnant?"

"No. Nobody never tell me so."

"Well, I could fix you up."

"You would do that? T'ank you, Mary Ann."

Molly Harry gathered up her cleaning things and climbed the stairs to the master's bedroom. She was content with her life. She felt sorry for Judy Ann out in the fields as she knew that the whip was part of the daily life for many of the field slaves, but in the house, and being the master's woman, she was protected. Since Harry had been born, the master had been very good to both of them, making sure that Harry had clothes and toys to play with, while she had nice clothes and extra portions of food.

She heard talk that the men who had been found guilty of taking part in the rebellion the year before had been executed. She felt sorry for them, but she could not fully understand how they wanted freedom so badly that they would die to get it. Her life was good. What would she do if she was free? She couldn't begin to answer that question. After all, she had never even thought about it and since the master had come and made her his woman she had no reason to think about it.

She had heard that he had freed Eliza and two other slaves that she didn't know when he was in England. How come he free Eliza? Why he didn' free her and Harry? But then, wha' she would do if she was free? It would be any different than how it was now? She ain' had nowhere to go and, anyway, she was happy to live in her little hut at Vaucluse.

***

Henry Peter dropped his empty coin bag on the table next to his bed. He had lost all his money today, the last to that pirate Sam Lord whose cock had beaten his. That was precisely why he only carried what he could afford to lose. He was determined never to find himself in such debt that he had to put his plantation into Chancery as his father had.

Things were going to get harder. He could see it coming. The registration of their slaves was only the beginning. There was a lot of pressure from England to abolish slavery and he did not know how long it would be before parliament would cave in to the pressure. He would fight that with all he had. Maybe he should have stayed in the House of Assembly, but it really was a waste of time voting on things like people's salaries and obeah laws when they were crucial issues facing the island. Did they not see that?

He had owned Vaucluse for over a year now and it was doing well. They had had a good crop last year and he was hoping to repeat it this year. It was a solid plantation; all it needed was someone to make sure that everything ran efficiently and in good order. He now knew all the slaves, by face if not by name, and he had had no major trouble since the incident with Judy Ann. At least he could say that none of his had run off or been found in the cage. After all, they were well treated and had a fair amount of freedom. He had even set up Mary Joseph and Mary who he had manumitted while in England with a little house in St. Michael.

He had not had an episode recently and all was well. The trip to England had eased some of the restlessness that he had been beginning to feel. He had thought that owning Vaucluse would cure that part of him. What was it that was missing from his life? He couldn't name anything. Maybe he just had to keep discovering new things to satisfy the restlessness in him.

Which was why he was surprised that he was still content with Molly Harry. Apart from seeing to his every need, somehow she seemed to soothe his soul. She was never demanding, never quarrelsome, never annoying. She seemed content with life. He envied her. That made him laugh to himself. He envied his slave? But her life was uncomplicated. Everything she needed was provided for her. What did she have to worry about? She did not even seem to crave the freedom that had driven the rebels. Surely ignorance was bliss.

Thoughts of her now stirred desire in him and he hastened downstairs.

"Molly Harry," he called.

"Yes, Massa Henry." She appeared from around a corner.

"Get Jack to draw a bath for me and let me know when it's ready. I'll be in my office."

"Yes, massa," said Molly Harry.

Half an hour later, Molly knocked at the office door.

"You' bath ready now, massa."

"Good, come and wash my back for me and then we can retire to my room. I feel to spend the rest of the evening with you."

"Yes, massa."

"Molly Harry, do you ever think to say no to me?" he asked curiously. She looked at him strangely, not sure how to answer his question.

"I didn' know I could tell you no," she replied quietly. Henry Peter thought about her answer for a moment, realising that he was not sure how he felt about it. It meant that she never came to him of her own free will, which took away some of the pleasure of having her. But then again slavery took away free will. Should man have the right to take something that God had given? Something foreign and uncomfortable stirred in him, causing him to think about things he preferred not to. He ruthlessly suffocated the feeling lest light shone upon it and give it life.

***

Molly Harry pulled the sheet over their bare bodies and rested her head on the pillow next to the master's. Their breathing had returned to normal as their hearts resumed their regular beat. Molly smiled contentedly as she thought about the pleasure the master had given her and she him. How different it was from the first time she lay with him.

He was a good master. He had even brought back gifts for her from England – scented soaps, handkerchiefs, two new dresses and underclothes. The last he had said were for him as well.

"What you do in England, massa?" she dared to ask him.

"I spent some time socialising and I did a little business."

"I hear that you free' Eliza and two more slaves when you was in England," Molly Harry said matter-of-factly.

"Who told you that?"

"I hear you tellin' Mr. Cummins," she confessed.

A slight discomfort ran through Henry Peter as he replied. "Yes, it's true. It costs less to free slaves in Liverpool than in Barbados." He knew that was not what Molly Harry meant.

"Eliza goin' still help me with Harry even though she free?"

"Yes, of course," Henry Peter assured her.

She thought for a moment and asked, "You ever goin' free me and Harry?"

"What would you do, Molly Harry? Where would you go? I want to look after you and keep you safe."

"You right, massa," she agreed. "I know that you

goin' mek sure that me and Harry got everythin' we need."

"That I will, Molly. You never have to worry about anything. I will take care of both of you."

"Thank you, massa," she said contentedly.

Once again Henry Peter thanked Providence that he had slaves like Molly Harry who were happy to be taken care of. It made life much easier.

Chapter 11

June 10, 1819
Vaucluse Plantation

Henry Peter secured the documents in his drawer and closed it. He had purchased seven passages to England. John's family, their nanny and he would sail to Bristol in five days on board the Venus. By the time they arrived in England it should be in the height of summer and the weather would be pleasant.

Unfortunately, it would not be only a holiday for John and Mehetabel. He had set up a meeting for them with George Gibbs and Robert Bright, two wealthy merchants who operated in Bristol and did trade with the West Indies, so that they could discuss obtaining a mortgage to finance Four Square Plantation. They would meet them in Bristol before travelling up to Liverpool, but normally he would sail straight to Liverpool and spare himself the long carriage journey.

He was concerned that John had overextended himself by buying Four Square. After all, Four Square had about 170 slaves and Simmons another 270 (give or take a few) and he knew what it was like to run Vaucluse with well over 200. Slaves were a significant expense especially if you clothed and fed them properly to get the best out of them, which he did.

When John had told him about needing money and being prepared to mortgage Four Square he had started to look for financiers outside of Barbados. Since he knew that George Gibbs and Robert Bright were always looking for opportunities to make money, he had approached them and found them to be favourably disposed towards the idea. As Mehetabel would be jointly signing for the mortgage, they had decided to bring the whole family over in the summer, start the discussions and stay for a month while the weather was still bearable in England, before travelling back to Barbados.

John's children were now getting older and would be easier to travel with, he hoped. He believed that the eldest, Mary Thomas, was about 12, with three years between her and his name sake, Henry Peter, and another three between him and Philip Cadogan. He didn't know how they would like sailing, but that was not his problem; John and Mehty would have to entertain them for the three to four weeks they would be at sea.

He had more or less adjusted to the voyage, although he would be lying if he said that he enjoyed it. At least he could make use of the time to indulge in his favourite pastime of reading. The sea breeze also seemed to do him good since his episodes were almost gone now, thank God.

Although he had recently returned from Liverpool after manumitting one of his slaves who now took care of the house in Liverpool, he didn't want to be in Barbados for too long, especially during the crop season with all the trash and cane arrows that were known to trigger his asthma. The plantation was prospering and it looked to be another good harvest, so buying passages for John and his family was no great hardship. After all they had been through the last few years it was the least he could do. Besides, he was not too sure that they could afford it themselves, although John had offered to pay.

He would have to tell Molly Harry to start to get his clothes in order and pack for him to leave in five days. She had not been pleased when he told her that he was returning to England shortly after arriving. She did not understand his need to leave the country and seek respite in England every year. She had been particularly difficult this time, very likely because she was expecting another child. He had assured her that he would be back before the child was born and if he returned with John and his family he would be, if she had the child in September as she believed she would. Granted, that time of the year was not the best to cross the Atlantic where the dangers of encountering a hurricane were always present.

"Molly Harry," he bellowed through the open door of his office, knowing that she would be close by waiting to see if he needed anything.

"Yes, Massa Henry," she answered a few minutes later, poking her head around the door.

"Come in. I need you to start getting my clothes in order and packing a trunk for me or get Eliza to help you if you are not up to it. I will be leaving in five days."

"Massa Henry, you goin' 'way already? I din' know it was to be so quick." She sounded distraught. "But the baby comin' soon." She was quite large, considering she was supposed to have another three months before the child was due.

"Molly Harry, we have discussed this before. From what you told me, the baby will not be here before the end of September. I should be back before then. And in any case, I don't need to be here as I cannot do anything. You will be fine."

Tears filled Molly Harry's eyes. She would miss the master. He could be demanding sometimes and got vex at small things, but she liked him, maybe even loved him, and she would miss him.

"I gine miss you, massa," she admitted quietly.

"I will miss you too, Molly," he replied and was surprised that it was true. However, nothing could entice him to stay in Barbados for any length of time. He greatly appreciated his life in England and the acceptance that he enjoyed there. "Before you know it I will be back. Now make sure you take good care of yourself, see the nurse regularly and give me a healthy son when I return."

"Yes, massa. But what if it is a girl?"

"That's no girl, Molly Harry. I have a feeling about this one. It will be a boy."

Molly Harry smiled. That was just like the master. He always expected everything to turn out the way he planned it and it always seemed to. She wondered if it would always be that way.

***

The Wharf, Bridge Town

John and Mehetabel's children were practically jumping up and down with excitement. This was their first trip on a boat and they could hardly contain themselves. There was general excitement in the air as the ship was loaded up with foodstuff to sustain the passengers and the crew for the four or so weeks it would take to get across the Atlantic, hopefully less.

They would soon call the passengers to board, but until then, Henry Peter was content to enjoy the feeling of solid ground under his feet while he waited. He was thankful that he did not get sea sickness as he had seen how miserable it could make a person. He hoped that the others would be spared from it as well.

"I cannot believe we are all going to England," Mehetabel enthused. "Henry Peter, how can I ever thank you for your generosity?"

"You can thank me when we're safely across the Atlantic," Henry Peter joked.

"I heartily agree with Mehty, HP. You've been very generous to take the whole family out," John added. HP nodded, uncomfortable with the thanks.

"That's quite all right. Let us speak no more of it. Did you manage to finish the manumission you were arranging?" he asked John, changing the subject. "You could have done it in Liverpool, you know, for less money."

"Yes, I know, but I wanted to deal with it before I

left. I've asked John Allen to act as attorney for me. He will pay the church warden, Thomas Briggs, the fifty pounds to manumit my man Joe Goddard. He has been very faithful to me through the whole rebellion and all that."

"That's fine, then."

"All aboard!" shouted a crew member, causing the passengers to erupt into a flurry of activity with slaves being ordered to pick up trunks and other belongings to take them on board. The Simmons joined the queue of passengers, followed by the children's nanny who Mehetabel was taking with her. Henry Peter already had servants who looked after the house in Liverpool, but she preferred to have someone she was familiar with looking after the children.

Henry Peter looked around at the small room that would be his for the next few weeks. He smiled wryly, accepting that no matter how much money you had there was no such thing as a large and comfortable room on a boat. Perhaps in years to come there would be ships built that would only be for passengers and would offer more comfortable accommodations. At least he had a small porthole that he could open and allow the sea breeze to blow in.

He now had a few servants to look after him in England, but he would have liked to bring Molly Harry who catered to his every need. However, she was very pregnant and wouldn't be able to do much. Maybe he would bring her one day when Harry and the new baby were older, provided that it survived. There should be no reason why it should not, although infant deaths were quite common. However, he left instructions to make sure that Molly would receive the best food, plenty of rest and care from the nurses on the plantation. Contrary to the belief of the troublemakers in England who were trying to put an end to using slaves and had been successful in ending the trade so far, his slaves were well looked after.

Returning to the deck when he felt the ship lift anchor, he joined John and his family as well as the few passengers at the railing. He always liked to catch this last view of Barbados as the ship sailed from the wharf and headed first north and then east towards England. A love for his country stirred in his heart. He did indeed love Barbados and the plantation that he owned, Vaucluse. What he did not like were the aristocrats, the large landowners who looked down on planters like him because of their wealth and their ties to the English peerage. Indeed, some of them were titled Lords while his family had no title, but Vaucluse was one of the larger plantations on the island and he intended to expand it.

"How are you faring, Mehty?" he asked his sister-in-law, noticing her pale face.

"I am fair at present, but I fear that my stomach will not take well to the movement of the boat," she said, placing a hand on her roiling stomach.

"I'm sure the ship's cook can give you something to settle your stomach. You will likely not be the only passenger to suffer from sea sickness."

"I do not suppose you are affected by it," Mehetabel stated, "For you are always on the seas."

"No, thank God. He has seen fit to spare me from that. Bronchial asthma is my cross to bear."

"Have you had any episodes recently?" John asked, although he knew that Henry Peter did not like to discuss his weakness.

"One since harvest started. I fare much better in England. The climate and the air there seem to agree with me more."

"I am glad to hear that," John told him.

The buildings and people became like toys as the ship sailed further from the shore. The children chattered excitedly, barely able to stay still. Henry Peter looked on them indulgently, glad that he had been able to give them this trip even though it was primarily for business. While John could certainly make his own decisions, he would not have advised the purchase of Four Square so soon after buying Harrow from John Allen, for it was a substantial plantation and no doubt cost a lot to operate. He hoped it would not be his downfall.

***

July 10, 1819
Bristol, England

The Simmons family once again stood together on the deck of the Venus, this time as the port at Bristol drew nearer. The children could hardly contain their excitement and Henry Peter acknowledged a sharing of their excitement as he approached England once again. They would stay in Bristol for a few days so that John and Mehetabel could meet with Gibbs and Bright before they all took a carriage to his lodgings in Liverpool where they would stay for about a month. During that time they might come back down to London and visit other nearer parts of the country so that Mehetabel and the oldest child, Mary Thomas, could see some of the famous sights. He wasn't sure if the boys would be too interested, but he and John could find other activities to entertain them.

"Are you glad to be back, HP?" asked Mehetabel, sensing his quiet excitement.

"I am indeed," he answered.

"What makes you like England so much?"

"Well, apart from the milder weather, you will find that we are welcomed as equals by the peers of the realm and the gentry, unlike in Barbados."

"And so you should be, now that you own a large plantation in Barbados," John reminded him. "That makes you landed gentry," John joked.

"As are you," Henry Peter retorted.

"But rich in property and little else."

The port at Bristol had nothing on the Bridge Town port in terms of ships and people bustling around. As soon as the boat had docked, and their luggage brought off, they were able to find transportation to take them to a fine boarding house where they would stay before travelling to Liverpool.

On arriving at the Inn Henry Peter arranged for three rooms: one for Mehetabel and John, one for the children and their nanny and one for him. As it was quite late on Saturday, they would not be able to meet with the merchants and would have to wait until Monday to send word of their arrival as no one did any business on the Sabbath. He was sure Mehetabel would want to attend a service at the cathedral anyway. He and John headed to the bar for a drink and information while the women and children made their way to their rooms.

"I will have to wait until Monday to send word to

the offices of Gibbs, Son & Bright of our arrival and request a meeting with them for Tuesday," he told John. "Meanwhile, we should see what there is to do in Bristol tomorrow so that you will not die of ennui," he joked, retrieving a copy of *Bristol Mercury* from a pile at the end of the bar after they gave their order to the barman.

"Contrary to what you believe, HP, I am not in need of constant entertainment."

"I do not believe that at all, brother, but would you prefer being in with the children?" HP looked at him over the newspaper knowingly.

"Now that you mention it…" John started, "an outing is sounding rather good."

"How unfortunate," Henry Peter said, "it looks as if we just missed several performances by a Mr. Kean from Theatre Royal in Dury Lane. He had a series of shows that finished on Thursday."

"I am much saddened by that," John sighed dramatically, earning him a wry look from Henry Peter.

"I forgot that you are lacking in culture, but Mehetabel would have enjoyed it immensely, I am sure. No doubt there will be some other entertainment to be had." Calling the bartender over, he enquired as to whether there was any entertainment available on the Monday.

"I heard that a new musical is starting called 'The Heart of Mid-Lothian'. It is a benefit hosted by a Miss Desmond," he said.

"The heart of what? And a musical you say?" John almost groaned aloud. The bartender smiled in sympathy.

"I am sure your missus will enjoy it," he cajoled.

Turning to Henry Peter he advised him where they could purchase tickets for a box and find out the time for the show. "I heard that you came in on the Venus from Barbados," he continued.

John and Henry Peter nodded in agreement, taking a sip of their ale.

"I understand that it made the trip in just twenty-five days!"

"Yes, indeed," Henry Peter confirmed. "Thank God that travel between the West Indies and here is improving."

"And are you here on holiday or to do business?"

"Business," John said, draining his glass.

"Thank you for the information." Henry Peter added, draining his as well. He and John both stood and took their leave, not wanting to give the nosy bartender any more information than necessary.

.

Chapter 12

Three Days Later

Henry Peter, John and Mehetabel sat quietly in the carriage, lost in their own thoughts. They had left the children with their nanny while they went to their meeting at Gibbs, Son & Bright. Henry Peter tried not to show his concern about the mortgage. Although he was the one introducing John to the men, he wasn't very comfortable as the mortgage was likely to be quite substantial.

He glanced at Mehetabel who was looking out of the carriage with a worried expression on her countenance. That was one of the reasons he had no wish to marry. Not that he was averse to borrowing or lending money. In fact, he and John Allen had signed a mortgage with Farrell to buy Dunscombe two years ago and he had extended a mortgage to Charles Kyd Bishop for Reed's Bay before that. There was nothing wrong with borrowing or lending, but you had to manage your affairs well and make sure you paid on time.

"Tell me a little about these men we are going to meet, HP," Mehetabel asked, looking around as if she had read his thoughts.

"George Gibbs is just a few years younger than me. He used to be married to the daughter of the Hendys who are merchants from Barbados. Not sure if you know them. But I understand that she died several years ago, and he has since remarried. He was in partnership with his father in a company called George Gibbs & Son before they started up this partnership with Robert Bright, hence the name. I don't know Robert as well as he is several years younger than George and me, but they are both very decent men. Their families have been merchants for years and, from my observations, they are very successful." Mehetabel nodded her thanks and John patted her hand as if to reassure her.

"Do not look so worried, Mehty. All will be well. Once we get this money we will turn the plantations around and pay them back with no problem." She smiled briefly but didn't look overly convinced. "We haven't recovered properly since the riots set us back, as you would know, HP. Simmons alone had the greatest damage sustained of all the plantations." Henry Peter nodded sympathetically, although he had heard it all before. He felt that John needed to justify the reason why his plantations were in need of finance.

"Here we are," he announced as the carriage

pulled up outside a fine-looking establishment with a sign over a heavy panelled door that read "Gibbs, Son & Bright", confirming that they had reached their destination.

They were greeted by a receptionist and shown into a board room where George Gibbs and Robert Bright were waiting to meet them. Henry Peter made the introductions and soon they were seated and offered beverages.

"So, you came in on the Venus," George started off.

"Yes, Saturday," Henry Peter told him. "Did you have cargo on board?"

"No, ours came in on the Sarah."

"We also had a shipment in from Jamaica on the Clara, so we'll be busy this week clearing those," Robert added.

"Glad that you could see us today, then," Henry Peter replied.

"What can we do for you gentlemen and, of course, lady?" prompted George, bringing the discussion back to the business at hand.

"I will let John explain since I am only here to make introductions."

"I purchased Four Square Plantation a few years ago and shortly thereafter the riots happened, destroying significant amounts of my sugar crop and causing major damage to the property. My other property, Simmons, or Harrow as it was also known, was extensively damaged as well. Needless to say, those factors significantly curtailed my sugar exports that year and the next." The men nodded sympathetically as everyone knew the impact of the riots on Barbados.

"I submitted claims of nearly eleven thousand pounds in damages to the insurance company, but they paid a lot less than that and furthermore all our premiums went up the following year. As you can imagine, the cumulation of these setbacks has left me short of cash which I need to operate the plantation, so I'm looking to secure a mortgage over the property."

"How much are you looking for?" George asked him.

"Eleven thousand pounds."

George nodded without comment. According to Henry Peter, they had pockets to let so that sum was well within his means to lend, if he chose to.

The two men listened attentively and asked questions, including Mehetabel in their discussions, which raised her estimation of them. Although Robert Bright was only 24, she found him to be just as quick and knowledgeable about business as George. On the way over Henry Peter had told them that he had joined the company George Gibbs & Son when he was only 19 and he had lived and worked in Spain in another part of the business before returning to England and becoming a partner with the new firm.

"We will need some time to review the information you brought, John, and of course we will make our own discreet inquiries about the plantation. We do a lot of trade with Barbados and we have an attorney there, Charles Thomas Alleyne, who will act on our behalf if we go ahead with the mortgage. Once we are satisfied, we will disperse the funds as soon as all the legalities are in place," promised George, standing.

"We would greatly appreciate that," John replied, rising as well. Henry Peter and Mehetabel joined them and thanked the men for their time before following Robert to the door.

"I think that went rather well," declared John once they had settled in the carriage. "Thank you for the introduction, HP."

"Happy to do it."

"Yes, they seemed like gentlemen that we can trust," agreed Mehetabel.

"Well, now that we have got that out of the way, you can enjoy your holiday," Henry Peter declared. "We can leave for Liverpool tomorrow."

"How long will it take to get to Liverpool?" Mehetabel inquired, wondering how the children who could become restless between St. Philip and St. Thomas would manage and, more importantly, how Henry Peter would deal with their close proximity.

"At this time of the year it will take just over a day at a good clip, so we will stop at an inn along the way to have a meal and we will spend a night at another one."

Mehetabel issued a silent prayer that Henry Peter would be able to tolerate being closeted with the children for that length of time. She also worried at the cost of the trip although she knew that HP's pockets were well lined with coin.

On arriving at the boarding house Henry Peter and John headed to the bar for a drink as was their custom while Mehetabel went to check on the children. The talkative bartender was there again and on hearing that they were leaving for Liverpool the next day, wasted no time in telling them about a riot which had happened there only the day before.

"We heard the news only today. 'Twas the Orangemen who were marching when they were accosted by a group of Catholic migrants. They threw bricks at them and tore their flags and beat them with the sticks."

"Who are the Orangemen?" John asked, concerned.

"They are Protestants who belong to an oath-keeping society called the Orange Lodge, named after William of Orange who was a king of England, Ireland and Scotland. They were having their usual march that they do every July 12 when a group from 'the lower order of Irishmen', as the *Liverpool Mercury* called them, started to attack them. Thankfully, no lives were lost."

"I am glad to hear that. I trust that peace has been restored," Henry Peter stated.

"Yes, indeed. Some of the Irishmen were arrested and are to be brought to trial."

"That is reassuring."

"No need to worry. I am sure that all will be back to normal by the time you get there."

"Thank you for that, as I would not like my family to be in any danger," John said.

"No danger of that," he was assured.

As John and Henry Peter mounted the stairs to their rooms a while later Henry couldn't help but remark with a cynical smile, "And they think that we are uncivilised in the colonies!"

Two Days Later
Lord Street, Liverpool

"We are not too far away now," Henry Peter assured Mehetabel who was almost at her wit's end trying to keep the two older children occupied. Thankfully, the youngest one was fast asleep across her lap. She threw a grateful smile at him.

"This is Lord Street," he informed them.

Lord Street was quite a wide street with red brick buildings lining both sides of the road. Many of the buildings had glass block windows at the front, hinting at the wares behind them. Smoke escaped from the chimneys on the shingled roofs, drifting into a clear sky and dissipating quickly. Men and women thronged the sidewalks while horse drawn carts, horses and donkeys meandered along the road. Mehetabel found it all rather pleasing.

"I do like the look of those brick buildings," she said, peering out of the window.

"Are we there yet?" asked Henry Peter's namesake.

"Just a few minutes more," answered his uncle in a remarkably patient voice. "Once we get to the end of this road we will be on Church Street and then my lodgings are just around the corner."

"Thank God," breathed John, who was as little accustomed to the long journeys as his children and had never been one to sit still for too long. Henry Peter smiled indulgently.

"What do you do for entertainment when you are here, HP?" asked Mehetabel.

"I tend to do a great deal of socialising as there is

always some dinner or musicale," he answered. "We also have a Theatre Royal that presents some fairly decent shows, so I am a frequent visitor of that establishment. I will take you to one of the shows," he promised.

"Oh, that would be lovely," she enthused. "I very much enjoyed the musical that we saw in Bristol."

"And what is there for my pleasure?" interjected John, who had barely survived the musical with his sanity intact.

"Oh, there are all kinds of entertainment. We have horse racing, there are various clubs and there is always a card party happening, although I encourage you to stay away from those."

"I wouldn't mind a visit to the races," John perked up.

"I also entertain quite a bit as I have made several acquaintances who always seem eager for my company and to hear news of the colonies whenever I come back."

"And why wouldn't they be eager for your company, HP? You can be quite sociable when you put your mind to it," teased Mehetabel.

"Yes, provided you are not set on matchmaking me with one of your young lady friends," he retorted wryly. Mehetabel smiled at him before reverting to the picturesque scene outside the carriage.

"Here we are," Henry Peter announced as the carriage pulled up to an attractive red brick house of two storeys. Before long they were in the foyer where Henry Peter was warmly welcomed back by a coloured servant who he introduced as William Richards and a stout English woman aptly named Mrs. Pounder who he said was the housekeeper.

Henry Peter left her to show Mehetabel, the children and their nanny to their rooms while he and John removed themselves to the library where he poured them each a snifter of brandy.

"This seems remarkably comfortable, HP," John said appreciatively, looking around at the well-appointed library.

"It's not Vaucluse, but it suits me well when I am here."

"And your man William Richards? Is he from Vaucluse? I can't say I recognise him."

"Yes, he used to be a carpenter there, but I have found better use for him here. I manumitted him in March, not long before I set out for Barbados. As I told you, it is much less than the fifty pounds they charge in Barbados."

"I know you're never one to spend a bad penny," John teased him.

"That's why I have so many to spend when I need to," Henry Peter remarked drily. John did not know if that remark was aimed at him, so he held his peace. After all, he was really in no position to defend himself when he had very few pennies to spend at the moment, bad or otherwise.

***

A Few Days Later

Henry Peter looked around the room as his guests mingled and chatted with each other. He had arranged the dinner party so that John and Mehetabel could meet some of his friends and acquaintances in the area. The group was made up of members of the gentry and merchants who were becoming more accepted since, in many cases, they had far more money than the landowners. The Gibbs and Brights were prime examples of merchants who had done extremely well for themselves, with businesses not only in Liverpool and Brighton but also in Spain. Being a landowner himself with a profitable sugar plantation, he was accepted by both.

"Has anything interesting happened in my absence?" he asked to those gathered.

"You've only been gone three months, Henry Peter," answered his friend Julian. "I find it quite amazing that you only left in April and are already back in July, having spent a month in Barbados as well."

"I'm becoming very fond of the Venus as it is very fast. We took only 25 days to get here with the help of some brisk trade winds and just a little longer than that to get to Barbados."

"Speaking of sailing to the West Indies, you missed the Annual Meeting of the West India Association last month," another friend said.

"Not a great miss," Henry Peter assured him.

"Oh, and Richard Lyster has died."

"Who is he? The name sounds familiar," Henry Peter mused.

"He was one of the parliamentary representatives for Shrewsbury."

"Oh, yes. Now I recall. Any good news?"

"William Blundell of Crosby House has a son."

"Congrats to him."

"In case you're interested, there is a residence near the sea that was offered for sale while you were away. I understand it hasn't been sold, in case you are looking for a more permanent property."

"Near the sea you say? Hmm, maybe I will take a look at it."

"And what of news from Barbados?" someone asked him.

"Nothing of significance to report. Thankfully, no more riots or such like. We do have a new Speaker of the House of Assembly. John Beckles, who was the Speaker since 1804, has now stepped down and Thomas Griffith is the new Speaker."

"You were in the House at one time, weren't you, Henry Peter?"

"Yes, for two terms representing the parish of St. Philip."

"I understand that you have to be a significant landowner to be eligible to hold a seat in the House. Is that right?"

"Indeed, but some of the smaller plantation holders have started to get more involved."

"And what about you, John?"

"Politics is not for me. One very vocal and controversial person in the family is enough," he joked, causing the men to join him in laughter. "And I'm sure that we have not heard the last from Henry Peter." John prophesied.

Chapter 13

"Massa Simmons, Molly Harry got another boy. He real sweet," Mary Ann announced from the doorway of his office.

"Thank you, Mary Ann. I will come and see him shortly. How is Molly Harry?"

"She good. Restin' now but this one was easier than the last one."

"I'm glad to hear that."

Henry Peter had returned from England just over a week ago and Molly Harry had been very happy that he would be there for the birth of her second child. Harry was now three and was running all over the place and giving Eliza quite a time chasing him. Although she was now free, she continued to live in

147

the house and helped Molly Harry to look after Harry. Henry Peter had been convinced that the child would be a boy even though Molly Harry had said she felt it was a girl.

What would he name this boy? Henry Peter put away the ledger he was working on and got up to go and see the newest addition to the Vaucluse family. Mary Ann opened the door of Molly Harry's hut before he even reached it and he was soon looking upon the child that he had no doubt was his. This one was fairer than Harry, with a small thatch of straight hair that would no doubt curl later. Molly Harry was proudly holding him against her bosom.

"Massa Henry, you was right. It is another boy," she announced, smiling tiredly.

"So I see. Well done, Molly Harry," he praised.

"He got blue eyes," she added, "but Hannah tell me they goin' change colour when he get older."

"Very likely, but he is a handsome boy." To Henry Peter he had the look of John Allen when he was born. He had been fourteen years old at the time and not overly interested in the baby, but he and John Allen had grown closer as they got older and had done a lot of business together, Dunscombe being the most sizeable property they had bought together. He would call him John, John Alleyne.

"I'm going to call him John Alleyne," he told Molly Harry.

"John Alleyne?" she repeated, looking at the baby. "That sound good," she agreed with a smile.

"Rest now. I am going back to my office to record his birth."

"Alright, massa," she said tiredly.

"Look after her," he told Mary Ann as she came

from the other room to take the baby from Molly Harry and put it in the cradle that he had had made for Harry.

"Yes, massa," she answered.

In a few minutes Henry Peter was back at his desk. His slave ledger had recorded twelve new births since Harry. The abolition of the slave trade would not hurt Vaucluse while he had healthy female slaves who kept breeding. Not that he considered the boys in that category. After all, they were his flesh and blood, so they would not be put to work in the house and certainly not in the fields. He added John Alleyne's information:

September 16, 1819
Birth
Coloured boy named John Alleyne

He would have to see about getting them baptised before he went back to England or maybe he would come back in time for the start of the harvest next year and do it then. He had had no objection to his slaves being baptised over the years and he would make sure that his boys were as well, even if he wasn't a big churchgoer. Already Harry was three and should have been baptised before, but he would make sure that they were both taken to St. Thomas Parish Church when John Alleyne was a little older. He remembered how long John and Mehetabel took to baptised their children. My goodness, they had been walking and talking by then.

He wondered how John was getting on now that he was back. He was glad that he had been able to give them the holiday in England and introduce them to Gibbs and Bright, but he knew that it would likely take a while for them to get the money they needed. After all, the men would want their attorney here to visit Four Square to determine if all was as John had said and then it would take a while before the papers were drawn up and the money transferred. He couldn't help him right now because he needed to watch his output of cash as anything could happen to devastate a plantation.

Thankfully, Vaucluse was doing well. In fact, all the plantations in Barbados were thriving, as the harvest had been good. The island had exported over 19,000 hogsheads and just about 7,000 tierces of sugar that year, the most hogsheads in fourteen years. Hopefully, Four Square and Harrow had a good year as well.

***

October 13, 1819
Vaucluse Plantation

The gale force winds whipped the trees soundly, stripping off leaves and small branches and blowing them far from their original location. The sound of it whistling through the cracks in the shutters was quite eerie and Henry Peter was glad that he had instructed Hannah to see that Molly Harry and the children had been brought into the house. The baby would be ignorant of what was happening, but he was sure that Harry would be terrified and maybe Molly Harry as well.

Of all the things he missed about Barbados, the

hurricane season was not one of them. When he had come in to buy Dunscombe in September two years ago there had been a distressing gale the next month that did serious injury to the shipping in the island before going on to devastate St. Lucia. There had been another gale last year while he was in England, although it had not done as much damage. It seemed that every year there was some force of nature to contend with, but that was the fate of the Caribbean. He should have gone back to England sooner, but there was nothing worse than meeting a hurricane at sea, so he would now remain until early December.

Peering at his pocket watch, he noticed that it was after noon, but his office was darkened by the shutters covering the windows and even when he had looked out the small window at the back of the house earlier it had looked as if the sun had never risen. The wind had been blowing ferociously for the last two hours with the rain driving down in torrents. While they were safe at Vaucluse because of the elevation of the land, he knew that parts of the island would soon be flooded if the rain continued in this vein.

The storm continued all day and into the following morning. Henry Peter spent most of the time in his office reading by the light of two lamps. Sounds of breaking tree limbs and flying missiles being blown against the house continued incessantly. The house servants huddled together in the back rooms while Molly Harry and the children bedded down in one of the bedrooms, together with Eliza who slept on a pallet on the floor. He smiled to himself as he imagined what Mehetabel would say to that arrangement.

When there was a break in the weather on the

second day, Henry Peter, tired of being cooped up in the house, ventured outside to inspect the plantation. He was shocked at the damage to the crops and many of the slave huts since the plantation house had been relatively untouched. The slaves had taken shelter in the barns and the sugar works, but they would have to wait until the storm passed before any repairs could be made to their homes.

Word came later that day, by one of the militia men who had come up from Bridge Town, that torrential rains had filled up the natural water-courses from St. Michael, St. George and from a part of St. Philip and the rushing water had swept away the Constitution Bridge which Henry Peter knew had been built at a substantial cost. He reported that in Broad Street water had risen to three or four feet and in some places as high as five feet, resulting in the flooding of the ground floor of every house that had managed to withstand the fierce wind. Two vessels, the Superior from New Brunswick and the Three Sisters from St. Vincent, had both been wrecked at Needham's Point and the military had been able to rescue all but two of the crew members.

Henry Peter thanked Providence that Vaucluse had not feared as badly as others, especially when he heard some of the tales of tragedy. The sugar works of many plantations had been damaged and several of the buildings at Foster Hall in St. Joseph had sunk under the earth and a wood below Hackleton's Cliff had slid down to the spot where the buildings at Foster Hall had stood.

Even more disturbing was the report that the ground under Dr. Bascom's house in St. Thomas had given away, leaving the house almost buried beneath the mud. Thankfully, the family were not in residence or their lives would certainly have been lost. It was being said that such destruction had not been seen since the Great Hurricane of 1780, which he could barely remember as he had been only four years old at the time.

This was life in the islands. They were constantly challenged by diseases, pests to ravage their crops or natural disasters, but they were a hardy people. They would put their hand to the task of rebuilding. They had no other choice.

***

March 5, 1820
St. Thomas Parish Church

Henry Peter greeted his friend William Grant Ellis outside of St. Thomas Parish Church. William owned land in St. Thomas as well and they had gotten to know each other when he had moved into the parish. Whenever he was in Barbados for any length of time they would meet for a drink and catch up on what was happening in the island. Like him, William was not married so they had that in common as well.

"Henry Peter, I am not accustomed to seeing you grace the door of this church," he joked.

"I am having two of my boys baptised today," he gestured to where Molly Harry and Eliza were tending the children until the parishioners left the church.

"You make a practice of baptising your slaves?"

"Yes, indeed. Over the years I have had many baptised and this year four so far."

"And you attend the baptisms?"

"Not as a rule, but Harry and John Alleyne are mine," Henry Peter answered.

William turned to look at them again. "Few men own their coloured offspring," he commented.

"I have no wife to shame with my coloured children."

"Nor I. But from what I hear, your sister's husband, Sir Reynold, would highly disapprove of your conduct."

"Very true," Henry Peter chuckled. "It is just as well that I do not seek his approval. He is very proud of the fact that he produces no coloured children on his plantations and I am happy for Rebecca. He would find it somewhat discomfiting if he knew that I have adopted the Alleyne name for one of my boys."

"You are without qualms about anything, HP," William chuckled. "I have to admit to also having a coloured son, Thomas, but as his mother is a free coloured woman, I may escape Sir Reynold's disapproval."

"Not that you would lose any sleep if you did. We are two of a kind."

"Indeed. So how many slaves do you have at Vaucluse now?"

"About two hundred and fifty. What about you?"

"About a quarter of what you have at Vaucluse and, unlike you, I have not baptised them."

"You should give it some thought. I find that those who attend to religious instruction and seek to be baptised are most industrious and trustworthy. When they ask me to have their children baptised I can only see the good in it, so I also approve the baptism of many of the children."

"I have not made it a practice among my slaves, but perhaps it is something I should start."

"I highly recommend it. It is good for them and makes them easier to deal with."

"Well, I will leave you to your appointment with the priest. Do stop by for a drink before you take off to England again."

"I will be gone next week, but I will be back in a few months and I will see you then."

***

July 13, 1820
St. Michael, Barbados

"I cannot believe how long this mortgage has taken to come through," John complained to Henry Peter as they entered the St. Michael precinct.

"I had not thought it would take so long myself. But the storm of last year delayed many things in the island, as you know."

"Indeed. You saw for yourself how we fared at Harrow and Four Square, but it could have been worse."

"At least you were not as unfortunate as Thomas Yard at Foster Hall and many others who lost everything."

"That's true, but I just wish I could catch my hand and work my plantations without a slave revolt or a storm. These incidents have certainly compounded my problems," he sighed wearily.

"I sympathise with you, John. I am sorry that I have not been able to help you more. John Allen and

I are still trying to turn around Dunscombe and make a profit from it as it had far too many negroes for such a small plantation. And as you said, the storm did not help. We have had to rebuild many of the slave houses and the sugar works was extensively damaged. We may well have to give it up."

"You don't have to explain yourself, HP. I do not think for one minute that you ought to help me, but I know that you would do it if you could. It's just that I've had to expend money when I could ill afford it, so I am very glad that this mortgage indenture is finally ready for signing."

They were interrupted by a clerk who came to tell them that it was John's turn to appear before Henry Bishop who was the Chief Judge for the precinct.

"Well, let me go and sign away my life," joked John.

"Let's hope it doesn't come to that," Henry Peter replied soberly, feeling very responsible for arranging this transaction for John. He really hoped that he would be able to meet the obligations of the loan.

Before long, John had signed the papers to confer judgement to Gibbs and Bright in the penal sum of twenty-two thousand pounds to secure payment of eleven thousand pounds for Four Square.

"I find myself in need of a drink," he said when they had left the precinct.

"Let us go and have a meal at the King's Arms and you can have a drink," Henry Peter suggested.

When their meal was before them and John had taken a fortifying sip of his brandy, Henry Peter sought to change the subject by telling him about some of the events in England. He had just started to share an amusing anecdote to lift John's spirits when

John interrupted him.

"Here comes Francis Barrow," John said, raising his hand in acknowledgement to Francis who had just come in.

"Hello, gentlemen." Henry Peter and John stood to greet Francis who had stopped at their table.

"Hello, Francis. Please join us," Henry Peter invited. "I take it that you know John, my brother."

"Yes, we are acquainted. How are you doing, John?"

"I am very well, thank you."

"It is quite the coincidence that we should see you today as I was just talking to John about Dunscombe." He turned to John and added, "When we bought Dunscombe from James Farrell we sold quite a number of the slaves to Francis and his partner John Leslie."

"Yes, indeed."

"So, how many children are you up to now, Francis?"

Francis laughed and told John that he and his wife, Sarah, had ten children. John whistled.

"I do believe we have enough now," he joked. "Did you recently get back from England?" he asked Henry Peter.

"Yes, last month."

"Is the country still in mourning for King George?" he asked. "You know we didn't hear a thing in Barbados until March and he had been dead for nearly two months by then."

"Yes, I heard that. I left the island just before the news arrived, so it wasn't until I reached England that I heard. By that time the Prince of Wales had been sworn in as King George the Fourth."

"Sarah and I are thinking of moving to England with the children."

"Whereabouts?"

"We are thinking about Bath."

"Well, I will be sure to look you up when I come down to Bristol."

"That would be good. I would enjoy seeing a familiar face."

"Gentlemen, I must be heading to St. Philip now. It was good to see you again, Francis, and HP, I will see you soon." John stood up and shook hands with his new acquaintance before taking his leave. He had to stop by the bank where he was told the funds would be deposited to his account. Hopefully, he would be able to turn around Four Square. He would certainly have enough money to do it, provided that no further tragedy struck.

Chapter 14

July 28, 1826
Barbados

Henry Peter looked at the approaching coastline of Barbados. This was one visit that he was not particularly looking forward to. His manager, William Doyle, had written to him to update him on the condition of the plantation as usual. While it was a common occurrence, what was different this time was that he had informed him that Molly Harry had died shortly after she had birthed a child in April. She had apparently never fully recovered from the birth and died a week later.

He had come back to the island the year before and signed an indenture on his birthday, May 17, to take out a small mortgage on Vaucluse, conferring judgement to Margaret Goodridge for the penal sum

159

of £3,000 to secure £1,500. Molly Harry had not been pregnant then, at least not to show. The child was not his, for he had not had relations with her on that trip. He had not expected her to keep herself for him though, as he now lived mostly in England and she was still young and attractive. He felt a pang as he thought about her. She would only have been about twenty-five, half his age since he had turned fifty that May, and she was already dead.

His mind drifted back to the last time he had seen her. He was in his office when she had knocked cautiously and waited until he bid her enter.

"I could come in, Massa Henry?" she had asked from the doorway.

"Of course, Molly Harry. Everything all right?" he had asked.

"Yes." She had seemed to hesitate for a moment before she blurted out, "I could get baptise, Massa Henry? Dina, Best, Station, Sonny and Mary Beth get baptise last year and Harry and John Alleyne get baptise ever since."

"That is true. You understand what baptism means, Molly Harry?"

"Yes, massa."

"Then, you may certainly get baptised." He wondered now if she had been pregnant at that time and if that was why she sought to put her life in order.

"Thank you, massa. And thank you for makin' sure that Harry and John Alleyne always got whatever they need and for the man you send to teach them. Both of them could read and write real good now."

"I'm glad to hear that, Molly. I told you that I would make sure they would have every opportunity.

You never have to worry about them." Those were the last words he had said to her and he hoped that she took them with her to the grave. He would keep his word.

He wondered how they were doing. Harry would now be ten and John Alleyne only seven. He had been only three when his father had died so he did not remember him at all. However, even being an adult when his mother had passed in England, he had felt the pain of loss, so he could well imagine how the boys were feeling. It was that that caused him to book a passage as soon as he had heard. He saw them but once a year when he visited the island, but he always made provision for their welfare and their education as he had promised Molly Harry. He knew that the housekeeper Betsy Jane, the house negro Mary Ann and the other domestics would look after them, but they would be devastated by the loss of their mother.

Within an hour the boat had docked and Henry Peter was on his way to Vaucluse. Thankfully, the weather was good although the rainy season had started, and he hoped that this would be a year that Barbados would be spared a hurricane. The last major gale had been the one he experienced in 1819 and a few had passed close in the last few years, but thankfully, they had been spared from major bad weather. He still kept abreast of what was happening in the island from the *Mercury* which his manager, William Doyle, mailed to him regularly. After all, what happened in the island affected Vaucluse and Vaucluse provided his living.

About three years ago there had been some unrest in the island among the slave population who had thought, once again, that their emancipation was imminent. He wasn't surprised because Wilberforce and Clarkson had been agitating for the abolition of slavery for years in England and word had gotten back to the island.

Naturally, he had read Wilberforce's pamphlet "Appeal to the Religion, Justice and Humanity of the Inhabitants of the British Empire in Behalf of the Negro Slaves in the West Indies". He had dismissed it because the appeal was surely not to him for he was not one to treat his slaves as brute beasts. Had he not baptised more than a hundred of them over the years? And though he was mostly absent now, he knew that Doyle was a good and fair manager. However, he had made a significant investment to purchase them and he was certainly not willing to lose his investment without a fight. Those agitators in the British Parliament had no understanding of what it took to run a sugar plantation and wanted to remove his workforce from him. That kind of talk of freedom only caused the negroes to become rebellious.

The unrest among the slaves had forced Sir Henry Warde, the Governor-in-Chief of the island, to publish a proclamation in the *Mercury* warning the slaves that they had erroneously heard that they were soon to be freed. He remembered what had happened in 1816 when they had thought that. Thankfully, his attorney seemed to have no trouble at Vaucluse which was the only property he now owned, or had an interest in. Four years ago, he had transferred the small mortgage he held on Reed's Bay to his colleague Thomas Lee and his partners Nicholas Farmer, George Haynes and William Foderingham, all of whom were merchants from Liverpool, and he and John Allen also no longer owned Dunscombe. The

English merchants were certainly getting their hands on a number of plantations on the island. He hoped that John was managing to hold on to his.

Everything was changing. Towards the end of 1823, Sir John Beckles, who he had served with in the House of Assembly, had passed away. It was akin to the end of an era in Barbados, as he had represented St. Michael in the House for 37 years and had been Speaker for fifteen of those years. The Speaker was now Robert Haynes from Bath Plantation who had represented St. John in the House of Assembly when he represented St. Philip. That seemed like a lifetime ago.

As the carriage he'd hired passed through St. Michael close to where his daughter Mary Ann and her mother lived, he made a mental note to visit her on this trip. He also needed to visit John and Mehetabel and he hadn't seen his half-sisters for some time. He was not sure why these thoughts were in his mind today. Maybe Molly Harry's death had made him more aware of the frailty of life and the importance of family, especially since neither his father nor his brother, Philip, had lived to thirty. Who knew how many more years he had.

***

The boys were overjoyed to see Henry Peter, since he had been there a year ago. It must have seemed a long time to them. Underneath the joy on their faces he could see sorrow lurking in their eyes. He was thankful that they had his housekeeper and the house slaves to comfort them and friends to distract them.

"Boys, I am very sorry to hear about your mother," Henry Peter said in his direct way. They nodded sadly, the joy disappearing from their faces at the fresh reminder of her death. "Who has been looking after you?"

"Betsy Jane, Eliza and Mary Ann," they answered.

"I am glad. I will always make sure you have someone to look after you, even if I am not here. Now come and tell me what has been happening since I was here last?"

"Harry and Elisha had a fight," John Alleyne reported with relish.

"A fight? Why?" Henry Peter looked at Harry sternly. "And who is Elisha?"

"One of the boys who works in the fields," John Alleyne supplied.

"He started it," Harry complained. "He and Duchess were asking how come they are the same age as John Alleyne and me and they have to work and we don't."

"What did you say to that?"

"I didn't get the chance to say anything because he pushed me and I pushed him back…"

"And they started fighting," John Alleyne finished excitedly.

"Harry, fighting is for people of little intelligence who do not know how to use words to diffuse a situation," Henry Peter explained. The boys naturally looked puzzled. "Do not fight unless it is to save your life or protect someone else's," Henry Peter instructed. They seemed to understand this better.

"So, why don't we have to work like the other children? Duchess is seven like John Alleyne and she still has to pick weeds."

"You do not have to work because you are special and I have greater things for you to do than work in the fields. That is for the slaves to do. Your job is to learn, as I promised your mother. Now, tell me what you have learned recently and let me hear how well you can read. Learning is very important; it is what separates men in life." They looked at him in puzzlement again, but he knew that they would come to understand what he meant when they got older.

Henry Peter spent the rest of the day looking over the plantation with Doyle, speaking to the slaves that he came across, many of whom he had purchased with the plantation as well as a few he had brought with him. He was saddened over the nineteen slaves they had lost since the last report, but they had had almost double the number of births, so the plantation was doing well. Last year the island had produced 22,545 hogsheads of sugar, second only to that produced in 1823, which had been the highest in twenty years. While tierces of sugar were down a little, the number of bales of cotton had been at their highest since 1805. Surely, England should be pleased that Barbados was continuing to help her to feather her nest and should be encouraged to leave well enough alone.

The next day he decided to pay a visit on Mary Ann and sent a message ahead to announce his visit lest he ride all the way to St. Michael to find that she was not at home. When he arrived he was somewhat taken aback to discover that she had become (seemingly in the last two years) a beautiful, mature young woman with a bloom in her cheeks.

"My dear, you look to be in the peak of health."

"Thank you. I am only now feeling more like

myself."

"Have you been ailing?"

She hesitated before saying, "Only in the mornings."

Henry Peter was not slow of mind and immediately caught her meaning. "Are you saying that you are with child?" He did not look pleased with the news.

"Yes. I am three months along. I am expecting to have the child in January."

"You are yet only sixteen," he chided before he caught himself in his own hypocrisy, as Molly Harry had been but fifteen when she birthed Harry. "Who is the father?"

"His name is William Morris. He is a merchant in town."

"Is he a free coloured?"

"No, he is white."

"Are you to marry?" Henry Peter asked. Mary Ann shook her head and looked down sadly, making her father soften towards her.

"You need not worry. I will see that you and the child are well taken care of."

"Thank you… Father." She added the title after a slight pause, looking at him as if for permission to use it.

Henry Peter nodded his acceptance "So, I am to be a grandfather," he acknowledged. The thought did not displease him; he was certainly old enough.

***

As the carriage pulled up to the great house at Four Square, nostalgia gripped Henry Peter. St. Philip was where he had spent the majority of his life, first at nearby Harrow Plantation when his father was alive and after his mother had remarried to John Allen Olton Sr. and then at his own properties. The house and yard looked well-kept so John and Mehetabel seemed to be doing a good job of keeping it up. When he was in the island he sometimes heard talk about John's slowness in paying his debts which concerned him somewhat.

Before he even reached the door it opened and Mehetabel and John met him on the porch with broad smiles.

"HP, good to see you," John greeted, shaking his hand and slapping him on the back.

"You also," he replied, turning to embrace Mehetabel.

"What brings you to these shores?" John asked him, leading the way inside.

"Plantation business," Henry Peter answered vaguely, aware of Mehetabel's presence.

"I will go and tell the girls to prepare some refreshment," she said, leaving to give them a few minutes alone.

"Your wife is a treasure," HP praised as she left them.

"Indeed. Now what kind of business are you here to see after?"

"Do you remember Molly Harry, the woman who is the mother of my two boys?" John nodded. "She died a few months ago shortly after giving birth to a girl. Not mine this time. I came back to see after the boys. See how they were doing and who is looking after them."

"That is very decent of you, HP. Some do not

acknowledge their offspring at all."

"I am not some," he smiled briefly. "Some are unable to because they have a wife. I have none, so I am not ashamed to name them as mine."

"I am very glad to see you, even if you are here for less than joyous reasons."

"How are things going?"

"They could be better, but at least we're not in Chancery," John assured him.

"Good, good. Although I don't know how long we will be able to go on as we have been because in England there is a great deal of pressure on the parliament to abolish slavery altogether. So many rumours are abounding about the way the slaves are treated in the colonies, and by those who have little knowledge of the truth."

"It is a constant source of worry to me. It is already hard to try to make a profit with the labour of the slaves, far less if we have to pay them!"

"That is why I am glad to leave it in the hands of Doyle and spend my time in England."

"How I wish I could do that!"

"Be careful that you do not worry yourself to death. I was thinking recently of how young our father and brother died. All of this has made me to appreciate life more."

"Well, you've made fifty, HP. That is old for our family."

"Indeed! Oh, and I am to be a grandfather," he announced.

"A grandfather?" John repeated in disbelief, searching his brain for how that was possible.

"Yes, my daughter Mary Ann is with child."

"I had forgotten about her. How old is she?"

"She is sixteen and will have the child next year. Some merchant in town is the father."

"Well, congratulations, I think."

Mehetabel rejoined them and they changed the topic of the conversation, lest she be appalled at Henry Peter's shameless acknowledgement of his reputed coloured children.

***

March 26, 1827
St. Michael

Dear Father

I asked your manager Mr. Doyle to send you this letter and he kindly agreed to send it with his next parcel to you.

On March 24 my son, your grandson, Henry Morris Simmons was baptised. He cried very loudly when the reverend put the water on his head so I think that he will have much to say in life and may be very bright as he is already very alert at two months. He looks like his father, with brown eyes and straight brown hair, but they may change as he gets older.

I am well, only a little tired. When you are next here I hope you will come and meet him.

Your daughter
Mary A Simmons

Chapter 15

"Mistress, mistress come quick!"

"What is it, Sally Betsy?" Mehetabel quickly got up from her seat on the veranda where she was sewing a dress for one of the house slaves. Sally was one of the coloured slaves who worked in the fields but would sometimes help out around the yard. Her eyes were now wide with panic. Mehetabel's heart felt as if it had stopped beating.

"William the carpenter say that the master collapse in the stables and the' carry he to the hospital. The nurse send somebody to get the doctor."

"Oh my God, I'm coming!" Mehetabel picked up

her skirt and ran from the veranda. Many different scenarios of what she would find flashed across her mind, but none prepared her to see John laid out on one of the beds, pale as death, as she rushed into the slave hospital.

"What happened? How is he?" she asked the nurse, picking up his hand. It felt lifeless in hers but still held warmth.

"John, John!" She urged him to open his eyes until the silence of the slaves who had gathered and the stillness of his chest told her what she could not believe.

"It must be he heart, mistress," the nurse said quietly. "By the time William bring he in he did already gone, but I still send for the doctor."

Mehetabel felt nothing but numbness and disbelief. Her eyes refused to leave John's chest as if expecting to see it rise with his next breath. She could not believe that he was gone. He had left the house only a short while ago to go to the stables to check on a horse that he was selling. He had told her he got an offer he couldn't refuse, but she knew that was not the truth. Had worry about the plantations caused his heart to fail him?

"Oh, John," she cried, throwing herself on his chest. "It was not worth it. None of it was worth this."

The slaves looked on silently in sorrow, but no one was brave enough to try to separate her from the body of her husband. When the doctor came he was the one who gently but firmly lifted her away and gave her into the care of the housekeeper. His heart hurt for her as she would have to tell the children and deal with the situation. He wondered if either of

John's brothers, Henry Peter or John Allen, was here to help with the burden, for she would need help.

***

February 10, 1828
Four Square, St. Philip

> *Dear Henry Peter*
> *I do not even know how to put the words on the paper, but it is with deep regret that I am forced to write you to tell you that John passed away suddenly two days ago. The doctor said it was his heart. I have not been able to bring myself to write of it before as I have been beside myself with grief. I still cannot believe it and I keep expecting him to walk through the door at any time. I have not even been of comfort to the children. Henry Peter is quite the young man at nineteen now and he has suddenly grown up and is handling things well. Rebecca has also come over and been a great help and comfort.*
> *I know that this will be a shock to you and you will no doubt regret that you cannot be here for his burial, but when you are next in Barbados I will go with you to his gravesite so that you may pay your respects. I am unable to write anymore at this time, but I promise to send you a longer letter when I am more myself. I do want to thank you for being the good brother you were to him and for being as a brother to me.*

> *Your dearest sister-in-law*
> *Mehetabel Ann Simmons*

Henry Peter stared at the letter in shock and disbelief. How was it that John could be dead? He was not yet fifty, two years his junior. Granted that their father and brother had died young, but he had thought he and John would grow old together. Grief choked him and sprang tears to his eyes. He felt more alone in that moment than he had ever felt in his life.

***

February 18, 1830
St. Michael, Barbados

Henry Peter waited impatiently to be called before John Alleyne Beckles, Chief Judge of His Majesty's Court of Pleas in the precinct of St. Michael. He could not help but remember sitting in the same precinct with John when he had come to sign the mortgage for Four Square many years ago. John had joked about signing away his life but perhaps that was what had killed him. He had not realised that he was in so much debt. Mehetabel would be forced to sell both Harrow and Four Square and, from what he had seen, they would only account for a portion of the debt. The plantations would go into Chancery; the very thing that he always feared for himself. His heart hurt for Mehetabel and grieved for John. He had come back as soon as he could get a passage on a ship to Barbados and had spent time at John's grave, comforting Mehetabel and the children, and helping Mehty get things in order. But then he had left in July to return to England so that he would be in time for John Allen's wedding to Mary Anne Sibun in August.

Today he was there to sign documents with James Neil for an additional mortgage over Vaucluse, but he was not concerned that he would be unable to repay it. It was not that he did not have assets, but he preferred to avail himself of the credit that was being offered so as to have his cash free for any opportunities that arose. Margaret Goodridge, who had held the first mortgage in the amount of £1,500 over Vaucluse since 1825, had assigned it by way of a writ to Neil, who had agreed to give him a further charge of £500 on the property and he would repay both amounts in a year.

The security included all the lands, the mansion, the outbuildings and the slaves, but he had taken care to include only 272 of the 280 slaves in the transaction. In the unlikely event that he was unable to repay the mortgage at the stipulated time, he did not want to risk losing Harry and John Alleyne, as well as some of his trusted slaves, to Neil.

Since he was in St. Michael he would stop by to visit Mary Ann and her son Henry Morris. He would be three years old by now and was no doubt quite a handful. He had instructed William Doyle to give Mary Ann a ten-year old slave girl, Mary Williams, last year (in trust) to help her out with Henry Morris. Henry Piggott had also given her (in trust) a girl of 23 years old with her two-year old child, but for a time only.

He wondered if Henry Piggott was Henry Morris' father but according to Mary Ann he was not so he was unsure why he would entrust her with two slaves. Perhaps he, too, was helping her out but for what reason, he did not know. Anyway, she was an adult and could well look after herself. He would continue to give her an allowance each year as was his custom. After all, she was his daughter.

Chapter 16

October 25, 1832
Lymington, Hampshire, England

"John Allen, I am sorely happy to see you!" Henry Peter greeted him. "Glad you could make the trip. I miss our exploits now that you have settled down and become a respectable married man."

John Allen laughed as he greeted his half-brother with a hug. "Do not let Mary Anne ever hear you talking of our exploits," he warned. "We've been married four years now, but she has little knowledge of my life in Barbados apart from the fact that I owned plantations. She is appalled that I used slaves for labour."

"I assume she is a supporter of abolition." John nodded. "How is she faring? No young ones on the way?"

"It does not look as if we are to be so blessed, but she is well. And how are you faring?"

"I am well, but my property in Barbados is under threat as you would know. You are fortunate that you sold Harrow and Hope to John – rest his soul – all of those years ago and that we no longer own Dunscombe, so you will not also be faced with the threat of losing your property because of these anti-slavery fanatics who are agitating for emancipation!"

"Yes, I read about it in the papers every day. They are getting much support, especially from the ladies. Mr. Buxton who, as you know, is the leader of the campaign in the House of Commons presents large bundles of signed petitions to the House with regularity."

"Blast the man! While I have no quarrel with the moral position of his theories, under no circumstances will I stand by idly and allow my property to be interfered with without some form of compensation!" HP declared as he led the way to his office where he poured two generous glasses of brandy.

"When are you going back to see your property? I believe you've been here a while," John remarked.

"I was there in May which was my first visit after the hurricane. To tell the truth, I am glad I was not there when it devastated the island. You cannot imagine the destruction. The house sustained substantial damage and all of the outbuildings were destroyed. I lost some slaves as well."

"How horrific!"

"Indeed. The destruction was too much to bear. I heard a story of one poor manager whose wife and child were buried under a building when it collapsed. Would you believe that when he managed to get their poor bodies out, not one slave on the estate would lift a finger to help build coffins to inter them? And he was one who was known for his kind usage of the slaves under his care. Other slaves looted and robbed their owners, leaving them with only the clothes on their backs. I tell you, they are not yet fitted for freedom."

"I had heard that there were about four thousand dead."

"That was the first estimate, but it turns out that just about sixteen hundred were killed or died of wounds sustained. Not a parish escaped damage, with St. Michael and St. Philip being the worst off. Most of the churches were destroyed and that included our parish church. The total losses for the island was nearly two and a half million pounds!"

John Allen whistled. "I cannot imagine what the island must look like now."

"Believe me, you would not want to. It has been over a year now, so I am sure that some of the rebuilding has taken place. I have a copy of a supplement to the London Gazette which carried Sir James Lyons' report to the Secretary of State for the Colonies a few months after the hurricane. It would give you a glimpse of the horror. Did you see it?"

"No, I can't say that I did. Can you put your hand on it?"

Henry Peter opened a drawer in his desk and lifted several documents until he found what he was searching for and handed the yellowing newspaper page to John Allen.

I have to acquaint your Lordship that, on the morning of the 11th of August, this flourishing and happy colony was visited by one of the most dreadful hurricanes ever experienced in the West Indies. On the evening of the 10th, the sun set on a landscape of the greatest beauty and fertility and rose on the following morning over an utter desolation and waste. The prospect at the break of day on the 11th instant, was that of January in Europe every tree if not entirely rooted up was deprived of its foliage and of many of its branches; every house within my view was levelled with the ground, or materially damaged; and every hour brought intelligence of the most lamentable accidents, and of very many shocking deaths.

The evening of the 10th instant was not remarkable for any peculiarity of appearance that I could observe, and everyone in my family went to bed without the least suspicion that any atmospherical changes were likely to disturb their rest. Soon after, however, it began to rain, accompanied with flashes of lightning and high wind; it appeared to me from the north and east; towards midnight the wind increased, and was more to the westward and south-west; the rain fell in torrents, and the lightning was vivid in the extreme; at one o'clock or thereabouts, it was first suspected by me, from its extreme violence, to be a hurricane, and not long after some of my servants came running into the house, saying that the roof of the kitchen had fallen in. Several poor people in the neighbourhood also took refuge in Government House, their wooden huts having been blown down. From about two o'clock till day broke, it is impossible to convey to your Lordship's mind any idea of the violence of the storm; no language of mine is adequate to express sufficiently its horrors. The noise of the wind through the apertures formed by it, the peals of thunder, and the rapidly repeated flashes of lightning (more like sheets of fire), and the impenetrable darkness which succeeded them, the crash of walls, roofs, and beams, were all mixed in appalling confusion, and the whole house shook to its very foundation; whether this last effect was produced by the force of the wind, or by an earthquake, supposed by many to have accompanied the storm, I am unable to decide; but the rents and fissures which are visible in the massive walls of this building, would lead one to suppose that the latter cause only could have produced them.

About this time, two o'clock, finding that Government House, which had been but recently repaired, was giving way, the officers of my staff, myself and servants, together with some unfortunate persons who had escaped from the neighbouring huts, took refuge in the cellar, where we remained in perfect safety, thank God, until the day dawned: had we continued in the rooms above-stairs, or indeed in any other part of the house, there is little doubt our lives must have been sacrificed, from the ruinous appearance presented in the morning. The tempest did not entirely cease, nor the atmosphere clear up, until about nine o'clock in the morning of the 11th, and then it was we became more sensible of the calamities and heart-breaking consequences of this most awful scourge. Whole families were buried in ruins. Fortunately, some of the churches were found less injured than any other buildings (although many are destroyed), and they were instantly thrown open for the reception of the wounded and maimed. Medical aid was procured with all the haste which the encumbered state of the streets and roads would permit, for many trees and houses had fallen across the public ways, and much obstructed our intercourse.

Under these most distressing and appalling circumstances, it is wonderful with what equanimity and fortitude everyone seems to bear his loss, and this affords some little consolation to my mind. But I cannot hide from my view the awful prospects of want and destitution, accompanied as it may be with pestilence, which must naturally result from such a general and wide-spread calamity.

179

No estimate of damage done, or loss sustained, can be at present formed with any degree of accuracy, or even surmised; suffice it to say that there is no exaggeration to the picture I have drawn; and that as soon as any correct opinion can be formed upon the subject, your Lordship shall be duly apprised of it.

I must not omit to add that the barracks and hospitals of St. Ann's are in a state of complete dilapidation and ruin; and I have been under the necessity of ordering the troops under canvas. No deaths have occurred among the officers, with the exception of one gentleman of the Commissariat Department, a Mr. Planner, who was entombed with three of his children, a female relative, and two servants, in the ruins of his house. The number of soldiers killed, however, of the corps composing the garrison, viz. the Royal Artillery, the 35th and 36th regiments, amounts by this day's return, to 36; and very many accidents of a serious nature have also been sustained by the troops.

I have called a meeting of the legislature for Monday the 15th instant, the earliest moment which I could hope to collect them together. In the meantime, the most wealthy and influential inhabitants are making every effort to relieve the poor, houseless and destitute. The sacred work of charity has begun and will be encouraged and assisted by every means in my power; and under circumstances of such grievous and awful calamity, I look forward with hope and confidence to the sympathies of the Mother Country.

I will not conclude this dispatch without giving your Lordship the assurance, that my determination is, as well as those who surround me, to meet our accumulated evils with resolution and fortitude, and to exert our best efforts to assuage and mitigate, to the utmost of our abilities, every distress which may present itself. The task may be arduous, but it will be continued with unshrinking perseverance, so long as it may please Almighty Providence to afford us health and strength to *do so.*

I have the honour to be, &c.,
(Signed)
JAMES LYON.
The Right Hon. Viscount Goderich, &c.

P.S. It has escaped me to mention that the few ships in Carlisle Bay were driven high on the strand, but fortunately no lives lost. How far this hurricane may have extended, I have hitherto had no means of ascertaining.

"My God, this is horrific. Rebecca wrote to me about it, but I had no idea of the extent of the devastation. She and Reynold sustained a lot of damage at Alleyndale Hall and River, but thankfully their lives were spared."

"How are my dear half-sister and the Baron?"

"They are as well as can be expected after the hurricane."

"How many children do they have now? I think I lost count after five."

"They have seven in all, having lost two in infancy. It seems that they have called it quits now, as the last one is four, I believe."

"I am going back next month to see how the rebuilding is coming and to check on the plantation, so I will make it a point to visit them. Before I leave, though, I will be sending a very pointed letter to the Right Honourable Earl Grey."

"The Prime Minister and head of the Whig party?" John Allen asked in surprise.

"Yes, indeed. I need to make known my position on the freeing of my slaves without the thought of adequate compensation. The rumours about the so-called horrors of slavery are rife and everyone is being tarred with the same brush! It is those lies that are inciting the abolitionists to call for emancipation."

"That is the truth. However, I know that you look after your slaves very well."

"Indeed I do, but my protests seem to be falling on deaf ears. Anyway, I shall finish the letter in the next few days. I'm getting Cousins on Duke Street to print it and I will have it delivered before I depart for Barbados."

"Good for you. You always were one to speak your mind, even when you were in the House of Assembly in Barbados," John reminisced. Henry Peter chuckled.

"So, how is your employment going?" Henry Peter changed the subject.

"It certainly is a change from owning plantations. Being a solicitor's writing clerk is not the height of excitement, and to tell the truth it barely meets our needs. Anyway, enough about me. How is Vaucluse faring or how was it faring before the hurricane, at any rate? Obviously good."

"I cannot complain. The plantation has done very well despite the circumstances, which is why this talk of emancipation pains me so. Our plantations will be further devastated, as if the natural disasters that we constantly face and the low price of sugar are not bad enough! I don't see how Barbados can possibly survive emancipation. It will be the end of the island as we know it and London cannot pretend that it will not hurt it as well."

"I totally agree. I remember what a time I had with Hope before I sold it to Robert Reece and that was before the difficulties with sugar and everything else that you are experiencing now."

"That is the truth. I must tell you that I am looking for somewhere else to live and start afresh. To that end, I am planning a visit to Upper Canada, with a view of making it my future residence if the soil, climate and other advantages are such as I have been reading from those who live there."

"Upper Canada? That is rather drastic."

"I feel the need for a complete change."

"What will do you with Vaucluse? Sell it?"

"No, I don't plan to sell it. It is still generating a nice profit. Sufficient to keep me well enough in England and to buy some land in Canada."

"Who will you leave it all to? John's sons?"

"I have not given it much thought, to tell the truth," Henry Peter admitted.

"HP, what are you now? You were fourteen when I was born so that makes you…" John started calculating in his head.

"Fifty-six," HP supplied with a smile. "You never were the best with figures," he joked. "I suppose I should give some thought to that. If I sell it, I will need to make provisions for the boys."

"Which boys?" John queried.

"My boys. Harry and John Alleyne."

"I had forgotten about them to be perfectly honest. How old are they now?"

"Harry would be sixteen and John Alleyne about thirteen. They are good boys. Doing well with their studies."

"Do they work on the plantation?"

"No, of course not. In fact, I am planning to emancipate them soon, whether or not the act is passed. At present a tutor comes in to teach them. School was somewhat of a problem for them."

"You know, HP, if anyone up here got wind of the fact that you have two children from a slave woman –"

"Three," Henry Peter interrupted. "There is Mary Ann as well."

"Yes, well, as I was saying, if anyone got wind of that, you would have no credibility. They would paint you as the typical slave owner who ravaged his slaves and got them with child, against their will."

Henry Peter looked uncomfortable with that description for a moment before he pulled himself together and said: "Well, I'll have to hope that no one finds out, won't I? Besides, I would hardly say that I ravaged my slaves. I'm far too civilised for that."

Chapter 17

Henry Peter picked up some papers from his desk and handed them to John Allen. "This is the beginning of my letter. Read it and let me know what you think." John began, reading the letter aloud.

TO
THE RIGHT HONOURABLE EARL GREY
FIRST LORD OF THE TREASURY, &c.

MY LORD,
On the eve of my departure from England, again to visit my estate in the West Indies, and of course, as an integral part of it, my negro slaves, those beings whom ignorance and falsehood represent as miserable and whom mistaken philanthropy would really render so, I have ventured to address your Lordship, solemnly to protest against any interference with my colonial property, without receiving ample compensation,

especially as this property is quite as much sanctioned by law as your own. I make no apology for this address as there is not a man in England who entertains higher sentiments of respect for your Lordship than myself. I have been wont in private conversation, when the peerage of this country was spoken of, to dwell with delight upon the virtues that adorn your character, and to hold up your Lordship as a model of the true dignity of a British Peer, one, which in my opinion, had not its equal in England. I have more than once maintained that there was a more genuine stamp of true nobility in all your actions, your words, in your very aspect, and in your whole deportment, than could be exhibited to the eye that should survey leisurely the assembled majesty of those, of whom your Lordship, by your virtue, consistency and talent, deserves to be the chief.

John Allen paused and looked up from his reading with a smirk. "Laying it on rather thick there aren't you, HP?" he teased.

"I'm just smoothing the way for what comes next because, as you will see, I in no way intend to be diplomatic in the use of my words. The time for diplomacy has long gone."

"Not that you have ever been diplomatic," John reminded him before continuing.

Entertaining these sentiments, I cannot believe that your Lordship seriously meditates any measure or arrangement by which my property is to be irretrievably injured, perhaps destroyed; because any such plan would of necessity render your own insecure and shake to its very foundations the tenure by which all description of property is upheld. It is neither in accordance with my taste, my inclination, or my feelings of moral propriety to be allowed to possess an undoubted and rightful property in my fellow man; and I beg in this respect to state that I agree in the moral position of Mr. Buxton's theories; but, my Lord, although Mr. Buxton may be considered by the Quakers and Shakers as a perfect oracle, I have the bad taste to prefer the legal opinion of the ignorant Lord Stowell to that profound sage Mr. Thomas Fowell Buxton; and Lord Stowell has pronounced in an able and elaborate judgement, that a slave is the undoubted property of his master.

"Oh, I do see what you mean by 'smoothing the way for what comes next'. You will certainly not be making a friend of Mr. Buxton. 'Quakers and Shakers'?"

"I have no desire to be friends with such a buffoon. How he can be a Member of Parliament is beyond me. And no doubt his views on slavery have been influenced by the Quakers, having married one. Everyone knows that, by definition, property is something that is owned by a person. I paid money for my slaves, therefore I own them. If my property can be taken from me simply by the passing of a law, then no property is secure. How can Buxton not see that?"

"I believe his argument is that a person cannot be the property of another person."

"Well, if they intend to change the law to make that so, they need to compensate me for the loss of my property. That is all I am saying. In truth, I do not consider it morally right to own my fellowman, which is what my slaves are, but according to the letter of the law, as it exists, I do own them. But as I say further down in the letter, it has always been my aim to treat my slaves as to render them slaves in name only. At no other plantation will you find slaves better treated than at Vaucluse."

"You do not have to convince me, HP. I am in complete agreement with you, but I have to tell you that you cannot win this emancipation war. It is almost a foregone conclusion. The most you can hope for is to be well compensated for the loss of your slaves."

"That is all I ask. Although I do believe that to emancipate slaves without preparing them for freedom will be a mistake. Anyway, I will continue to put forward my arguments and hope to be heard. This is the first letter, since I am sure it may require more than one to make my point."

"We have both emancipated slaves over the years, HP."

"True, and some have stayed with me although they were set free. Others, like my daughter Mary Ann, I have helped to get a start. I've even given her slaves to help her out. If or when emancipation comes and she has to free them, I will arrange for her to come to England and try to find a husband for her."

"You are always thinking ahead, HP," John Allen chuckled.

"I have to! What about coming to Canada with me?"

"I think I will pass. I am quite settled here and happy with my own Mary Anne. I could not drag her to the wilds of Canada."

"Fair enough. I have invited a friend that I met fairly recently to visit Barbados with me and then to go on to Canada to explore it. He is a physician by the name of Thomas Rolph."

"And he is prepared to just up and move to Canada?"

"I believe that he was planning to move to New South Wales in Australia, but perhaps it is my enthusiasm for Canada that has persuaded him to visit."

"You do have the gift of persuasion."

"How I wish I could persuade the Lord Earl Grey to come around to supporting my point of view."

"Tremendous pressure is being brought upon those in parliament to abolish slavery totally, so I am afraid your powers of persuasion will not work in this case."

"I fear you are right, which is why I am going to Canada. It may be a refuge for me when all hell breaks loose in Barbados."

John Allen picked up the letter again. "Let me continue. I am almost at the end."

It has been, my Lord, the aim, the bent, the tenor, the object of my whole life, so as to treat my negroes (from whom I derive all my comforts, and they in return derive all their comforts; yes my Lord, I say emphatically, all their comforts from me), as to render them but slaves in name. When I have heretofore returned to visit them, they have assembled together in groups, affectionately to give utterance to their joy on my return; and I hesitate not to assert that the welcome even of the Howick Tenantry could never have been more cordial than the hearty greeting and reception which I have hitherto invariably received at their hands, and which, my Lord, will never cease, from any diminution of kindness from me; but I fear, may, if the attempt at alienation should be successful, which the plans of our modern emancipists would render inevitable.

"'…that the welcome even of the Howick Tenantry could never have been more cordial…'?" John Allen gasped. "HP, mayhap you go too far."

"Howick Hall is the family seat of the Earls Grey, as you would know. All I am saying is that the greeting which my slaves afford me, more than likely, is more cordial than that of his tenants and they are free. What is wrong with that? You are almost at the end of what I have written so far."

I give to all persons whatever permission to visit my slaves at all times, and under any circumstances they think proper, and appeal to the Bishop of Barbados, whose theology is as consonant with my views and feelings as the politics of the Bishop of Exeter are with your own, I confidently appeal to him, trusting that he will – nothing extenuate nor set down aught in malice – and I am quite satisfied that he will testify to the uniform happiness, comfort, prosperity and gratitude of the negroes on my estate.

"What on earth does 'nothing extenuate nor set down aught in malice' mean, HP?"

"My boy, your education is sadly lacking. In that you are like John was, not interested in reading. It is a quote from the play Othello by Mister Shakespeare. It means not to make anything up or write anything untrue because of malice'. In other words, I am saying that I expect the Bishop to be fully honest and objective in his assessment of the condition of my slaves."

John looked at his half-brother in admiration. Henry Peter could always put them to shame with his superior knowledge and business acumen. He might not be able to stop the abolition of slavery, but if anyone could ensure that compensation was paid to the planters, he was sure it would be Henry Peter.

Chapter 18

December 20, 1832
On the Atlantic Ocean

I am relieved that we are finally in warmer latitudes and on our way to Barbados. The brig, Retrench, on which we sail, left Gravesend on November 17th and the first few days were horrendous as the fierce winds and heavy fog forced us to stop at several ports. I suffered most severely from sickness; my nervous system was so disturbed as to prevent me from sleeping and, even after landing, the tremulous and undulating rocking of the ship caused it to remain unabated for some time. We landed at Portsmouth on November 22nd and were delayed there for several days until we weighed anchor on December 5th and by December 7th we finally left the shores of England behind.

The calm weather and the beauty of the rising and setting of the sun have been somewhat of a balm. The grampusses *frisking about the ocean are very amusing with their frolicsome gambols. There are also many birds still around. The glare of the sea in a complete calm is somewhat disagreeable, the motion of the ship remains unpleasant and the perpetual flapping of the sails quite annoying.*

We have been in a calm for two days now with no wind. Here the brig lays, morning, noon and night, rocking and rolling on the huge, lazy ocean which, smooth as a polished mirror or a lady's brow, on the surface, still hove up and down with the ceaseless, majestic and very uncomfortable underswell of the Atlantic. It does my stomach no good.

Doctor Thomas Rolph lay his quill down and closed the bottle of ink but left the journal open to dry. He was intent on capturing every element of his trip, even the continual bouts of sea sickness. He considered himself indeed fortunate to have been invited to visit the estate of his good friend Henry Peter Simmons in Barbados and travel on to Canada with him. He was quite impressed that although Henry Peter knew him to be a supporter of the Whig party and was against slavery, he never obtruded the subject on him, but instead had invited him to Barbados to see his plantation for himself.

Climbing the companionway to make his way onto the deck, Thomas was happy to see Henry Peter in conversation with another gentleman whom they had discovered was on his way to visit Barbados for the first time. He was always eager to hear more about Barbados and looked forward to his arrival with great anticipation, for more reasons than one.

"Thomas, how are you faring today?" Henry Peter greeted him as he joined them.

"I am somewhat improved, but I must say that I

am eager for the wind to pick up again."

"So are we all," agreed their fellow passenger, Jonathan Millard. He was going to visit some relatives who owned a plantation on the island who were known to Henry Peter for, as he said, everybody knew everybody in Barbados. "One would think that since there is no wind the brig would be quite still, but it is still riding the waves quite a bit, isn't it, even though it is going nowhere," he mused.

"I am quite aware of that fact," Thomas replied, holding a hand to his much-abused stomach. Henry Peter gave a sympathetic smile, glad that he was not so affected since he crossed the Atlantic quite often and would hate to have to contend with sea sickness each time.

"I was just telling Jonathan that I used to have a small mortgage over Reed's Bay Plantation, where he will be staying, when it was owned by Charles Kyd Bishop."

"My word! What are the chances of that?" exclaimed Thomas.

"Please come and visit Reed's Bay when you've had time to settle down. Not that I have any right to be inviting you to my cousin's estate," Jonathan said humbly.

"You will find that the planters in Barbados, for the most part, are very appreciative of guests, especially those who bring news from the motherland, even though she is in the process of trying to abandon her children." Henry Peter couldn't help adding his bitter comment. An uncomfortable silence followed that was thankfully broken by excited shouts from the crew as a gentle breeze wafted into the sails, ruffling them a bit. The next gust was strong enough to fill the sails and this was accompanied by several cheers as the Retrench began to move forward again.

***

January 13, 1833
Off the Coast of Barbados

Henry Peter gazed with fondness upon the island that the Retrench drew increasingly close to. The lad who had gone up to the masthead to unfurl the sails had announced that it was in sight quite a while ago, to the relief of Thomas who was in a very enfeebled state.

"That there is Moncrieff, in the parish of St. John," Henry Peter indicated at the first point of land. "It has a signal station there that communicates with three other signal stations which I will take you to see."

"And those are coconut trees lining the shore?" Thomas asked, feeling his strength return just at the sight of land.

"Yes, they are but considerably fewer than were there before. The hurricane significantly decimated their numbers and it will take several years for them to return to their former glory. When I read an account of the hurricane it said that every tree, if not entirely uprooted, was deprived of its foliage and of many of its branches."

"It must have been terrifying!" exclaimed Thomas.

"Undoubtedly," agreed Henry Peter. "We will sail

around the southeast of the island, past St. Philip where Samuel Lord, the brother of my good friend John Thomas Lord who is now deceased, was rumoured to lure ships onto the reefs and relieve them of their treasures."

"Surely you jest!" Thomas exclaimed.

"I do not put anything past Sam Lord. He is quite the scoundrel."

"I say, this is wonderful," said Jonathan, joining them on deck.

"Indeed it is," Thomas agreed. "Even more so now that my departure from this instrument of torture is imminent." The two men laughed sympathetically.

"We will be rounding Needham's Point shortly and then we will be upon Carlisle Bay where we will drop anchor."

"Sweeter words I have never heard," Thomas assured them.

Carlisle Bay was not overly large but had many ships at anchor there, some waiting to take sugar to England. They were gaily decorated with colourful pendants and ensigns, making a beautiful picture as they bobbed on the waves. Thomas' eyes eagerly devoured the sights which Henry Peter pointed out as they sailed past.

Thomas was overjoyed when they dropped anchor at one o'clock and in short time they were off the boat and back on terra firma. His feet did not seem to realise that fact at once and for some time he imagined that he could still feel the swaying of the boat under his feet. He was gratified to step into the carriage that Henry Peter had procured to take them to Vaucluse after bidding Jonathan good-bye and agreeing to come by for a visit.

There was a companionable silence in the carriage, which was broken occasionally when Henry Peter pointed out something of interest or when Thomas asked one of his many questions. Thomas was fascinated at the sight of the neatly dressed negroes who were congregating in groups along the side of the road. Many of them were carrying baskets of fruit on their heads and appeared to be enjoying themselves.

He looked at Henry Peter in wonder and asked, "Are they slaves?" HP nodded and said most likely.

"And they are allowed to wonder free?"

"Yes. It is Sunday. They are probably on their way to the market to sell their produce. Many of them have small plots of land where they can grow their own food to sell. Mine certainly have that privilege. It enables them to earn a little money to buy things for themselves, although I provide everything that they need."

Thomas fell silent as he digested this information. Already he was aware that all was not as it was described in England. He decided to keep his eyes open and make notes of the occurrences he saw while on the island. He noted with delight the plantations they passed on the way to Vaucluse with their negro inhabitants milling around the yards, the richness and splendour of the flowers and trees, the windmills and sugar houses, all new and exciting to him.

"How far is your estate from Bridge Town?" Thomas asked after they had been travelling a while.

"About six miles. We are nearly there," Henry Peter answered. "It is at a high elevation so we will soon start to climb. You will enjoy the views from there."

"I am looking forward to it tremendously. I must say, the island looks very prosperous."

"An enormous amount of work has gone into it to rebuild it after the hurricane. However, prosperity will be hard to be maintained if England proclaims this Act."

"I believe it is more a case of 'when' than 'if,'" Thomas told him. "There have been very many petitions presented in parliament and so much agitation that the government will do what it will to appease the people."

"I am well aware of that, but I will continue to make my appeals."

"We have not discussed it, but you must know that I am a member of the Whig party and as such I, too, am against slavery."

"I am aware of that. Yet, you have never pushed your opinion on me and it is precisely for that reason I invited you to join me so that you can see first-hand that what I have said of my negroes is true." Thomas nodded without commenting.

"That there is a Moravian church," Henry Peter pointed to a large building with a smaller one to one side of the yard. "They have set up a school as well. Many of my negroes attend the church and some of their children go to the school."

"Indeed!" Thomas exclaimed, surprised. "I had no idea that you allowed your negroes to attend church."

"Yes indeed, and I find that those who attend are extremely sober and industrious."

"I would think that it is the instruction they receive."

"I agree. Many of my slaves have asked to be baptised and I would say upwards of one hundred have been baptised over the years that I have owned Vaucluse."

"Your slaves are baptised?" Thomas was shocked. "I do not understand," he said in a bewildered voice.

"What is it that you do not understand?"

"To baptise your negroes is to acknowledge that they have a soul capable of being saved. How then is it that you see nothing wrong with owning another soul?" This was as close to a confrontation about slavery as he had come to with Henry Peter. He waited for his reply, wondering if he had overstepped his bounds and offended his host.

"As I said in my letter to the Lord Earl Grey, I do agree that it is morally wrong to own my fellow man, which is how I see my negroes, but, according to the law, they are my property. When I bought Vaucluse I paid thirty thousand, two hundred and fifty pounds for it which included one hundred and ninety slaves as part of the property, so if I am forced to free them then I should be compensated for the loss of that property."

Thomas could see that Henry Peter was becoming quite stirred, but he did not see how he could claim that he saw his slaves as his fellowman and still have no issue with owning them, although he could see some merit in claiming recompense. He wisely held his opinion lest he stirred up his anger further, and instead decided to pay special attention to how the slaves at Vaucluse were treated to see if it bore out the claims made by Henry Peter.

"Here we are," Henry Peter announced as the carriage turned down a long driveway lined by thick trees. A grand plantation house stood at the end of the driveway, with a wide veranda spanning its width. Colourful flowers and shrubs grew in abundance around the front of the house, contrasting with its white walls. In the background Thomas could see a windmill and various outbuildings as well as what looked like it could be a stable. Several negroes were milling around the yard and, upon seeing the carriage appear, smiles broke out on their faces.

"Welcome to Vaucluse," Henry Peter said as the carriage drew to a halt. "I am happy to say that it has been restored to its pre-hurricane state, although many plantations have not been so fortunate."

Thomas alighted and looked around him curiously. He was looking forward to his stay at Vaucluse and all it would reveal.

Two boys who looked to be teenagers came rushing from the house. They were light-skinned, one very fair in complexion and the other a bit darker. Their hair was curly and soft-looking. Thomas was surprised to see them hug Henry Peter in delight. He was even more surprised when Henry Peter turned to him and introduced them.

"These are my boys, Harry and John Alleyne."

They confidently told him that they were pleased to meet him. Thomas vaguely returned the greeting as he silently puzzled over the scenario. What did Henry Peter mean by his "boys"? Did he mean his slaves or were they, in fact, his children? The darker one's forehead seemed remarkably like Henry Peter's while the other one certainly had the look of him. He had not known Henry Peter to be married. Were these coloured boys from one of his slaves? He was no stranger to this accusation brought against the planters, but he never thought it of Henry Peter. He was even more confused than before. If Henry Peter had children, were they slaves and if they were, why would he not free them? 'This man is not what he seems,' he thought.

Chapter 19

Henry Peter sat in his office and listened intently to the boys' enthusiastic chatter, bringing him up to date on all that had happened since his last visit. He was amazed at how much they had grown and how intelligently they answered his questions. Their tutor was obviously doing an excellent job with them and one would never know that they were looked after by the housekeeper Betsy Jane and other domestics since their mother had died. He was proud of how confident and articulate they were. He made sure they had a good appreciation of reading, unlike his brother and step-brother. They had a lot of potential.

"Who is that man you brought with you?" John Alleyne, the more inquisitive of the two, asked. Henry Peter smiled fondly at him before answering. John Alleyne took after him more than Harry, and not just in looks. He could already tell that he outstripped his brother in intelligence.

"As I told you, his name is Thomas Rolph and he is a physician. He will be staying here for about three months, after which we will be going to explore the upper regions of Canada."

"Canada? All the way past the United States?" John Alleyne asked with excitement in his eyes.

"You're leaving again?" Harry asked wistfully.

"I will be here for a few months, but yes, then I'll be off to Canada."

"Can we come with you?" he asked.

"Sorry, not this time. I do not know what I will find. However, if the land is to my liking, I will buy some property there and then I will take you." That seemed to satisfy the boys. "Now I'm sure that I have some presents for you somewhere. Go to my room to see if you can find them."

He smiled as the boys took off with excited shouts. His smile eventually faded as his thoughts returned to the situation he had left in England. He had argued in his letter to the Lord Earl Grey that he should be compensated for his property and, according to the law, Harry and John Alleyne were his property. His heart gave a funny pain, causing him to absently rub the spot. They were not his property; they were his offspring. If his request for compensation was granted, he could not take compensation for his own children. He would emancipate them as soon as he was back in England.

He would take some time while he was here to show Rolph the island so that he could see for himself the state of slaves in Barbados. Meanwhile, he wouldn't mind a good cockfight. He grabbed a piece of paper from his desk and wet his quill to write an advertisement to put in the *Mercury* lest he forget. He wrote, inviting his friends to rally next Sunday at the cock pit with a bag of money in one hand and a great fighting cock in the other. That, at least, brought a smile to his face. There were still some pleasures to be had in Barbados.

For a moment Molly Harry came to his mind and he was surprised that he felt a tug on his heart at her loss even seven years after her death. He wondered if the children still missed her. They seemed quite happy, but how would he really know when he was so seldom here. He would really have to take them on his next trip. It was time they saw something other than Barbados because he did not want them growing up ignorant of the world.

A knock at the door brought his thoughts back to the present. It was Thomas, who had been shown to his room by the housekeeper and seemed to have freshened up and appeared keen to begin his Barbadian adventure.

"Henry Peter, I do hope I am not disturbing you," he began tentatively.

"Not at all," Henry Peter assured him. "Is everything to your liking?"

"Most assuredly. I could ask for nothing more."

"Good, good."

"How long have you owned the plantation?"

"My late brother John and I bought it early in 1816 and then he signed his share over to me. At the time it was four hundred and thirty-five acres and had one hundred and ninety slaves. I've managed to add to the acreage by acquiring adjoining lands and I now have nearly three hundred slaves."

"That is quite a significant number," Thomas

noted.

"Yes, and I take care of all of them well, even the ones who are old and are not able to work any longer."

"That is very good of you. I look forward to seeing some of them."

"By all means. Feel free to go wherever you desire on the plantation. I am sure that my friends will extend the same invitation to you. In fact, I was just contemplating where I should take you first."

"I believe that I have quite a few acquaintances on the island as well that I would like to visit, if that is agreeable to you."

"I will do my best to ensure that you manage to visit them all. I have just finished an advertisement to go into the *Mercury* to let my friends know that I am back and inviting them to meet at the cock pit next Sunday. No doubt we will be inundated with invitations once they read that."

"I take it that you are an enthusiast of the sport?" Thomas asked carefully. Henry Peter could see that he was not.

"Indeed I am, but I will not drag you to witness such a bloody sport with me. I am sure that you will have your share of invitations once it is known that you are staying with me."

"I look forward to seeing the island, although I am already impressed with what I have seen."

"This is the west of the island. I will take you to the eastern side of the island as well and the north. We will have to go on horseback much of the time. I take it that you ride?"

"Certainly, although I am a little out of practice."

"While we have a fairly decent road system, or we

used to before the hurricane, some parts of the island are best accessed on horseback."

Thomas nodded, looking as if he was debating whether to say something. Henry Peter took pity on him and asked, "Was there something you wanted to ask?"

Hesitating another moment to best phrase his question, Thomas cautiously asked, "When you introduced me to your boys, I was curious to know…"

"If they are really mine?" Henry Peter finished for him.

Thomas nodded, looking uncomfortable. "It is just that we have heard quite a lot about miscegenation in the colonies. It is quite frowned upon…" Again he trailed off, fearing that he had gone too far.

"Yes, well, it is a reality here in the Caribbean. I have three children from slave women. A daughter, Mary Ann, who I manumitted years ago and my sons, Harry and John Alleyne, from a woman named Molly Harry who was on the plantation when I bought it. She died seven years ago."

"And you…own your sons?" he asked awkwardly. "Not that it is my business, of course," he hastened to add.

"Yes, I do. But I just decided, as I was sitting here, to manumit them when I return to England. After all, it would be distasteful to be paid for my own offspring if our request for compensation is agreed to."

Thomas nodded in agreement. He found the whole idea of having children from your slaves distasteful. Did the slaves have any say in the matter?

Were they willing to lie with their masters or did they, in fact, have any choice? Needless to say, he was too polite to share his thoughts with his host. And perhaps he would not mention it in his observations either.

Chapter 20

Sunday, January 20, 1833

Henry Peter had been delighted when Edward Hinds from Westmoreland Plantation, not too distant from Vaucluse, invited Thomas to spend the day with him. He was therefore free to head to the sand pit with a pair of fighting cocks and spend some time with his friends while catching up on the gossip of what was happening in the island. He would also impress on them the need to rally together to insist on compensation for their slaves since it looked as if, in spite of his protests and the protest of others, emancipation was likely to happen sooner rather than later.

"I heard that you brought a house guest with you," one of his friends who was an officer of the St.

Andrew's militia told him.

"Yes. He is a physician by the name of Thomas Rolph. He is very keen to see the island and how we live here."

"No stomach for cockfighting?"

"Alas, no. Fortunately, he has gone to Westmoreland to spend the day with Edward Hinds."

"You must bring him for a visit."

"Indeed I will, although it is quite a journey. However, I am sure he will greatly appreciate the scenery that we will pass in order to get to your Mess Hall."

"We have had to erect a new one, since the old was totally destroyed in the hurricane."

"I must say, that hurricane wreaked havoc on the island. I am still seeing the evidence of it over a year later."

"It will certainly take a few years to rebuild all that was destroyed. The damage was tremendous. Six churches were demolished including your own St. Thomas Parish Church, as you would have seen. They haven't even begun the rebuilding yet."

"I know that the damage of the property destroyed, including slaves who lost their lives, was over two million pounds and it is believed that fifteen hundred people were killed."

"Some put the number as much as twenty-five hundred. I tell you, Henry Peter, you are lucky that you were not here. That hurricane put the fear of God into all of us."

"I cannot imagine the horror of it. I was here in May and things were a lot worse. We lost one hundred and sixteen slaves in St. Thomas and about twenty-eight at Vaucluse. We've had to rebuild all our outbuildings and the plantation house had substantial damage and parts had to be rebuilt."

"You have the devil's own luck, HP. Some people completely lost their houses."

"I am well aware of that! However, I'll be needing more than luck to convince the Prime Minister of England not to succumb to the pressure and pass the law to emancipate our slaves. Worse yet, without compensating us. This hurricane has set the country back years and emancipation will only be the nail in the coffin."

"The planters are fortunate to have you agitating on their behalf. Thankfully, I have no plantation to worry about."

"I almost wish I could say the same, but it is my plantation that affords me the life that I have, and I will fight to preserve it in any way I can. Speaking of which, I believe that the first set of cocks are ready to fight," Henry Peter declared, turning towards the cock pit. "I will see you in a week or so with my guest."

The excitement of the cock fights and the pleasure of seeing friends that he had not seen for several months made Henry Peter glad to be back in Barbados. He would visit Mehetabel and see how she was doing and if she needed help. Also, he had told John Allen he would visit their sister Rebecca. In spite of all that was going on, it was good to be back.

***

"Henry Peter, I had a most wonderful time today," Thomas enthused later that night. "So sorry that you did not join us. I trust your day was fine."

"Yes, indeed," smiled Henry Peter who had come home with a heavy purse.

"It was the occasion of Edward's daughter's birthday and his negroes put on a performance for the guests. I have never seen the like. When I reached his house, which he told me had been erected since the hurricane, there was a group of negroes very gaily attired with tasteful and pretty ornaments, dancing with the greatest agility, animation, and light-heartedness, and exhibiting, too, great elegance and precision in their steps."

Henry Peter nodded, silently amused at his exuberance and poetic descriptions.

"One man was singing and shaking a calabash half filled with the berries of a shrub, which I am told is called the English Plantain; another was playing an instrument like a tambourine,

and forming together admirable concord."

"I am glad that you enjoyed it."

"To tell the truth, I could not help but think that some might object to the dance taking place on a Sunday afternoon, but I do believe that the Sabbath should be as well a day of recreation as of devotion."

"I am in total agreement with you," said Henry Peter, who had thoroughly enjoyed his day of recreation at the sand pit. "I ran into several friends and acquaintances today, one of whom is an officer of the St. Andrew's militia. He has extended an invitation to bring you to dine with them in their new Mess Hall. It is in an area called Barbadian Scotland, which is so named because it has the look of some parts of Scotland. You will enjoy the views from there as well as on the journey."

"I am very much looking forward to that. I

cannot thank you enough for your kind invitation to visit Barbados. It has been very educational for me so far. I am making copious notes so that I can write a brief account about it afterwards."

"Don't mention it. I am glad that you have been able to take this opportunity and I certainly look forward to reading your account."

***

Tuesday, February 9, 1833

Tuesday morning dawned clear and bright; a perfect day to journey to the Scotland area on horseback. After leaving Vaucluse, Henry Peter led Thomas north through a thickly wooded and scenic valley called Porey Spring which had been owned by his friend William Robinson years before. He pointed in the direction of Dunscombe to show Thomas the plantation that he had owned with John Allen some sixteen years ago. Thomas remarked on the rocks and the shape of the trees, while Henry Peter listened with half an ear, letting him ramble on at length.

They continued their gradual ascent once they left Porey Springs until they eventually arrived at the summit of Mount Hillaby, the highest point on the island. Dismounting, they rested their horses while taking a few minutes to enjoy the view.

"Mount Hillaby is just over eleven hundred feet high," Henry Peter informed him. "Barbados is quite flat compared to some of the other islands in the West Indies."

"This is amazing," exclaimed Thomas as Henry

Peter pointed out the Scotland area in the distance. "It truly does like look Scotland with those mountains rising above each other. And the rocks look white and chalky where they aren't covered with that beautiful thick foliage. The sea looks to be far rougher than on the west coast as well."

"Yes, that is the side that faces the Atlantic Ocean, although Barbados is not actually in the Atlantic Ocean. Of course, you know that Barbados is the most easterly of the islands in the archipelago." Thomas nodded, having done considerable research before the trip.

In the distance, flowers of all descriptions could be seen and in between the clefts and hollows of the mountains, magnificent cabbage palms, plantain vines and small fields of sugar cane. To the south and west were plantation houses, evidenced by their factory towers, with thick foliage surrounding them. After enjoying the scenery, they mounted their horses and continued the trek to the Mess Hall.

On arriving at the newly built Mess Hall, Henry Peter introduced Thomas to Colonel Nathaniel Forte, the leader of the regiment and the Speaker of the House of Assembly and to his fellow officers. Since it was still not time for lunch, he offered to extend their ride for a while so that Thomas could get the full benefit of the scenery from that elevation, even though they were both somewhat fatigued. They rode along the coast by the sea for several miles, sandwiched between the wild and intimidating mountains in their various shapes and forms and the dazzling blue sea that threw up foamy waves when it crashed over huge rocks onto the sand.

They returned by a different route, this time

travelling on a road that was quite rough and very steep. The narrow pathway, running alongside disturbingly deep ravines, made Thomas quite dizzy. Some of the passes were through cavernous rocks which made the way quite dark and gloomy. However, at the end of the road they emerged into brilliant sunlight with a marvellous view of the valley in which the Mess Hall was located.

On making their way back to the Mess Hall, they were offered much welcomed drinks and treated to a sumptuous dinner. Thomas was delighted to recognise the surgeon of the regiment who was an old friend and fellow student that he knew from England.

"Thomas Rolph! What on earth are you doing in Barbados?" his friend greeted him.

"My word, this is a surprise. I did not even know you were here. I am in Barbados at the kind invitation of my friend Henry Peter Simmons."

"How long have you been here?"

"I arrived about three weeks ago and I have had the pleasure of seeing some of the island. This is the first time I have seen the militia."

"Every parish has a militia and we meet once a month in each parish. Our purpose is to protect the island against slave rebellions, especially after the one in 1816. Every free person between sixteen and sixty is eligible to join and serving is compulsory unless you can find a substitute."

"News of that rebellion certainly reached us in England and was probably instrumental in the beginning of the serious agitation for emancipation. Have you had any trouble since then?"

"Thankfully, no."

"Tomorrow I am having a cockfight at the ruins

of my old house," Colonel Forte announced. "It was destroyed in the hurricane," he added for Thomas' benefit. "Henry Peter, I know that you will not want to miss that, and you must bring Thomas, of course."

Henry Peter agreed enthusiastically, while Thomas nodded politely, although he could hardly credit the interest in such a sport.

Shortly after lunch Henry Peter announced that they should leave in order to make it back to Vaucluse while it was still light. Thomas readily agreed as he did not care to travel on some of the pathways that had brought them there without the benefit of proper light.

"Thank you very much for today," he told Henry Peter once they got on their way. "I have fallen in love with the beauty of this island. In fact, apart from the fact that you are owners of slaves, it reminds me very much of England."

"Indeed, we have adopted many of the customs of the mother country. Still, we have our own unique way of doing things as well, which I wish England would not try to interfere with. They will be cutting off their nose to spite their face, you mark my words."

Thomas diplomatically did not respond, for as much as he was beginning to like Barbados and his host, he was still very much against the institution of slavery.

***

Friday, February 19, 1833

I have been so busy that I have not written anything for

several days. I must not become lax lest I forget to record pertinent information about my trip.

On the 13th of February, I paid a visit to my friend, Dr. Ifil, at his residence called Mangrove Lodge, near Bridge Town. The house is one of the few that in a great measure escaped the destructive fury of the hurricane. It is beautifully embosomed in trees; round the house is a fine grove of lignumvitae trees and, immediately in front, a most magnificent umbrageous mangrove tree, the branches of which, stretching to the ground, have taken root and form a beautiful arcade round the parent tree. The house is named after this stately and majestic tree.

Today Henry Peter took me to Reed's Bay as promised, where we renewed our acquaintance with Jonathan Millard over breakfast. Reed's Bay is located between Hole Town and Speight's. The road from Vaucluse is on a gradual descent to Hole Town, and from there the road runs by the sea shore to Reed's Bay. While the ride is extremely pleasing, there are still a vast number of trees which the hurricane blew down and broke in every direction, shooting forth afresh in all the bloom and vigour of youth.

The extreme heat of the day induced me to taste, for the first time, the water of the green cocoa-nut. It contains an agreeable acid, and forms a delightful beverage, well calculated to slake the thirst induced by tropical heat.

After breakfast we drove on to Speight's Town on the west coast, a place of considerable importance, and although the ride was rendered somewhat oppressive from the dazzling whiteness of the sand upon the beach, it is one possessing a succession of pleasing and picturesque scenery. The sea views, the plantations, and the smiling seats which adorn the neighbourhood, give an air of great cheerfulness to the scene. To the right, a bold range of mountains, completely intersecting the island, forms a fine sight; and on the left, the sea shining with a sapphire hue beneath the morning sun, and the beach fringed with graceful

216

cocoa-nut trees forming a beautiful contrast. Speight's Town is a neat and well-built town, containing some good houses, but still exhibiting the desolating ravages of the last dreadful hurricane. The church was a complete mass of ruins.

In the garden of Reed's Bay, I observed a beautiful cherry tree, a species of malpighia, covered with a handsome looking red fruit, which I found was unfit to eat. There are also many fine breadfruit trees in this neighbourhood; they were then covered with fruit, which is esculent, and answers the purpose of bread. There are some varieties of gooseberry much employed for a cooling drink in fevers. I saw some varieties of the bean growing, trailed over lattice work, forming a beautiful vine, and producing an excellent vegetable.

Feeling sleep overcoming him, Thomas laid down his quill and smothered a yawn. He would continue in the morning. There was so much to see and to write about in Barbados, but he wondered if anyone would ever read these observations that he was recording. Perhaps they would prove useful to someone in future generations.

Chapter 21

February 23, 1833

"I am going to take you to St. Ann's today," Henry Peter announced over breakfast. "It is quite close to Carlisle Bay where we dropped anchor. It is the base of the British Regiment and was built in 1705. Unfortunately, the barracks fell during the hurricane and killed some of the troops and wounded upwards of one hundred."

"My God, that hurricane completely devastated the island."

"Yes, but we are a hardy people. Much of the rebuilding has started and we will pull through this. Whether we can survive emancipation on top of all this remains to be seen."

"I have heard that Barbados has never been

invaded by foreign troops."

"That has been due in a large part to the location of St. Ann's Fort as the central command point for the island's signal stations. You will also see the parade ground, which is rather magnificent, with several acres for the troops to carry out their exercise."

After a short stop at St. Ann's they drove to a little sea bathing village which Henry Peter informed him was called Worthing and which was frequented by invalids from Bridge Town for health and bathing. On the way, they passed a monument that had been erected in honour of those who perished in the barracks at St. Ann.

"In spite of having to deal with their own losses, soldiers from St. Ann's had to come out and keep order after the hurricane, as the slaves were looting. Order was not restored until one of them was shot."

"Looting? I can't imagine it of the peaceful souls that I have seen in our travels about the island."

"They are peaceful when they are under care, circumspection and surveillance as they are now, but what that brief interlude of freedom after the hurricane has shown is that they will make a miserable perversion of freedom if it were granted to them."

"I am not sure if you can compare the brief freedom they had after the hurricane with emancipation. While I am not condoning their behaviour, I can well imagine the fear and desperation they must have felt with most of the food and shelter on the island destroyed."

"It is not only the looting that concerns me, but the fact that many of them would not lift a finger to help save people buried under the rubble, some of whom were alive. These and other behaviours that I have read about and observed convince me that the negro is not yet fitted for his freedom."

"With all due respect, Henry Peter, but do you seek to take the place of God in deciding who is fit for freedom and who is not?"

"By no means do I seek to take the place of God!" Henry Peter protested angrily.

"I meant no offence," Thomas was quick to add. He decided not to voice his opinions to his host in the future, but he was at a loss to understand how Henry Peter appeared to treat his slaves well (at least he had observed no ill treatment so far) yet still insist that they were not fit for freedom. He felt that his arguments were more influenced by finances than belief.

"None taken, but I will point out to you and in my next letter to the Lord Earl Grey that the commission of crimes of great enormity in Barbados, except after the hurricane, is much less than any county of similar size in England. Furthermore, although accusations of cruelty have been made against us, never has a slave been imprisoned for six months for stealing a cabbage or nine months for stealing a faggot!"

"Are you suggesting that these things happen in England?"

"My good man, are you not living in that same country? These are the exclusive merits of free, happy and merciful England! In the words of Horace, it is very much a case of 'we neglect the things under our noses and, regardless of what is within reach, pursue what is remote'."

"I have heard of much greater atrocities than

being imprisoned for six months inflicted on slaves for small offences," argued Thomas.

"Do show me one the next time you see it," invited Henry Peter. Thomas could say nothing and nodded silently.

***

Henry Peter ushered the boys into his study where they sat before his great planter's desk. He smiled fondly at them, seeing aspects of his features in both of them. Before emancipation came, since it was looking as if he was fighting a losing battle, he would definitely free them himself and decide then what he would do with them. He wondered if they understood what was happening.

"I've had a good report from your tutor," Henry Peter praised them. As he had observed years before, John Alleyne was the one with the greater intellect, even though he was younger than his brother by three years. He had obviously inherited that from him, while Harry more likely took after his mother.

While they had no duties on the plantation, he wanted to make sure that they had some understanding of how it worked so he paid a tutor to come in and teach them not only the basic subjects, but also some of the knowledge they needed to understand how the plantation worked.

"Boys, you realise that according to the law, you are considered to be my slaves. But you realise, I hope, that you are not as slaves to me. You are my sons." They nodded silently. "Even in your baptism records you are not listed as belonging to Vaucluse as other slaves are. When I go back to England this time

I will manumit you. Do you know what that means?"

"Yes, it means to set us free." That was from John Alleyne.

"What will be different?" Harry asked him. "Aren't we already free? We still don't have to go in the fields and we don't work in the house either. We have better clothes and food than the other children. Aren't we free?"

"While you are free to do what you want on the plantation, according to the law you are not free. You belong to me, but I want to set you free."

"Don't you want to set everyone free?"

"Yes, in time, but I don't think the best thing is to set them free without teaching them how to handle that freedom."

The children looked puzzled, as they often did in their conversations, and Henry Peter could see that they did not understand what he meant. How were they to understand that when even the Members of Parliament in England did not or would not. Was he the only one who could see it?

***

Thomas opened his journal as he sat in his room back at Vaucluse Plantation. He had seen a lot of the island in the last two weeks. After leaving Worthing beach on the Saturday, they had returned round the Bay, over what Thomas considered to be a most miserable bridge, into Bridge Town and driven to his friend Dr. Cuttings for breakfast.

Thomas found him to be a very intelligent physician devoted both to the interests of science as well as to the prosperity of Barbados. He had spent three very enjoyable days in his company and in his comfortable mansion with its spacious rooms which were made cool by deep verandas. He had been glad for the time away from Vaucluse after his disagreement with Henry Peter. However, Henry Peter did not appear to hold it in his mind and had greeted him warmly on his return.

He picked up his quill to record the events of the last few days lest they escaped his memory.

Wednesday, February 27, 1833

This morning I breakfasted with the Hon. N. Forte, the Speaker of the House of Assembly, at his house on Bennett's estate, the ride to which embraces a view of the sea the entire distance. It is a very charming residence, admirably adapted for the climate; a beautiful avenue of trees has been recently planted along the road leading to the house.

He is a well informed and most hospitable man, precisely the character fitted for a Speaker of a public Assembly, possessing great patience, liberality, impartiality, knowledge, united with a most courteous deportment. He is so devotedly attached to Barbados that he has never quitted the island, even for a day, and from his long residence and general intelligence he has acquired a practical knowledge of the Colony, and possesses an intimate acquaintance with its wants, its

interests, and its inhabitants: he has always so discharged his duty, as to have secured to him the lasting esteem, confidence and regard of all parties in the island.

After writing at length detailed descriptions of his visits to various parts of the island, he stood to stretch his legs before continuing. Lunch must soon be ready, as his growling stomach indicated, but he wanted to bring his journal up to date.

Monday, March 4, 1833

I accompanied a party to visit one of the greatest natural curiosities in the Island, a deep and extensive cavern, termed Cole's Cave. It is situated in the parish of St. Thomas. The entrance to it is on the side of a steep hill, upon an estate called Walk's. The great abundance of rock here is very remarkable; the roads are carried through deep ravines, and the sides of the rocks being embellished with stalactitical columns, renders their appearance very singular and striking. Amid the crags of the rocks, trees are constantly jutting out and the beauty and profusion of the wild flowers astonishing. The entrance to the cavern is difficult, being very precipitous and rugged. We were escorted by two guides who took good care to be well furnished with lights. The huge rock, forming the canopy to the entrance of the cavern, has a similar appearance to Thorpe Cloud in Dove Dale, Derbyshire. At a short distance from the entrance to the cave you arrive at a spring of water, boldly gushing from the rock, and continues throughout its subterranean course, forming large pools of water, sufficiently spacious to enjoy the pleasure of bathing…

Thomas paused to recall how glad he was that his guides had a good number of lights for he would not have wished to experience the cave in its natural darkness. Before he could continue there was a knock at the door and the housekeeper informed him that Master Simmons was waiting for him to join him for lunch. He asked her to convey a message that he would be there shortly.

Henry Peter was already seated at the small table on the veranda which was a wonderful place to have lunch. Not that he noticed his surroundings for he had just received a disturbing letter from John Allen confessing that he had spent three days in debtor's prison early in January. He had not known that things were so bad with John Allen for he had said nothing when he came to see him not long before he left. He could have done something to help him, after all he was his brother. How his mother must have turned in her grave to know that her son had spent any number of days in prison for failing to pay his debts.

"I hope I didn't keep you waiting long," Thomas apologised. "I was recording my observations of the places I have visited in the last few weeks before my memory fails me." Henry came back to the present with a start as Thomas' voice intruded on his thoughts.

"Not at all," he answered vaguely, collecting his thoughts. "And how are you finding your visit?"

"It has exceeded my expectations," Thomas enthused. "I have seen and done so many things, I hope I do the island justice as I try to capture them in my journal."

"I will take you to see the signal station at Gun Hill next week," Henry Peter promised. "We will go on horseback. The road is through a deep ravine and the view of Vaucluse from that glen is truly remarkable. It was travelling through there one day to look around the plantation before I signed the deed of purchase that made me decide to change the name from Yorkshire Hall to Vaucluse."

"Why Vaucluse?"

"At the time I was very ill with bronchial asthma, which thankfully has now passed. My doctor advised me to move from St. Philip where I was living at the time and find an estate in either St. Thomas or St. Joseph where the air would be clearer. When I was coming to inspect the plantation, I looked at the rolling hills and the lush foliage that covered them which made the plantation look like a retreat to me."

"Ah, you named it after Petrarch's Vaucluse in France," Thomas finished, smiling approvingly.

"Yes."

"It is well suited to its name. You have a truly beautiful estate, Henry Peter. I have not even had the chance to discover all of it as I have been out constantly with one or the other of my friends, and I appreciate you taking the time to accompany me to other estates as well."

"Please feel free to investigate the estate at your leisure. Go anywhere you like and talk to any of the negroes you desire. I have nothing to hide."

"You have been more than accommodating. You have my sincere gratitude."

"It is my pleasure and also to my benefit for you to see the island for yourself so that you can write the truth, which is totally different from what the abolitionists are claiming."

"I am not sure if my humble writings will have any impact, but I certainly will do my best to be objective in my account."

***

Good Friday, April 5, 1833

"Thomas, as it is Good Friday, would you like to

attend services?" Henry Peter offered.

"I would be very pleased to do so, but I see that the parish church is still in ruins."

"You can attend the Moravian church that I showed you on our way here."

"They are of sound doctrine, so I would be happy to fellowship with them. How long have they been in the island?"

"Since about 1768. They first met at a place called Bunker's Hill, very near to here, until about 1799 when they built the new church which is called Sharon. Like many of the churches, it was destroyed in the hurricane but was re-opened for services last Sunday."

"I would be most gratified to attend service and experience the Moravian traditions. Is this the church where your negroes are baptised?"

"No. The Moravians baptise, but mine are mainly baptised by the Church of England. However, many seem to prefer the Moravian services. As I mentioned to you before, the ones that attend I find to be extremely sober and industrious."

"That is very good. I would be most appreciative to be able to pass Good Friday service there and, of course, make some observations for my journal."

"By all means. I will get one of the men to take you in the carriage."

"I take it that you will not be accompanying me?"

"Not on this occasion, no. I am sure, though, that some of my negroes will be in attendance as they have the day off, since it is a solemn day."

***

On returning several hours later, Thomas immediately sought a few minutes to make his observations in his journal. He had spent a few minutes speaking to the Reverend after the service and he had furnished him with some interesting information about the school that they had established. He doubted that Henry Peter's sons attended it. He had not had much interaction with them on his visit, but in the brief meeting on his arrival, they had seemed very educated and well spoken, so perhaps they had a tutor.

I attended the service at the new Moravian Church, lately erected in the parish of St. Thomas, and which had been only opened for worship on the preceding Sunday. The chapel is an octagonal building and has a very neat and imposing appearance: a row of young cabbage trees, areca oleracea, were just planted and will form a fine avenue when they attain their growth. It is capable of containing one thousand persons. There were a vast number of negroes present who seemed to pay great attention and joined in the exercises of devotion with much apparent feeling of piety. The service consists, principally, in singing hymns, a very acceptable mode of worship to the negroes who are so passionately fond of music; but between the singing portions of the service they have prayers, preaching and reading. The Moravians have also a large school for the instruction of coloured children, and they labour in their vocation most meritoriously. There is likewise another establishment in the parish of St. John. Their teachers are greatly esteemed for their unostentatious merits and as they inculcate most strongly the necessity of industrious habits and virtuous principles, and the merits of good works, they prove useful and admirable instructors of the negro race.

Thomas put down his quill once more as he got up to go down for lunch. Barbados was continually surprising him.   It was not at all what he had expected. Still, he had not seen everything yet. Who knew what he would discover?

Chapter 22

Thomas could hardly credit that his time at Vaucluse was almost over, but he and Henry Peter would be setting out for New York and then on to Upper Canada in just a few days. While he had visited several estates and sites on the island, most of his four months had been spent at Vaucluse where he had freedom to go wherever he chose and at any time he wanted. He had also had the benefit of seeing canes being harvested and processed and he was well satisfied that everything was as Henry Peter had told him.

They now sat on the veranda surveying the yard and the garden that they could see in the setting sun. Crickets chirped in the background, a noise that Thomas immediately noticed when he first arrived on the island, but which he no longer heard unless he listened intently. His journal lay next to him as he had been making his last few observations before Henry Peter joined him.

"Henry Peter, I know I have said it before, but I really thank you for inviting me to stay at Vaucluse for these four months. I have seen for myself the condition of the slaves in Barbados and it is not as reported in England, at least not in the places I have been. You have a fine estate and your slaves seem to be well looked after."

"Well thank you, Thomas. I am proud of it. I have near to six hundred acres and about three hundred negroes now, so it is one of the largest in the island. It is very well-kept and has been prosperous although I cannot claim all the responsibility since, as you know, I reside in England quite a lot of the time."

"How many acres are in use?"

"Every year we plant about sixty acres in cane and reap one hundred and thirty acres as we have canes growing at different stages. But we also plant yams, guinea corn, Indian corn, eddoes, sweet potatoes, and various sorts of peas. Some we raise for our own use and some we sell to the other islands."

"I have gone all over the plantation and I have counted your negroes," Thomas informed him. He opened the journal to the last page where he had made his notes. "There were four masons, three carpenters, three coopers, four domestics, three male and two female superintendents of the field, sixty field labourers in the first gang, fifty in the second gang, twenty-five in the third, eight watchmen, six cooks, two sick nurses, eleven tending the cattle, calves, three tending the goats and pigs, one groom, two women in charge of children, a hundred and fifteen old infirm people, infants and young children, and six invalids." Henry Peter nodded as he went through his list.

"That sounds about right, and I challenge any of the abolitionists in England to show me one of the peasants in their tenantries who has the kind of care and provision that my negroes have here," Henry Peter pointed out.

"In truth, I cannot," agreed Thomas. "I was truly surprised, not only at the condition of your negroes but at the number and condition of their houses. I counted eighty of them, with a separate kitchen in nearly every house. I also did not expect them to be permitted to keep pigs, goats and poultry for themselves and to have a piece of land to cultivate."

"Yes, indeed. Most of them have about half an acre and they are able to earn a little money for themselves by selling some of the produce from their land."

"One of them who is obviously very industrious told me that he had made on an average ten pounds per annum by raising ginger and starch from his portion of ground, and that he had amassed more than a hundred pounds."

Henry Peter nodded.

"I am not saying that slaves are unable to provide for themselves, but they have to be taught to do so. My protest is against freeing them without proper instruction. While they have that here at Vaucluse, all are not so fortunate."

"Speaking of fortunate, I was pleasantly surprised to find on your estate a hospital, of all things. Furthermore, the building is comfortable, roomy and well ventilated. When I visited it, I spoke to the medical practitioner who seemed to be very skilled.

He told me that your negroes are carefully attended in sickness, or on receiving any injury from accident. He said he is employed to attend day and night and nurses are provided to take charge of them. I was made to understand that whatever is ordered by him is at once procured." Thomas recounted his findings as if Henry Peter was not already aware of them.

"I am not one to advocate ill-treating slaves. That is more to be found in America and in some of the other islands, my findings tell me. I and many of the planters here are followers of Henry Drax's methods of providing well for his negroes and keeping them in good health. It breeds loyalty in them and they work better if they are well-fed and cared for."

"I have observed that they work from six to six, but they have time out from their labour for their meals, making their time of labour only nine hours."

"You would have seen that they have Saturday and Sunday off and, if they ask the manager, they are allowed to attend a funeral or go to market and sell their own stock."

Thomas nodded to indicate that he had seen this for himself.

"I have also noticed that in addition to the meals which they have in common, they also have a weekly allowance of provisions, ten pints of Guinea corn, or thirteen pints of Indian corn. If in roots, yams, eddoes, or potatoes, thirty pounds; and one pound of salt fish to each negro."

"If you were here at Christmas you would see how bountifully regaled they are. You would have seen for yourself on Good Friday that they were permitted to abstain from work and that is also so for other solemn days".

"Henry Peter, I must say that I still do not advocate slavery; however, it is but justice to say that I have never seen such happiness and prosperity amongst any body of labourers as amongst the negro population of this island and those at Vaucluse in particular. They do not seem to feel the hardship of want. I have seen no distress by the cares of a starving family and wife; they are secure in the possession of a comfortable house and know not the misery of seeing their family and children driven from the shelter of their roof by the cruelty of a creditor."

"Can the peasantry of England claim that?" demanded Henry Peter again, shaking his head.

"No, but neither is a value put to them and their names listed in a ledger like a piece of furniture, nor are they owned by anyone."

To that Henry Peter had no argument, for he could not argue with the truth.

***

June 1833
Ancaster, Ontario, Upper Canada

Henry Peter was happy to arrive in Ancaster for it was beginning to feel as if the journey was without end. The latter part had left him battered and bruised when he and Thomas had travelled by stage coach on a most miserable road from Lockport to Youngstown to take the steamboat that brought them to Upper Canada.

If he was glad to be at the end of the journey he could well imagine that Thomas was doubly so, as he had suffered from several bouts of sea sickness on the journey through the Caribbean. After leaving Barbados they had sailed past St. Lucia where they admired the twin peaks of the Pitons before passing Martinique. They had stopped at Dominica and got becalmed near Guadeloupe. The boat had passed between Montserrat and Antigua before heading towards the Virgin Islands and then on to the United States.

They had arrived in the United States on April 23, some six days after weighing anchor in Carlisle Bay. At St. Thomas in the Virgin Islands they had boarded a schooner by the name of Vernon for the trip to Philadelphia. From Philadelphia, they had travelled over land until they eventually reached New York on May 13 and had been delighted to see what a beautiful city it was. They had then left New York in a large and beautiful steam-boat named the De Witt Clinton, in honour (they were told) of one of the best and most enterprising governors that ever presided over that state.

They had travelled along the scenic Hudson River, coming to Albany five days after they left New York. They had found Albany to be pleasing in appearance, being well-built with some handsome structures. Leaving Albany, they had travelled along various canals in boats, making slow progress because of damage made to the banks of the canal and the aqueducts due to a recent flood in that part of the country.

The interruption to their progress had enabled them to enquire of many English farmers who were settled along the shores about the country and its prospects, and Thomas had been particularly gratified to hear of the prosperity they were all experiencing. They discovered that many of the travellers in boats that shared the canals were also on their way to Canada.

The excursion along the canal had been made doubly interesting by the neat new houses along its banks, the well cultivated fields, the gently rising hills adorned with trees and the large orchards with the peach, apple, and pear trees covered with lovely blossoms. The canal itself was almost choked with boats conveying passengers and their goods to new homes.

Both he and Thomas had been encouraged by the richness of the land and while the cattle did not have the same appearance of wellbeing, the horses were not so bad. They had travelled to Rochester and then on to Lockport to see the new roads being built, one of which would go to Buffalo. Leaving Lockport, they had travelled by road to Youngstown. The roads had been in such poor condition that they many times found themselves in danger of being thrown from the stage coach and the constant jolting had left them with many bruises. Thankfully, on June 3 after the bruising journey, they had boarded a steamboat to Upper Canada where they settled in a place called Ancaster.

Henry Peter and Thomas found lodgings and spent some days getting to know the people of Ancaster and observing the land.

"I am thinking to purchase some land around the village. I saw a good piece on a hill that is several hundred acres, although not all is usable. But I will also invest in a piece of land in the village and lay out a street and sell it off in smaller parcels," Henry Peter announced. "I have been talking to two gentlemen by the name of Horatio Gates and James Leslie who have about seventy acres to sell at a very good price. It is big enough that I can sell it in many smaller lots and recoup my investment at a profit."

"It is good to have the money to invest in land here as it is so cheap. The most I can do is to buy one of the lots that you will sell, so please give me first refusal when you are ready," Thomas told him.

"By all means, Thomas," he promised.

"Providence must have caused me to meet up with you, for I had planned to seek out my living in New South Wales until you spoke to me of your plans to visit Upper Canada in order to make it your future residence."

"Indeed," Henry Peter agreed. "It was very sporting of you to agree to visit Vaucluse before you came here and to see for yourself that the abolitionists err in their belief about slavery in the colonies, or at least in Barbados."

"While I have not seen the atrocities that have been described, I must say that I still am not in agreement with human beings being owned by another."

"I, too, am not in favour of it, but as I have stated in my letter to the Lord of the Treasury, according to the law – which I did not make myself – they are my possession so if I am to give them up I should be compensated."

"I am all for compensation if it means the end to slavery."

"When I return to England I intend to emancipate my two sons and three other slaves in the event that the emancipation law does pass, although I will continue to advocate against it."

"Why would you emancipate your sons and others if they are to be free anyway?"

"It is mainly because of the planned apprenticeship period of six years, which means that if I do not emancipate them they will be required to apprentice for the plantation. Besides, my boys have never worked on the plantation and, in any case, I would not want to receive money for my own children if the compensation comes through."

"That is understandable. When you leave I will open my practice for there is no doubt need for a doctor in the village. I will need to impose on you to take some correspondence to my wife and to bring her with you on your return."

"You may rely on me to do both."

Chapter 23

September 1833
Surrey, England

"Henry Peter, it is good to see you. I take it that you received my letter when you were in Barbados?"

"Yes indeed, John Allen, and I was horrified to hear that you had spent three days in debtor's prison! Our mother must have turned in her grave. Why did you not say something to me?"

"To tell the truth, HP, I did not think for one moment that that scoundrel Charles Walker would have me thrown into prison like a common criminal for a few pounds! Anyway, that is all settled now so you need not concern yourself. As for you, I did not expect you back in England as yet for I thought you would settle a while in Upper Canada."

"That is my intention, but I have some business I need to deal with in England first and that is the emancipation of my sons and a few others."

"What has prompted that after so long? And has not the law already passed for all slaves to be emancipated?"

"It is to my detriment that it has passed, but it has not yet been enacted. I have decided to emancipate my sons now for, in the event that we are compensated, I seem not to have it in me to be compensated for my own sons."

"Understandable. How did you find Upper Canada?"

"It was all that I had hoped. The land is spacious and fertile and, most importantly, it is extremely affordable. I have arranged to purchase seventy acres in the village of Ancaster for just six hundred and thirty-five pounds when I return in two months."

"Six hundred and thirty-five pounds? That's preposterous!" John sputtered.

"It is, considering that I sold six acres of Vaucluse land to William Doyle for five hundred and thirteen pounds two years ago. I will lay a road and cut it into smaller parcels that I will sell off eleven or twelve pounds an acre. That will give me a modest profit. I also plan to buy a substantial acreage and build a decent house there."

"HP, I admire your business acumen tremendously. You have always had a gift for planning far ahead and making your plans come to fruition."

"That is why I decided to explore the region of Canada, for I knew that despite all of my arguments to the contrary, abolition would happen. Still, I had to try. I wrote a second letter to the Lord Earl Grey over a month ago, this one of greater length, documenting my findings to convince him that the negro is not yet fitted for his freedom. That is all for naught now anyway."

The door opened and John Allen's wife Mary greeted Henry Peter.

"Henry Peter, I could not help but hear what you said as I came in. What on earth do you mean that the negro is not fitted for his freedom?"

John Allen braced himself for the heated discussion which he knew was about to unfold.

"I was just telling John Allen that I had written a letter to the Lord Earl Grey. In it I told him that I believe the negro's organisation – defective alike both in his moral and intellectual capacities – renders him unfit for freedom. I did, however, say that over time I believe this impediment can be removed."

"I do not understand. From what I have heard, you have freed slaves before and yet you say they do not have the moral or intellectual capacity to be fit for freedom?"

"It is true that I have freed slaves over the years but generally in exceptional circumstances. However, I am about to emancipate my sons but–"

"You have sons who are slaves?" she interrupted, shocked at this. Henry Peter realised, too late, that John Allen must not have shared that particularly sensitive information with her.

"Yes, their mother was a woman on Vaucluse. As I was saying, I do not think negroes are beyond hope, but time is needed to cultivate virtuous habits and industrious pursuits in them."

"In all the years you have benefitted from that

horrible, oppressive system you did not think to cultivate these virtuous habits and industrious pursuits in your slaves?"

John Allen stirred uncomfortably. He knew that he should have intervened as soon as the conversation began.

"On the contrary, many of my slaves have benefitted from being baptised and attending services at the Moravian church near to the plantation. Some of the children even attend school. I have also provided small plots of land for them to cultivate for their own use, either to consume the crops or to sell them."

"So, how can you say that they are not fit for freedom?"

"I do not necessarily mean my own. I mean negroes in general."

"You say that slaves are defective in their morals and yet you have sons from a slave woman who, for all I know, did not consent to having relations with you. You say that they need to be industrious and yet they grow their own food for consumption and for sale on plots of land that you provide. Henry Peter Simmons, you are either the biggest hypocrite alive or you do not know what you truly believe!"

"I think you've said enough, my dear," John intervened, taking her by the arm and leading her towards the door. "Perhaps you could see about arranging some refreshments for my brother who is also our guest," he said, stressing the last word. She went willingly, not keen to stay in Henry Peter's company much longer. "I do apologise, HP," John Allen said once the door was closed, "but I have told you on occasion of Mary's views on slavery."

"You do not need to apologise for your wife, John Allen. She is entitled to speak her mind as I am free to speak mine. I am no longer fighting to prevent the emancipation of my slaves as it is a foregone conclusion. What I now seek, as I did in my first letter, is compensation for the loss I will experience when it happens."

***

March 18, 1834
Vaucluse Plantation, Barbados

Joseph Bayley put down his pen and sighed with relief as he flexed his fingers. He had just completed the Slave Returns for Vaucluse Plantation where he was acting as Henry Peter's attorney. He had recorded the names of 285 slaves plus the three that had been forgotten from 1829 and 1832, then the twenty-four new births and eleven deaths since 1832 and finally the five slaves (Harry, John Alleyne, Henry Wellington, Margaret and Sam Fleming) that Henry Peter had manumitted in Liverpool and the one girl, Sarah Frances, who he had instructed was to be gifted to his daughter, Mary Ann. That left a total of 295 slaves; 105 more than were at Vaucluse when Henry Peter bought the plantation eighteen years ago.

Joseph knew that Harry and John Alleyne were Henry Peter's coloured sons, as he made no secret of the fact, but he was not sure who Henry Wellington and Margaret were. He figured that if they were also Henry Peter's he would have claimed them as his own. It was not his business to ask such questions, only to record the names. Sam Fleming, a black slave, had also been manumitted. Previous records showed that he used to keep the cattle but he was no longer assigned to any work, possibly due to an injury. Perhaps that was why he had been manumitted. His children and the other two that were manumitted were not assigned to either the field or the house either; they had privileged status. He wondered if emancipation would mean anything to the two boys, for they were slaves in name only, as they had all the privileges that their father's money afforded them.

This would be the last return because the news had come from England last year that on the 1st of August all the slaves were to be emancipated. He didn't know what would come of the island when that happened. Henry Peter had purchased land in Canada and seemed to have plans to move there for he had asked him in his last letter to begin to make enquiries to see whether anyone would be interested in leasing Vaucluse for a time. He was not of a mind to sell, but he did not appear to want to have to deal with the apprenticeship system that was being forced on the planters. The slaves would continue to be bound to the plantation and were to continue to work there for a period of six years. He, too, wished he had the wherewithal to leave Barbados until things settled down again, if they would. They certainly would never be like they were before.

At least he had some good news that he could send to Henry Peter with a copy of this last record. George Hewitt, who was one of the wealthiest attorneys on the island, had expressed an interest in leasing Vaucluse. He owned Bloomsbury Plantation in St. Thomas as well as land in St. George. Vaucluse, at 582 acres with 295 slaves, was a fine, profitable plantation and would be a good addition for him. He would no doubt have to pay a substantial rent to lease it from Henry Peter Simmons.

***

August 1, 1834
Vaucluse Plantation

There was a buzz of excitement around the yard in Vaucluse coupled with a sense of confusion. The slaves were not in the fields as was their custom at this time of the day but milled around in the yard talking excitedly; some were even singing and dancing.

"What is happening?" Margaret, one of the young coloured slaves asked.

"We free today, that is wha' happenin'," Mary Ann answered. "Nobody can' make we work if we don' want to," she added.

"I never used to work before so I was always free?"

"No, girl. It is just that you and you brother, Henry Wellington, was treated the same way as Harry and John Alleyne, the master sons, but wunna only get free last year."

"What you tellin' the girl that nobody can't make we work ain' true, you know," David, one of the house servants, explained on overhearing the conversation. "You don't understand this apprenticeship t'ing. Although we not slaves no more we still got to work for the plantation, but we is to get time to work for we self too." At that, Margaret wondered off, uninterested in talk that was of no importance to her for, apparently, she had been free already.

"So, how come the ones in the yard ain' wukkin' today?" Mary Ann continued.

"The manager must be giving them a little time to celebrate."

"How long this apprentice thing is to be for?"

"They say six years for we."

"Wuhloss, that long. And then wha' is to happen?"

"We will be free free but we goin' got to make we own way. Work for somebody or get a piece of land somehow and work it, not that the' got any land 'bout here that nobody don' own."

"What I could do now but keep house? I don' know what I would do and I old now. I is fifty-seven years. I did very good with how t'ings was. The master don' be 'bout here much and we ain' had nobody to trouble we."

"Girl, that alright for you and me in the house, but wha' bout them that does work in the fields from sunup to sundown? And here ain' even bad, but the' got some other plantations that the managers ain' no sweet bread. We got it good."

"Praise the Lord. I only hopin' it stay so."

"The master must be goin' come in soon. I wonder what he goin' do with the plantation now? I did hear that he didn' want slaves to be free."

"Wha' you expect? It is the free labour that does give he the money to live big up in England you know."

"That is the truth."

***

May 6, 1835
Vaucluse Plantation

Henry Peter signed his name to the lease with his usual flourish and passed it to George Hewitt for his signature before his friends Thomas Lee and James Thomas Rogers added theirs as witnesses. He had agreed to lease Vaucluse to George Hewitt from the 1st of July for five years. He stood up and shook hands with George to seal the deal and poured drinks for the gentlemen.

"Congratulations on leasing Vaucluse, George," Thomas told him.

"You should be congratulating Henry Peter, for the rent I have to pay him of thirty-five hundred pounds a year for the first three years and then three thousand pounds a year for the next two is no small sum."

"Vaucluse is well able to provide you with profits above that, George, have no doubt," HP assured him.

"I am certain it will, or I would not have entered into the lease. Or it could before the apprenticeship system. I will now have to see if I can get the slaves to continue to produce as much now that they are free."

"I am sure that you are well up to the task," Henry Peter told him.

"Who are these non-praedials and praedials that you have excluded from the lease agreement?" George asked him.

"I am taking my house servant, David, with me

and the others are trusted servants who will look after my boys while I'm away. The field slave Sarah is too old now to work and the girl Molly Harry or Molly Grace – as she is called – is a half-sister to my boys and will live with them."

"Henry Peter, you are very good at hiding a big heart," his good friend James Rogers complimented him. They were a year apart in age and had known each other since they were children. Henry Peter was godfather to his son, John Henry.

"Let us not go too far now, my friend," Henry Peter denied. "How are the wedding plans coming?" Henry Peter quickly changed the subject which made him uncomfortable. John Henry was to marry his fiancée Margaret Frances Carew in less than a month.

"Good. John Henry has got himself a good girl there. Hopefully, they will give me many grandchildren."

"Your son John Henry is the sexton at St. Paul's chapel, correct?" George asked him.

"Yes, that's right."

"Good boy," George praised. "So, is it back to England for you, Henry Peter?" George asked him.

"My dear man, have you not heard that our friend Henry Peter has purchased land in Upper Canada?" Thomas Lee asked him, looking at Henry Peter admiringly.

"Indeed?" George looked very interested. His admiration for Henry Peter grew.

"Yes, I have purchased two pieces."

"Is the land there reasonably priced?"

"Yes, indeed. So much so that I bought seventy acres which I have divided and started to re-sell and I plan to purchase a large parcel of about eight hundred acres on which I will build a house."

"Eight hundred?" George whistled.

"I will not develop all of it. Canada is truly a vast land and very fertile. The crops are plentiful, but the cattle are lacking, and I have not observed many sheep. Once I settle, I will see what I can bring to the country."

"That sounds most lucrative. I commend you on your foresight, Henry Peter. If I were of a nature to seek adventure I would join you in Canada but, alas, Barbados will always be home to me."

***

September 30, 1835
Ancaster, Ontario, Canada

A meeting of the inhabitants of Ancaster and its vicinity is requested on Monday Evening, October 5, at 7 o'clock, at the tavern of Mr. Rousseau, to take into consideration the best method to be adopted in consequence of a gift of H.P. Simmons, Esq. of two village lots for the erection of a schoolhouse and a reading room for the reception of 250 volumes of the most approved works in literature and in history, the gift of the same gentleman to the village of Ancaster forever. P.S. Mr. Simmons, having laid out a new street through the village of Ancaster, has several village lots to dispose of on application to him at Ancaster.

Henry Peter folded the *Dundas Weekly Post* newspaper of the day before and put it on the table with a feeling of satisfaction. Much had been accomplished since his arrival at the beginning of July, almost a year since his last visit. The town had developed nicely in his absence and Thomas had opened his medical practice since August of the year they arrived. This trip Henry Peter had brought Thomas' wife with him, together with David his servant and another lady who was a friend of the Rolphs from England. Thomas and his wife had been among the first to purchase one of the lots that he had put on sale after laying the road. He already had quite a number of persons who had signed up to purchase lots, so he could well afford to donate two of them to the town.

He had always valued education and was an avid reader, so he was happy to provide the lots for a schoolhouse and a library to be erected. He could certainly spare the volumes from his wide collection which he had brought from Vaucluse, since he would not be visiting it for the next five years and he had no desire to leave them behind.

He would begin the construction of his house on the hill shortly. He already had plans drawn up of what he wanted, and he could picture it with its high ceilings and large windows to let in the light and appreciate the view. He would of course have stables built and import some quality horses, as the few he had seen were of an inferior breed. He would also bring in some Dishley sheep and some Norfolk hogs. The sheep had long, heavy fleece which would be good for producing wool, with the added benefit of having very meaty carcasses for mutton. He had read about the breeding techniques of Robert Bakewell which had led to the production of this excellent breed of sheep.

He would miss both Barbados and England, but

he intended to make the most of this new life in Ancaster, Canada. He would build a house that would be the talk of the town and leave a legacy through his donations which would provide for the betterment of the inhabitants of Ancaster.

Chapter 24

June 20, 1839
Hellingly, Sussex, England

"James, do you take Mary Ann to be your wife? Do you promise to love, honour, cherish and protect her, forsaking all others and holding only to her forevermore?"

"I do."

"Mary Ann, do you take James to be your husband? Do you promise to love, honour, cherish and protect him, forsaking all others and holding only to him forevermore?"

"I do."

"Please repeat these vows after me."

Henry Peter listened with one ear as James and Mary Ann repeated their vows after the minister. He was happy that he had arranged for them to meet and that Mary Ann would be married and have someone to take care of her. Having had Henry Morris, who was now twelve years old, they had agreed to say that she was a widow in order to maintain her respectability. James Baber was five years younger than her and a second son, but she had done well. He was well pleased.

George Hewitt had just over a year left on the lease of Vaucluse, after which he would return to Barbados and see the state of the country now that the indenture period had been shortened to four years. He still seemed able to pay the lease so the labourers must still be producing well. He was actually beginning to miss Barbados. Canada was fine and he liked England too but maybe his old bones needed the warmth of Barbados. Besides, he wanted to die in the land where he was born and it was three years since he had passed his sixtieth birthday, so he did not know how much longer he had.

The minister finished the service and in little time, the couple had signed the register. His daughter was now the wife and responsibility of James Baber Esquire. Looking at her, beautiful in her wedding dress, no one would ever suspect that she had once been a slave who he had freed twenty years ago. She was well read and bred as any gently reared white girl. He had done well by her. She would be fine.

"I am proud of you," he whispered in her ear.

Tears filled her eyes as she replied: "Everything I am, I owe to you. Thank you, Father."

Henry Peter's heart swelled with love for his daughter as he handed her over to her husband to have and to hold.

***

June 28, 1839
Rochester, Kent, England

Henry Peter looked around the room trying to smother his boredom. He really did not feel to be at the house party, but he had promised his good friend Martin Bailey to attend. He was surprised at how melancholy he was feeling since Mary Ann had married James last week. He was happy for her, but for some reason he now felt lonely, which was ridiculous given he had been alone his whole life. The last time he had felt like that was when John had died. He must be getting old after all. Who would have thought he would live so long when most of his family had died so early?

"HP, allow me to introduce you to Edward Young and his wife Isabella. As soon as Isabella heard that you were from Barbados she was intrigued and begged me to introduce you."

"Uncle Martin, you do me no credit," protested Isabella, blushing.

"Edward, Isabella, this is Henry Peter Simmons who has become a good friend to me. Isabella is a great friend of my daughter Annabel. She is also like a daughter to me, which is why I have no qualms in causing her embarrassment," he teased her.

"That you have," she confirmed. "I am honoured to meet you," she added to Henry Peter.

"The honour is mine," insisted Henry Peter, gallantly bowing over her hand before shaking her husband's.

Isabella Young was a tall woman of slender build with rich brown hair and a healthy complexion, as if she liked to be outdoors. She wouldn't be described as a great beauty, but her face was arresting and he couldn't help but be intrigued by the slightly haunted look he glimpsed in the eyes that met his briefly, which seemed to contrast with her forthright manner. Her husband was the opposite, being a short stocky fellow. He was not a bad looking man but had a serious demeanour and cold eyes which his brief, polite smile did not bother to trouble. Henry Peter quickly summed him up as one of those men who resented the fact that Providence had denied him more inches in stature. He had come across men of his ilk before, so he wasn't surprised to see the possessive hand he kept on his wife's lower back, holding her close to his side.

"I will leave you to get acquainted while I greet my other guests," Martin announced, bowing slightly before he took his leave.

"I understand that you own a plantation in Barbados," Young challenged, somewhat abruptly.

"Indeed I do, though it has been leased out for the last four years."

"I suppose you owned slaves as well." His wife started to protest at his tone but was quelled by a harsh look from her husband.

"I did indeed," admitted Henry Peter, without any qualms. "They came with the plantation when I bought it and I added to their number over the years. They are all now free, of course."

"As they should be," declared Edward.

"Believe me, my slaves were more advantaged

than the poor here in England."

"How could being owned by someone be of any advantage?" asked Edward rudely.

"Well, at least they were well-fed, clothed and housed unlike some of your poor, in spite of the freedom that you say they have."

"What is the name of your plantation?" Isabella cut in hurriedly before the conversation could escalate into a quarrel. She knew that Edward did not really care about the plight of slaves, but he liked to argue and he could be quite rude when he got started.

"Vaucluse," Henry Peter answered politely, repressing the annoyance he felt towards her husband.

"Vaucluse?" she repeated delightedly. "As in Petrarch's retreat?"

Henry Peter looked at her in surprise as if he was seeing her afresh. He felt a stirring of interest, as a woman who was as well read as he was rare in his experience.

"You read Petrarch?" he asked. She nodded almost shyly.

"I used to read widely, but do not have much opportunity anymore," she admitted wistfully. Henry Peter wondered what prevented her from reading.

"I have to admit that I miss my library considerably as I, too, am an avid reader. I did bring some of my favourite books with me, though. Do you share the same passion?" he asked her husband politely.

"I cannot say that I find it necessary to read about things that have no bearing on reality. I also believe that there are other things that women can employ themselves with in the home of more importance than reading, even if there are no children to see after," he added almost accusingly, giving HP a glimpse into their situation.

"Well, we certainly differ in that opinion," Henry Peter asserted and saw Edward visibly bristle and open his mouth to reply. He hid a smile that he had managed to rouse the man so easily yet again.

"Was your plantation always called Vaucluse?" Isabella interrupted again, obviously trying to avert another confrontation. Henry Peter took pity on her and recounted how he had come to change the name from Yorkshire Hall.

"What a lovely story. Vaucluse certainly sounds like a beautiful place." She barely concealed the wistfulness in her voice, as if she would love to visit it but knew it would never be.

"It certainly is. Nearly six hundred acres of fertile countryside in the middle of the island with views of the south and west of the island."

"Oh, how I would love to see it." The words slipped almost involuntarily from Isabella's lips.

"Well, that is unlikely to ever happen. Please excuse us, Mr. Simmons, we do not want to monopolise your time. Come along, Isabella." He nodded to Henry Peter before guiding his wife away with the hand that was still resting on her back.

Isabella made a helpless gesture towards Henry Peter as her husband shepherded her away. Henry Peter was surprised at the pang he felt on her departure. He would have liked to talk more with her. Imagine her knowing about Petrarch's retreat. Even as he made his way to speak to an acquaintance, he wondered how he could talk to her again without the dampening presence of her husband.

Next Day

Isabella sat in the garden of Annabel Linton's house. This was one of the few places that Edward allowed her to go and she gladly escaped to spend some time with her friend where she could be herself. She was beginning to wonder what that meant, for she hardly recognised the person she had become. Who was this quiet, cowering woman? She used to be an adventurous, lively young woman who was as comfortable curled up with a good book as racing across the countryside astride a horse in a very unladylike manner. Edward had practically destroyed that person with his harsh words and heavy hand. Meeting Henry Peter Simmons last night had stirred something in her. A yearning for adventure and freedom once again. She would have loved to see his plantation in Barbados.

"Your father's party was very enjoyable," she ventured to Annabel who sat with her feet tucked up next to her.

"It was?" Her friend looked sceptical. She had been and had not found it overly enjoyable.

"Well, I met a very interesting man."

"Oh really? Who would that be? And where was Edward in all this?" she teased, not knowing Edward for who he truly was.

"It wasn't like that," Isabelle assured her. "His name is Henry Peter Simmons."

"Oh, he's one of my father's old business associates."

"I didn't suppose him to be so old. There is

something quite youthful about him," Isabella defended.

"Youthful? I wouldn't have said that. He is likely older than my father! He owns a huge plantation in Barbados and property in Upper Canada. Apparently, he is quite wealthy."

"Indeed?" She didn't have to do much to prompt Annabel to continue, as she had a bit of a loquacious nature.

"Yes. He married off his daughter just last week to a farmer from Hellingly in Sussex by the name of Barber or Baber or some such. It is quite scandalous really, for she is his illegitimate, coloured daughter who was apparently born of one of his slave women!" Her eyes opened wider with each disclosure.

"Really?" Isabella exclaimed, intrigued in spite of herself.

"Yes, and he seems to have no shame about it. My father said that he gave her away at the wedding, bold as you please, and signed the register as her father. Disgraceful situation, if you ask me. In fact, he has two coloured sons as well and he does not hide it."

"Does he have a wife? And does she not mind?" Isabella asked.

"No. He has never married. My father says he cannot understand why. He is certainly wealthy enough to support a wife."

"Maybe he has never met anyone that he could spend his life with."

"Or maybe he has not met anyone who would want to spend her life with him!" she exclaimed. "I find him rather opinionated and brash. He actually spoke to you? He rarely speaks to me on the occasions that I see him. Not that I want him to," she added.

"Yes, we spoke briefly. And I found him quite interesting."

"What could be so interesting?" Not waiting for a reply, she said, "And to make matters worse, he was a slave owner! I once overheard my father talking to him about some letters he wrote to the Lord of the Treasury before slavery was abolished, trying to get his support against emancipation!"

"He must have had his reasons," Isabella defended.

"Isabella! There can be no good reason, apart from the fact that he would have been out of pocket. I think it's disgraceful."

"Well, I am glad that those poor slaves were freed as well, but he did tell us that he paid for them when he bought the plantation, so to him abolition would have meant loss of his assets."

"I can't believe you're defending him, Isabella!"

"I'm not defending him. And anyway, he reads Petrarch." The non-sequitur had Annabel at a loss.

"What?" she asked, looking blankly at Isabella.

"He named his plantation Vaucluse, after the retreat of the poet and philosopher Petrarch."

"And that makes him interesting?"

"Never mind. Let us speak of something else. How are Robert and the children?"

At that Annabel perked up. Isabelle was glad for her friend but felt a pang of envy that her own marriage was so far from the happy one that her friend was blessed with.

"They are wonderful. The nurse is looking after the children so that I can have some time with you.

Why don't you stay for tea? My father is coming over and is bringing the dreadful Henry Peter who is staying with him. You can speak to him at length if you so desire."

Isabella eagerly accepted, then said, "I am not sure if Edward would want me to stay. Although he has gone to the races and won't be home until late."

"Well, write him a note and I will get one of the servants to take it around to your house and give it to one of your servants."

"Yes, I will do that." With that decision, she felt a leap of excitement at the thought of being able to speak freely to Henry Peter Simmons without her husband intervening.

Several Hours Later

"Father, Mr. Simmons, welcome," greeted Annabel as they were shown into the parlour by the butler.

"Thank you for entertaining us, dear," her father said, kissing her cheek.

"Yes. Thank you for your hospitality," agreed Henry Peter.

"You are both welcome. This is my friend Isabella Young." Annabel drew his attention to Isabella who had been partly hidden behind her on the sofa. Henry Peter's eyes conveyed his pleasure at seeing Isabella again, all the more so with her husband apparently absent.

"We met last night. Lovely to see you again, Mrs. Young," he greeted, moving to bow over the hand she extended.

"Isabella, this is a nice surprise," Mr. Bailey said. "I am so glad to see you two days in a row. We don't see enough of you. That husband of yours is very selfish with your company," he joked.

Isabella smiled, knowing that he had no idea how true that was. Edward would no doubt be annoyed that she was not at home waiting for him, especially if he knew that Henry Peter Simmons was present. She certainly had no plans of informing him of that.

"I will call for tea now that you have arrived. Robert won't be able to join us as he has some business that may keep him late."

Henry Peter sat next to Isabella on the sofa, leaving Martin to take one of the side chairs. He was delighted to see her again and looked forward to speaking more with her.

"I seem to recall that we have reading in common," he began. "What have you read recently?"

"I have to confess that I have not read anything much of late."

"Well, tell me then which of Petrarch's poems is your favourite?"

"You assume I have read Petrarch because I knew of Vaucluse?" she asked. "Perhaps I am only a student of poets and philosophers and not of their poetry."

"That would be like admiring a dressmaker and not enjoying the dresses that she crafts."

"Indeed it would," she laughed. "I suppose I hesitate because I do not want to seem like a romantic fool. My favourite is the one that he was reputed to have written the day he saw the mysterious Laura."

"'*It was on that day when the sun's ray was darkened in*

pity for his Maker when I was taken, and I did not defend myself against it, for your lovely eyes, Lady, bound me." Henry Peter quoted, looking into Isabella's eyes.

Isabella's heart raced at the intensity in Henry Peter's eyes before she reminded herself that he was simply falling into the role of the poet.

"'It did not seem to me a time to guard myself against Love's blows; so I went on confident, unsuspecting; from that, my troubles started, amongst the public sorrows,'" he continued.

"'Love discovered me all weaponless and opened the way to the heart through the eyes, which are made the passageways and doors of tears,'" she joined in.

Before either could complete the poem, Martin interrupted. "For heaven's sake, enough of that drivel. And you a serious businessman, Henry Peter," he teased.

"Philistine!" they said together and, looking at each other in surprise, burst into laughter. Sobering first, Isabella was taken aback at the ease she felt with this man who was practically a stranger to her. Henry Peter looked at her and felt that he could, for the first time in his life, identify with Petrarch as he regarded one who was perhaps his own Laura. She, too, was out of his reach and not just by the gulf of years that separated them, but because someone else had already been given the gift of her.

Chapter 25

"Thank you for having us, Annabel, but I must get Henry Peter home as he is travelling back to Lymington early in the morning."

"Oh, you are from Lymington? I had assumed you were from Sussex," Isabella blurted out, before realising she would only have based her assumption on information from Annabel.

"Yes. I was in Sussex for the marriage of my daughter and I decided to visit Martin a few days before going home as I had not seen him recently."

Annabel caught her eye and her look seemed to say, 'See what I mean? No shame.'

"Oh." Isabella did not know what else to say. For some reason she felt at a loss that Henry Peter lived over 100 miles away, which meant she was unlikely to see him again.

"Take me to see my grandchildren, Annabel, before I go," her father demanded, heading towards the stairs with a murmured excuse.

Henry Peter was grateful to his friend for the few moments alone with Isabella.

"It is the damnedest thing, pardon my language, but I feel as if I have known you for a long time," he said bluntly.

"I feel the same and no offense taken. I have heard worse."

Henry Peter reached into his jacket and proffered a card. "Please take my card in case you ever need anything."

"What could I possibly need?" she asked, taking the card from him and slipping it into her reticule. They looked at each other and unspoken words passed between them.

"One never knows. Perhaps one day you may want to visit Barbados."

"There is not the slightest chance of that happening. My husband has no desire for adventure and I am afraid that he would never consent to me having one without him."

"If I were ever so fortunate as him to have a wife such as you, I might feel the same way."

"No, I'm sure you wouldn't." Isabella looked down shyly.

Henry Peter swore at himself for flirting with her. She was a married woman and less than half his age. How he wished that he was younger and she was not married. However, if wishes were horses, beggars would ride. He had better put such thoughts behind him and get on with his life.

"Do you still visit Barbados?" she asked to fill the uncomfortable silence.

"I have not been to Barbados since I leased my

plantation in 1835. The lease will finish next year and I will return to see how things are. Meanwhile, I purchased some property in Upper Canada and I have a house there. I travel between here and there quite often."

"Canada? You certainly are adventurous! What made you buy property in Canada?"

"I heard a lot of good things about it from people who were living there. Land is very cheap compared to Barbados so I was able to buy more acres than I have at Vaucluse, although only about a quarter of it is developed. And I did not want to be in Barbados after emancipation."

"So, what do you grow on the land?"

"I grow various crops and there is an abundance of all kinds of fruit, but I recently brought in some Daisley sheep for mutton and wool and also Norfolk hogs for pork."

They were interrupted by Annabel and her father returning and Isabella and Henry Peter were left once again with the feeling that they had not exhausted all that they had to say. As they said their goodbyes, they both were reminded of the poem they had shared and its meaning.

***

Young Household
Rochester, Kent

Edward Young lounged on the sofa in the parlour looking deceptively relaxed. In truth, he was seething with anger and frustration. He had had a bad run of luck at the races and he had come home to be handed a note from Isabella by a servant saying that she would be having tea with her friend Annabel. It was long past the time that tea should be finished and she was not home as yet. She would be sorry if she didn't get home soon.

The sound of the front door and her voice in the foyer alerted him that she was home. He made an effort to relax and sat up, not wanting to be at a disadvantage by lying down.

"Hello, Edward. I'm sorry to be late. I thought you would still be out. Annabel sends her regards." Isabella clamped her mouth shut, aware that she was rambling on to cover her nervousness. It was not as if speaking with Henry Peter Simmons was a sin of some kind.

"I came home expecting to find you and instead I received your note. What made you think that you could stay for tea?"

She could smell alcohol on his breath from where she was. She would have to tread carefully.

"I am sorry. I saw no harm since I knew you would not be home."

"But as you see, I am home and I have been here for several hours."

"I am sorry," she said again.

"What were you doing? Who was there?"

"I was having tea. Annabel's father came over to have tea with her." She deliberately refrained from telling him of the other visitor, knowing that might throw him into a fit of unnatural jealousy that she could do without. She tamped down the guilt that she felt at the deception, but she knew from experience that it was better to withhold the truth than suffer the consequences of her honesty.

"Have you eaten already?" She changed the subject.

"No. I was waiting for you. You arrived just in time, for I had given you another five minutes."

Isabella knew that he was not only referring to going ahead without her. Relief washed over her at the escape.

"I will just pop upstairs and freshen up. I will be right back." She paused, waiting for his nod of dismissal and hurried from the room clutching her reticule, eager to find a safe place to hide Henry Peter's card. She hated herself for the frightened woman she had become. She could not continue this way or she would never find her way back to who she was. When she had married Edward she was a spirited, adventurous woman just two years past her twentieth birthday, but he had almost crushed her spirit with his harsh words and heavy hands. She had to get away from him. The card seemed to burn her hand as she pushed it into the back of a drawer. Maybe she would take up Henry Peter on his offer of help. A burst of excitement mixed with terror battled in her as she contemplated the unthinkable. Dare she leave her husband and escape to Barbados?

***

July 19, 1839
Rochester, Kent

Dear Mr. Simmons
Please excuse my boldness in sending you this letter and in presuming that you remember me, but you gave me your card at

Annabel Linton's house and told me that if I ever needed help I should contact you. Well, I need help to keep my sanity. That may sound a bit dramatic. What I mean is that I need someone to talk to who shares some of the same passions as I do and reading seems to be something we share. I hope you do not mind if I write you from time to time and share what I've been reading. I must confess that I sneaked to the library, without my husband's knowledge, and borrowed a book of Petrarch's poems. I have just finished reading 'Per fare una leggiadra sua vendetta' or in English: 'To make a graceful act of revenge.'

You may know how it begins:

> *"To make a graceful act of revenge, and punish a thousand wrongs in a single day,*
> *Love secretly took up his bow again, like a man who waits the time and place to strike."*

How I wish I could punish a thousand wrongs done against me in a single day. Maybe that day will come. Until then, I hope you will reply (I shall have to be careful to intercept the mail) and share with me your favourite poem of the one whose retreat your plantation's name shares.

> *Your friend (Hopefully)*
> *Isabella Young*

Henry Peter was both surprised and delighted to receive the letter he held. He had thought about Isabella Young endlessly this last month and had chided himself for being a fool of the highest order. He had no desire to be another Petrarch and spend his life pining for a woman who would never be his.

And now here he held a letter in his hands which made a rare smile grace his face as he read the poem she had shared and pictured her stealing off to the library. The smile fell from his face as he re-read the words that she had sneaked to the library without her husband's knowledge. Anger pushed away the pleasure he had received from reading the letter at the thought that she had to sneak out to borrow a book. What manner of man was she married to? He reached into the drawer for a sheet of paper and dipped his pen in ink to reply.

August 4, 1839
Lymington, Hampshire

Dear Isabella (I feel I am old enough to take the liberty of addressing you by your Christian name).

I was delighted to receive your letter, as I must confess that you have crossed my mind on several occasions since we met. It pains to hear that you have to sneak out to go to the library when I have hundreds of books that I would love you to have the liberty to read. I am at a loss as to why your husband would not want you to read. It is beyond comprehension. I am of the opinion that knowledge is what separates men from beasts. I trust that you are not married to a complete beast.

As for the poem, I can completely understand how Petrarch felt for:

"My power was constricted in my heart,
making defence there, and in my eyes,
when the mortal blow descended there,
where all other arrows had been blunted.
So, confused by the first assault,

it had no opportunity or strength
to take up arms when they were needed,
or withdraw me shrewdly to the high,
steep hill, out of the torment,
from which it wishes to save me now but cannot."

You will, of course, recognise that as the conclusion of the poem that you referred to in your letter. I, too, would revenge every wrong done to you in a single day. In fact, my heart pains at the thought of any wrong done to you and my offer of help remains, should you need it.

Your friend
Henry Peter Simmons

***

Isabella practically grabbed the mail from the hands of her servant as she had been rushing to collect the mail every day before the maid received it. The poor girl looked at her in bewilderment.

"Sorry, Sarah. I didn't mean to snatch, but I am expecting a letter."

"That's alright, missus. I was just about to bring them up to you."

"Thanks." She waited until the maid walked away before sifting through the letters with shaking hands. When she saw the one addressed to her in a strong, masculine script she dropped the others on the table and hurried to her room with her treasure. She read it over several times, barely daring to believe what it implied. Was he only finishing the poem because she wrote of it or was he using it to say something else? How much was he willing to help if she needed it?

Edward had been very good lately so maybe she was being dramatic, as he often accused her of being. She eagerly took a sheet of paper to respond to the letter.

It was to be the first of several letters that went between the two. With each one they discovered more about each other and were delighted to find that they not only shared a passion for reading but also for riding. Of course, she had not ridden for several years, but the desire to fly across fields of green grass on the back of a well-bred horse stirred in her again as he described riding through fields and glens in Barbados and in Canada on his horse Somonocodrom that he kept there. She had teased him about the peculiar name. He would soon be returning to Barbados (as his lease was coming to an end) to deal with his plantation before going back to Canada. She didn't know how she would survive.

It was bound to happen sometime and the day that Isabella found Edward with her letters in his hand and his face deceptively calm, she knew that if she survived his fury she would have to leave. She had no idea how he had found the letters she had so carefully hid at the back of her cupboard in an old bag, or how he even suspected they were there. Before she even opened her mouth to try to fumble an explanation he was on her and her world exploded in pain.

***

"Mister Simmons, there is a lady at the door who says that she needs to see you." Henry Peter was finishing off a few letters before he went to a club.

"A lady? Who is it, David?" He had no idea who

would be calling on him.

"She didn't give me her name, but she don' look so good. I put her in the parlour. In fact, she look like somebody beat she bad and she said to tell you that she need that help now."

He had barely finished speaking when Henry Peter was on his feet and out the door. The sight that greeted him made his heart ache in one instant and begin to race with anger in the next. Isabella's face was covered in bruises, one eye was purple and her lip was swollen.

"My dear," his voice cracked as he gently pulled her head to his chest and hugged her. That caused the dam that had been holding her together to break and she wept all the tears that she had been holding back for the last five years.

"That beast does not deserve you, my Laura. I am taking you to Vaucluse. It will be your retreat also."

Chapter 26

November 5, 1841
Vaucluse Plantation, Barbados

Henry Peter spread the parchment before him and dipped his pen in ink. He was about to write out his last will and testament. He was amazed that he had lived so long, considering he had battled with bronchial asthma so many times, crossed the Atlantic, sometimes during storms, and survived the trips to Canada, particularly in the earlier days. He was now sixty-five years old and had amassed a fortune in property and assets. He needed to document who he wanted it to be left to in order to make sure that those he cared about would be taken care of.

This is the last will and testament of me, Henry Peter Simmons, of the parish of Saint Thomas and island abovesaid Esquire hereby revoking and making void all former and other wills and codicils by me at any time heretofore made. I direct my just debts and funeral and testamentary expenses to be fully paid and satisfied by my Executors hereinafter named as soon as possible after my death. I give and bequeath to Elizabeth Jane Bazwell and her assigns for and during the term of her natural life one annuity or (near) yearly sum of ten pounds recent money of the Island of Barbados to be paid to her in four equal quarterly payments.

Betsy Jane had been his faithful servant who had been with him during that first asthma attack. He had brought her with him to Vaucluse where she had stayed through all the years and had helped to raise the boys.

I give and bequeath to my natural and reputed coloured daughter Mary Ann Baber, the wife of James Baber Junior Esquire of Leelands in England (late Mary Ann Simmons, spinster), during her natural life one annuity or (near) yearly sum of fifty pounds sterling money of Great Britain to be paid to her by four equal quarterly payments.

Although Mary Ann had been married two years now, they were by no means wealthy so he would ensure that she continued to have the same allowance he had given her from the time he had emancipated her and her mother.

I give and bequeath to Sarah Simmons Harper Rogers, the daughter of Henry Rogers Esquire the son of James Thomas Rogers Esquire, the sum of two thousand pounds sterling money of Great Britain when she attains the age of twenty one years, the interest of which said sum of two thousand pounds to be computed at the rate of six percent per annum from the day of my decrease I direct paid to the father or qualified guardian of the said Sarah Simmons Harper Rogers until she attains the age of twenty one years for her education, support and maintenance and in case of the death of the said Sarah Simmons Harper Rogers under the age of twenty one years then I direct the said sum of two thousand pounds to sink into and form part of the residual of my estate.

John Henry, his godson, and his wife Margaret had had a daughter, Sarah, three years earlier. She was a beautiful and intelligent child, and while he did not see her very often, he had wanted to ensure that she had every opportunity to be educated and well maintained and so he had decided to make a significant provision for her as they would not be able to.

I give and bequeath to my friend Isabella Young, the wife of Edward Young of the city of Rochester in the county of Kent in England (late Isabella Akers, spinster) now resident at my plantation called Vaucluse in the island of Barbados, her living and residence in my dwelling house in the said plantation together with the use of my wines, linens and furniture, china (glass plate and plated articles) and also the stabling and all our out offices attached to the said dwelling house and the garden and orchards attached to the same for and during the term of her natural life should she prefer living in Barbados and I further give and bequeath unto the said Isabella Young the carriage and two horses which I now give and direct that she be allowed to keep for stalling on my said plantation two horses which are to be supplied with fodder and litter and also two feeds of corn of four pints each per day at the expense of my said plantation Vaucluse and that my said dwelling house and the out offices attached hereto be kept in good and tenantable order and repair at the expense of my said plantation and to the satisfaction of the said Isabella Young and further give and bequeath unto the said Isabella Young one annuity or (near) yearly sum of four hundred pounds current money of the island of Barbados for and during the term of her natural life.

Isabella. Henry Peter smiled as he thought about her. She had brought joy to these last two years of his life, especially since she had bravely left her husband and all that she knew and moved to Barbados. She took to the island as if she had lived here all her life as he had known she would. She loved Vaucluse and they spent hours riding all over the plantation and exploring the countryside. They had so many things in common, the greatest being reading, and so they spent many evenings discussing books they had read and sometimes arguing their points. He had never been intimate with her. Contrary to what people thought about their relationship, he respected the fact that she was still married, and, like Petrarch's Laura, she was untouchable to him. Not to mention that he was sixty-five to her twenty-nine. She had her whole life ahead of her and he would make sure that she lacked for nothing. He had better add something to ensure that her husband could not get his hands on her allowance.

... and not to be subject or liable to the debts, control, interference or engagements of her present or any future husband with whom she might intermarry.

He added a number of provisions to ensure that Isabella's annuity was protected. He finally stipulated that a suit of mourning clothes be provided for Betsy Jane and a few of the other slaves to wear at his funeral. Finally, he addressed what was to be done with the remainder of his property.

All the Rest Residue and remainder of my estate and property real personal or mixed, whether in possession, reversion, remainder or expectancy in this island, in England, in Upper Canada in the British Province of North America and elsewhere subject to the payment of the said several annuities and the legacy hereinbefore bequeathed, I give devise and bequeath the same and every part thereof (in which I include any principal sum reserved for payment of the annuities hereinbefore bequeathed when the same shall respectively fall in and cease) to my two natural coloured and reputed sons Harry Simmons and John Alleyne Simmons who are both registered as being baptised in the parish of St. Thomas on the fifth day of March one thousand eight hundred and twenty and are the sons of a woman on my plantation Vaucluse named Molly Harry (now deceased) and their heirs, executors, administrators and assignees to be equally divided between them share and share alike and to take as tenants in common and not as joint tenants and in case of the death of either of them the said Harry Simmons and John Alleyne Simmons in my lifetime then I give devise and bequeath the proportion of my said estate hereby given devised or bequeathed to him so dying as aforesaid unto the survivor of them the said Harry Simmons and John Alleyne Simmons his heirs, executors and administrators and assignees forever.

He had kept his promise made all of those years ago to Molly Harry that he would make sure that the boys could read and do even more than that. John Alleyne had the quicker brain, but both had been well educated and, although they had never been assigned to work in either the fields or the house, he had made sure that they understood how the plantation worked and how to maintain the records. They would be the executors of his will and he would make sure that they gave Isabella free reign of the house, grounds and buildings.

I nominate and appoint my said sons Harry Simmons and John Alleyne Simmons Executors of this my will in testimony whereof I the said Henry Peter Simmons have hereinto set my hand and affixed my seal this fifth day of November in the year of our Lord one thousand eight hundred and forty-one.

Henry Peter left the will unsigned. He would go over it with his friends James Hinkson and Sam Husbands and get them to witness it for him. So, that was that. His life's work shared among the people that he cared for most. He was glad that he had been given another chance at life all those years ago when he'd had his first asthma attack and he had thought he was going to die. He had not lived a perfect life, but he had done as he had vowed and kept his plantation from going into Chancery.

He had a beautiful property in Canada, a thriving plantation in Barbados in the most beautiful part of the country and he had lived in the best lodgings when in England. He had provided a living for hundreds of slaves and then for them as freemen after the apprenticeship system was discontinued in 1838. He had even leased small pieces of land to those who asked and ensured that all had work. His time, he felt sure, was almost over and it had been a life well lived. Not everyone would agree with some of the things he had said and done, but when had he ever cared what anyone thought of him. All that was left now was to answer to his Maker. Would he be weighed in the balance and found wanting or would his kindness over the years be credited to his account? Only time would tell.

***

Barbados Mercury
February 25, 1843

Died. – On 19 inst. at Vaucluse Estate, Henry Peter Simmons, Esq. A large flock of wild birds passed over this island yesterday. It was a singular occurrence at this time of the year.

***

Henry Peter Simmons (1776 – 1843)
His grave can be found in the roundabout at Countryside in Vaucluse.
It is a very friendly grave and is the site of many of the neighbourhood's events.

Postscript

Although I ended *Vaucluse* with the death of Henry Peter Simmons, who was also notably absent from the plantation in the apprenticeship period, I have been asked what happened after emancipation and if the plantation was run by Henry Peter's sons. As I said in the book, Henry Peter leased Vaucluse to George Hewitt from July 1, 1835 to July 1, 1840. His children were emancipated before slavery was abolished, but I do not know where they were during this period. They were apparently back at Vaucluse when he made his will in 1841.

The average number of hogheads of sugar produced in Barbados between 1835 and 1840 was 25,549 while the average number of puncheons of molasses was 6,252. Those numbers compared very favourably with the pre-emancipation period. However, it should be noted that by 1840 and 1841 only 13,319 and 16,714 hogsheads of sugar, respectively, were produced. It was suggested that the productivity of the labour force decreased as the labourers now had access to their own plots of land on which they could grow their own food and therefore could not be incentivised to work hard for the plantations.

During the apprenticeship period, the number of slave marriages increased and this was also the case at Vaucluse. One of the slaves who married was Samuel Welch Simmons who became the undermanager of Vaucluse by 1839. An extract from his will written in 1855 is as follows:

Will of Samuel Welch Simmons : RB4/76/156, March 19th 1855. Entered 20th June 1856

Wife: Hannah Simmons. Unexpired lease granted by former kind master Henry Peter Simmons on 2 acres (a peppercorn lease) part of Vaucluse Plantation along with dwelling house and buildings thereon.

I am uncertain what happened to Harry Simmons as he seems to have disappeared and there is no record of his death and Vaucluse was shown as being owned by John Alleyne Simmons. John Alleyne sold the property in Ancaster, Canada to James Russell in 1848. He married Caroline Gresham in January 1855 in Biggleswade, Bedfordshire, England. The Greshams seemed to have been friends with the Rolphs since an 1881 census listed Elizabeth Whitbread (Thomas Rolph's sister in law) as the head of the house in Shefford, Bedfordshire, her sister Frances Rolph (Thomas Rolph's widow) as a member of the household and Caroline Simmons as a visitor, so perhaps that is how John Alleyne and Caroline met.

Caroline came from Chicksands in Bedforshire which was very close to Shefford. Her father, Robert Gresham, was listed in an 1851 census as a tanner with 18 labourers and a farmer with 460 acres and 30 labourers. They had a French governess and six servants, so they seemed to be quite wealthy.

John Alleyne and Caroline had three children: Henry Ellis Gresham Simmons who was born in England on November 26, 1855, Caroline Marie Simmons who was baptised in St. Thomas, Barbados in October 1857 and Frances Alleyne Simmons who died in England in July of 1860 at a year and a half. A John Alleyne Simmons represented St. Thomas in the House of Assembly in 1857-58 and 1858-59 and could well be the same person, as the family lived at Vaucluse in that period. John Alleyne died on May 31, 1860 at St. Leonard's-on-Sea, Sussex, England.

How successful the plantation was after Henry Peter died is not known, but it never went into Chancery as so many other plantations did in that era, so it appeared to have held its own. The Hughes-Queree Index of Plantations shows it as being sold to an A. Ashby in 1870 for £27,500.

Other Historical Novels by Donna Every

The Price of Freedom
He owned her and was prepared to give her freedom, but was she prepared to pay the price? An exciting, page turning historical novel set in Barbados and Carolina in 1696.

Free in the City
Free in the City is a compelling story of forbidden love between Thomas Edwards and his mulatto slave mistress, Sarah, set in Barbados in the late 1600s. This is the prequel/sequel to The Price of Freedom.

Free at Last
William Edwards is banished to Jamaica, a land where the slavery is brutal and the maroons are fierce. He finally meets his match in this book, the final in The Acreage Series.

Made in the USA
Columbia, SC
20 January 2019